THE FOLLOWERS

*Christopher Nicole titles available from
Severn House Large Print*

Poor Darling
The Pursuit
The Search
The Voyage

THE FOLLOWERS

Christopher Nicole

Severn House Large Print
London & New York

This first large print edition published in Great Britain 2005 by
SEVERN HOUSE LARGE PRINT BOOKS LTD of
9-15 High Street, Sutton, Surrey, SM1 1DF.
First world regular print edition published 2004 by
Severn House Publishers, London and New York.
This first large print edition published in the USA 2006 by
SEVERN HOUSE PUBLISHERS INC., of
595 Madison Avenue, New York, NY 10022.

British Library Cataloguing in Publication Data

Nicole, Christopher
    The followers. - Large print ed.
    1.   Jones, Jessica (Fictitious character) - Fiction
    2.   Policewomen - England - Fiction
    3.   Missing persons - Investigation - Fiction
    4.   Suspense fiction
    5.   Large type books
    I.   Title
    823.9'14 [F]

    ISBN-10:   0-7278-7473-X

Printed and bound in Great Britain by
MPG Books Ltd, Bodmin, Cornwall.

'Behold, I was shapen in wickedness.'
The Book of Common Prayer

Prologue

Six Years Ago

Matthieu strode up and down the ante-chamber, his anxiety plain to see. Of medium height, he was powerfully built, as he had heavy features beneath his thinning pale brown hair. He looked capable of extreme violence, as Kanem well knew. Thus Kanem was equally anxious, not because of what was happening in the operating theatre, or what was going to happen after the operation; he feared a premature explosion on the part of his boss.

In contrast to his employer, Kanem was tall and thin. His features were a classic mixture of his Arab-Mandingo ancestry, and were normally quiet. Only his dark eyes were alive and usually sparkling. Today his eyes were sombre. For all his faith, he did not believe in what was happening beyond the closed door. His fingers drummed on the valise he had placed on the floor beside his chair.

'In the name of God!' Matthieu said. 'What can be taking so long?'

'It is in the *hands* of God that matters,'

Kanem ventured.

Matthieu turned towards him, and he gave an ingratiating smile. 'Must they all go? She is a pretty girl, that nurse.'

Matthieu snorted. 'One day that weakness of yours is going to get you into trouble. At last.' The door opened. 'Well?' he demanded.

De Groot stripped off his gloves, pulled the mask from his face. 'We are bringing her round now.'

'So soon?'

'She will feel almost nothing. A slight soreness. That is the beauty of the keyhole.'

'And the operation?'

The surgeon smiled. He had thin, narrow features to go with his thin, narrow body. 'I would say it has been a success. Of course, we will not be able to tell just how successful for some time. Perhaps six years.'

'Six *years*?'

'Of course. In all other respects the child is normal, and his development will be normal. There is one point. His head will grow somewhat larger than normal. Thus I strongly recommend delivery by Caesarean section. Otherwise it will not only be painful for your wife, but even dangerous. I will perform the operation myself, if you wish, when the time is right. But once he is born, why, he will develop with absolute normality – physically. Traces of his genius may be evident from the age of three, but I cannot guarantee it. You must be patient, my friend. But the mere fact that such an operation has been carried out is a resounding triumph for the medical profession.' His smile widened. 'And for me.'

The nurse appeared from the doorway. 'Mrs Matthieu wishes to see her husband.' She smiled at Kanem. She could tell he found her attractive.

Matthieu looked at De Groot. 'Of course,' the doctor said.

'And Coleby?'

'He is still unconscious. It will be some time before he can be brought round.'

Matthieu nodded and entered the theatre, followed by the nurse and the doctor; Kanem remained in the waiting room. There were three other people present, standing, two nurses and the anaesthetist.

Lying on adjoining trolleys were two people. One was a man, his eyes shut, his head bandaged, his breathing stertorous. On the second trolley there was a woman. Her hair was concealed beneath a cap, so that only her features were revealed, but these were exquisite, small and delicate, fitting perfectly into the oval of pale brown flesh.

'My darling!' Matthieu stood beside her and held her hand. 'How do you feel?'

'I do not know, yet.' Her voice was low, and liquid.

He touched her swollen stomach. 'Is there any pain?'

'I wish to scratch. But they will not let me.'

'You will be able to, soon enough.'

Her fingers were suddenly tight on his. 'The operation...'

'De Groot says it has been entirely successful. Although of course we will have to wait on the results.'

Claudine Matthieu's eyes drifted left and right, taking in the other people in the room. 'But we cannot wait that long,' she said softly. 'The business must be completed.'

'It will be. Do you doubt my resolution?'

Her gaze came back to him, and, disconcertingly, she did not speak for several seconds. Then she said, 'It must be done now. If one word of this were to be known...'

'No one will ever know,' Matthieu promised. 'And it will be done, very shortly. You must not worry, my dearest. I have organized everything.'

Claudine gave him another long stare. 'Then do it, and get me out of here.'

Matthieu squeezed her hand and stepped away from the trolley on which she lay. De Groot had waited by the door. 'What happens now?' Matthieu asked.

'Your wife will be transferred to a private ward, and will remain there for, oh, perhaps two days.'

'Is there any danger?'

'None at all. This is merely a routine precautionary measure.'

'So she *could* go home now.'

'She could. But I would prefer her not to. When I said there is no danger, I meant in a general medical sense. But any surgical operation is attended by some slight risk. This can be eliminated by constant supervision

10

and care over the critical period, which, as I say, will be the next couple of days.'

'I am sure you are right,' Matthieu agreed. 'And who will carry out this constant supervision?'

'Why, members of my staff, of course.'

'These people here?'

'Partly. But they have to be relieved. I do assure you, Mr Matthieu, that your wife will be in no danger.'

'I was thinking of the secrecy we require.'

'That is taken care of. No one knows who your wife is. She is registered as Mrs Smith, here for a minor operation. My people are absolutely reliable. When Mrs Smith leaves the clinic, she will simply disappear. Until and unless you wish to make the operation public. Actually, I would like to discuss this with you.'

Matthieu jerked his head at the still unconscious man. 'What about him?'

'Well...' De Groot pulled his nose. 'He also came in for a routine operation. When he wakes up, the operation will have been carried out. Unfortunately, there will have been an error in the administering of the anaesthetic, and he will have suffered irreversible brain damage. I accept there will be a great scandal, and my reputation will probably be ruined, or at least that of my clinic. But that is why you are paying me ten million dollars.'

'We cannot allow him to wake up at all.'

De Groot frowned. 'Nothing in our contract mentions murder.'

11

'An error in the anaesthetic, as you say. He just will not wake up. Be real, Doctor. You have a man of Coleby's international stature in your clinic and destroy his brain through a surgical error? The press would be crawling all over the place in an hour.'

'Would they not do that if he died on the table?'

'These things happen. There will be an outcry, and, as you say, your reputation will be ruined. But there will be nothing anyone can find in an autopsy to suggest anything more than a dreadful error. If he is released from hospital a cretin, more and more people are going to start considering what might really have happened.'

De Groot glanced at his staff, who were listening. 'I think we would require additional payment for that.'

'Yes,' Matthieu said, thoughtfully.

'But we must also discuss how and when the news of this operation can be revealed to the medical world,' De Groot went on.

'It can never be revealed. You signed a contract to that effect.'

'I did. But in view of what you wish me to do, that contract will have to be redrawn. In fact, it might be possible for me to accept that in place of more money. Do you realize that I have just performed the most remarkable operation in medical history? Its implications are immense. The prospects it opens up are unlimited. It conjures up visions of immortality.'

'And you could get the Nobel Prize. They might even release you from prison, temporarily, to go to Oslo to collect it. Sadly, you signed a contract. You are going to have to carry your magnificent secret to your grave.' His turn to glance at the waiting staff. 'As will they.'

De Groot's face stiffened. 'Well, then, a further twenty million.'

'For killing one man? Even such a man? I think your brain has deteriorated even quicker than Coleby's.'

'That is the price of my silence. And that of my people.'

'You are wrong, Doctor. This discussion has in any event been academic. If you had been at all reasonable I might have chosen a different course. But...' Matthieu looked past De Groot at Kanem, standing in the doorway, and nodded. At the same time he drew a silenced automatic pistol from the deep pocket of his coat, and from a range of six inches shot De Groot through the heart. The doctor uttered no sound, other than the thump as he collapsed to the floor.

Matthieu turned to face the other three people, who were staring at him in consternation. Kanem now stood beside him, also holding a silenced pistol. Between them they fired six times, before any of their victims could move. The three bodies struck the floor virtually together. Kanem turned to the pretty nurse, who was standing behind him, momentarily paralysed with horror. Now she

13

came to, and turned herself, desperately, towards the door. Kanem caught her by the shoulder, pulled her back to him, and shot her through the back of the head, pushing her away from him again to prevent himself being spattered by blood. She struck the floor with a thump. 'What a waste,' he remarked, and went forward to examine the other bodies, firing twice more at close range.

Matthieu pocketed his pistol and took out his mobile. 'Bring the car round.' He stood beside his wife.

'That was well done,' she said. 'Where are my clothes?'

Matthieu shook his head. 'The doctor said you needed to be careful for a day or two. We shall wheel you out of here.'

'What about this one?' Kanem stood above the unconscious Coleby.

'He will go up in the explosion,' Matthieu said. Kanem nodded, went into the antechamber and returned with the valise. This he placed on the floor next to the corpses, opened it to reveal a solid interior and several dials. 'Half an hour,' Matthieu said.

Kanem set the clock. Matthieu spread a blanket over Claudine. Kanem joined him, and between them they rolled the trolley out of the theatre and across the antechamber. This door they locked behind them, then rolled the trolley to the lift. They descended to the lobby on the ground floor. 'There is no ambulance ordered,' said one of the two orderlies on duty. 'It may take a little time.'

'We have our own transport,' Matthieu explained. 'Dr De Groot said it would be all right.'

'I'll just have to log the patient out.' The orderly went behind his desk, while Claudine smiled at his partner.

'Smith,' Matthieu said.

The orderly ran his finger down the list. 'Oh, yes. Margaret Smith. Exploratory surgery.' He raised his head.

'It was entirely successful,' Matthieu explained.

'My congratulations, sir. Will you sign?'

Matthieu signed the name John Smith. 'Have a nice day,' he recommended. 'What's left of it.'

Kanem wheeled Claudine out into the gathering winter darkness, accompanied by the other orderly. 'Our people should be doing this,' the orderly remarked.

'I am in a hurry to get home,' Claudine explained.

The limousine was waiting, the rear doors open. The chauffeur and Kanem lifted Claudine from the trolley and laid her on the bed waiting in the back of the huge vehicle. 'Thank you so much,' Matthieu said, and got in beside his wife. Kanem sat in the front beside the driver. The orderly wheeled the trolley back into the hospital lobby. 'Move it,' Matthieu said, looking at his watch.

The limousine rolled down the drive to the gates. The watchman peered at them, then saluted and pressed a button. The car drove

15

through and the gates clicked shut. 'That,' Matthieu said, 'was a damned near run thing.' As they swung round the corner, out of sight of the clinic, there was a huge explosion from behind them.

One

Today

'The commander will see you now,' Mrs Norton said, peering over the top of her glasses at Detective-Sergeant Jessica Jones. The pair of them had never liked each other, and from the secretary's aura of prim satisfaction, Jessica knew she was going to hear the worst.

She stood up, a trim if decidedly small figure in the blue skirt and white blouse of the Metropolitan Police, her yellow hair, which she wore shoulder-length when off duty, confined in a tight bun beneath her hat, isolating her face. But this merely enhanced the softly crisp features which were close to beauty; perhaps, she thought, knowing she was being catty, part of Mrs Norton's angst was sheer jealousy.

She gave a little tap on the inner door, opened it, stepped through, and came to attention. 'JJ,' Commander Adams said, expansively. 'Good to see you. You're looking well.'

'I am feeling well, sir,' Jessica said, carefully.

'Well, come in, come in,' Adams said. 'Sit down.' Jessica obeyed, just as carefully. The commander had always reminded her of a bloodhound, his large head seeming to droop between his shoulders rather than his ears, and bloodhounds are not by nature designed either to smile or look benevolent. The tension in her brain increased. 'That's a splendid tan.'

'It's beginning to fade.'

'Well, I suppose that's a good thing. Can't have you catching skin cancer, eh?'

Jessica refrained from pointing out that one does not 'catch' skin cancer, or indeed any other sort of cancer. 'No, sir.'

Adams turned over the first sheet in the folder that lay open on his desk. 'I assume you have seen a copy of this?'

'I have, sir.'

'And what do you think of it?'

'That Mr Gresham has drawn several unsubstantiated conclusions.'

'It's a matter of perception,' the commander suggested, mildly. 'And attitude. Perception of attitude,' he added, warming to his theme. 'Mr Gresham is one of our leading psychiatrists. He is concerned with attitudes. And he does have facts to support his hypothesis. As for instance, you did shoot those three fishermen on that island.'

'I killed those men in self-defence. And they were not fishermen; they were pirates.'

'According to the two that survived, they were harmless fishermen who had gone to

18

your rescue.'

'May I remind you, sir, that the court in the Marquesas did not agree with them? They were sent to prison; I was entirely exonerated.'

'What bothers Mr Gresham is that when questioned, you said you would do it again.'

'Of course I would do it again, sir. Those men attacked me.'

'They were armed only with knives. You had an assault rifle.'

'I had an assault rifle, sir, because I took it away from one of them. If I hadn't shot them, they would have taken it back.'

'I have no doubt that you were provoked, JJ. But your reaction comes across as somewhat, shall I say, negative. I blame it on that assignment you were sent on as part of an SAS unit. They gave you the idea that it is acceptable to shoot first and ask questions afterwards.'

'They were the finest body of men I have ever known, sir.'

'And then, of course, being blown up in Alicante...'

'That was before I was seconded to the SAS, sir.'

'No doubt. But being blown up can affect one's mentality, don't you agree? Gives one a different perception.'

If he uses that word again, Jessica thought, I am going to wring his neck. Although the commander was twice her size, she had no doubt that, thanks to her intensive training, she could do it. It was an attractive daydream.

But she merely said, quietly, 'Are you suggesting that I am mad, sir?'

'Oh, good heavens, no, JJ. But it is a matter of attitude. What about those men you shot in the London siege?'

'I was endeavouring to rescue the Princess Karina, sir. And only one of them died.'

'You sound sorry about that.'

'I didn't care for any of those thugs.'

'Quite. And then that business in Colombia, shooting down an entire helicopter full of people.'

'It was full of drug-running bastards, sir, who were engaged in dropping bombs upon me and my colleagues. I consider that I was fully justified in returning fire.'

'And in hitting their fuel tank?'

'I was not aiming at the fuel tank, sir. It was dark. I just wanted to discourage them.'

'Attitude and perception, combined with your remarkable ability with anything that can be considered a lethal weapon. The fact is, JJ, questions are being asked, and not only by Mr Gresham. The media are becoming interested. Mention the name of Detective-Sergeant Jones and their ears prick up. Who has she been shooting now? Our various clients are even more interested. Some actually request you. It apparently makes them feel safer. Others, and I am afraid they are in a large majority, don't want you under any circumstances; they are afraid that with you protecting them they will wind up in the middle of a shoot-out. And frankly, not all of your colleagues wish to be on your team, either. They also are not sure they wish to find themselves shooting people to avoid being shot at. There is even a murmur that there may be a question in the House, something like, can the minister confirm that the Special Branch Protection Unit employs a shoot-to-kill policy. That would be intensely embarrassing.'

'I would hate to embarrass the department, sir.'

'Of course you would. So I know you will agree with me when I suggest that you should drop out of sight, just for a while.'

'Sir?'

'I think, in the first place, you should take a month's holiday. Find a nice beach somewhere and restore your sun tan.'

'Aren't you afraid that will increase the risk of my developing skin cancer?'

The commander was impervious to sarcasm. 'I don't think just one more month will be all that dangerous.'

'I should also point out that for the past four months I have done very little else than lie about in the sun.'

'Except when shooting fishermen-turned-pirates, eh?'

'Very droll, sir. I am merely suggesting that questions may well be asked about the amount of leave I have been enjoying. Or at least time off work.'

'Oh, come now, JJ. You were kidnapped by a very dangerous criminal.' He held up his

21

finger as she would have spoken. 'I am not going to get into the peculiar relationship you seem to have formed with the man, nor do I wish to discuss your absurd theory that he was not guilty of the crime for which he was first convicted. He was certainly guilty of kidnap, assault, and, ah ... rape.'

'With respect, sir, Lomas did not rape me.'

'I have said that I do not intend to discuss it. Whatever happened, for those months you were held a captive against your will. That is not a vacation. Now, then. You will take a month's leave, starting today.'

'And when questions *are* asked, the word will be that I have been suspended on full pay ... It will be full pay?'

'Of course it will be full pay. And I will have the balls off any man, or woman, who says you have been suspended.'

'You may find the second half of that promise difficult to implement, sir, but thank you, anyway. A month's leave. Very good, sir. And when I come back...?'

'I am going to recommend you for promotion to inspector. It's due. How old are you?'

'I shall be thirty-eight on my next birthday, sir.'

'Good heavens! You don't look it.'

'Thank you, sir.'

'And how long have you been on the force?'

'Sixteen years, sir.'

'Good lord! You should have been an inspector long ago.'

'You did wish to recommend me, sir, three

22

years ago. But I declined.'

'Why?'

'I like my job, sir.'

'You mean shooting people.'

Jessica sighed. 'Protection, sir.'

'Well, you are overdue for promotion, and you are going to get it.'

'You mean I'm to spend my time making up duty rosters instead of being in the field.'

'Ah ... we shall have to discuss that. When you return from holiday.'

'With respect, sir, I would like to discuss it now.'

'JJ, you are a damned difficult woman. I don't know how Lawson puts up with you.'

'He doesn't, always.'

'Is that why you've never married? I know it's none of my business. However, the future ... You will be an inspector, and I think in the first instance you should replace Inspector Harriman. He is due to retire in six months' time.'

'Inspector Harriman is in charge of Departmental Records, sir.'

'That is exactly it. A huge job. A highly responsible job. I know you will be a great success at it.' Jessica gazed at him. 'You'll get used to the idea. But first, that month's leave. Enjoy yourself. And remember, JJ, that we're all on your side.'

Jessica stood up, saluted, and left the office. 'You'll have to have a new uniform,' Mrs Norton suggested.

'You know,' Jessica said, 'there is something

23

I have always wanted to ask you. Is there a Mr Norton?'

'Good lord, no. I got rid of him years ago.'

'What a lucky fellow.' Jessica went to the lifts.

It was nearly one, but Jessica did not feel like eating. She took a taxi home; she did not feel like rubbing shoulders with people on a tube or a bus, either.

Fortunately, the flat in Clapham was empty; she also did not feel like encountering Tom at this moment. She threw her cap in the corner, and threw herself across the bed, on her stomach, kicking off her shoes as she did so. Why haven't you got married? Adams had asked. But she had been married, once, and it hadn't worked out.

Was that the reason she had never married Tom? She didn't think so. When they had first got together the idea of being Jessica Lawson had been quite appealing. He was an attractive man, and there had also been the gratitude factor. Tom had already been in the Special Branch, and it had been thanks to his lobbying of his superiors that she had followed him off the beat and into the Protection Unit, a line of work she loved, whatever the dangers.

But the idea of marriage had dwindled over the several years they had shared a flat. Tom was good in bed, sometimes, could be excellent company, sometimes, and they liked the same music and films, mostly. But there

24

was nothing else. He was dead against children, and she was growing desperate; she felt that time was running out. And recently, the jealousy factor had crept in. They were both sergeants – which meant that she had been promoted more recently than him – but she had also stolen the headlines. On the odd occasion they had worked together, he had supported her loyally. But there was the rub. In the eyes of the department, and occasionally even the world, *he* had been supporting *her*. Whatever the truth of the situation, there appeared to be something irresistibly fascinating about a diminutive blonde – she was only five feet four inches tall – taking her place in a man's world of crime and violence, if necessary with guns blazing, and proving herself the best. She was proud of the reputation she had achieved over the past few years, and if a lot of people, including, sadly, her boss, felt that she was too willing to go out on a limb, she had also earned several commendations for her courage and determination.

But she could understand Tom's feelings. What he was going to say when he learned that she was stepping up a rank above him, even if at the same time it meant that her career in protection was over, just didn't bear contemplating. Which was the nub of the matter. She didn't want to leave the Protection Unit and spend the rest of her life sitting behind a desk, even if it did involve promotion.

And then there was Andrea.

Andrea was the only person she actually felt like speaking with at the moment. She used her mobile. 'Hi.' Andrea's voice always sounded as if she had just awakened from a sexy dream and couldn't wait to turn dreams into reality. She was a continuous bone of contention between Jessica and Tom. He couldn't fault the number of times the two women had worked together: Andie was the best back-up on the force, and had a reputation only inferior to that of Jessica herself. But he had doubts about her sexuality. Jessica knew he was justified, but she also knew that however often Andrea had made it clear that she would like to get together in an emotional sense, she had never dared cross the bounds of professional friendship; she regarded Jessica as the best in the business, and was always proud to be part of her squad. Which was never going to happen again!

'Hi,' she said.

'JJ! How lovely to hear from you. I was just thinking about you.'

'Snap! You on duty?'

'I'm at Heathrow seeing his nibs off. What a fart! Have we got something?'

'I'd like a chat. Call me when you're free.'

'You got it.'

Jessica took off her uniform – as Mrs Norton had said, that too could be on its way out – had a shower, put on a dressing gown, and listened to the door open.

Tom was a large, rugged-looking man who

26

was every bit as tough as he looked. 'Hi, sweetheart.' He gave her a hug and a kiss, both perfunctory. 'How'd it go?' He knew her interview with the commander had been that morning.

'I'm to take a month's leave.'

'You talking about a suspension?'

'I'm talking about leave. I'm to find a nice quiet beach and lie on it.'

'Haven't you been doing just that for the past four months?'

'Look, can it.'

'Okay, okay. So you're swanning off somewhere for a month. Damnation. When I went looking for you on that desert island I was told that was my leave. Shit! Where's lunch?' His inner man was always very dear to his heart.

'I wasn't hungry.'

He studied her for a moment – he knew her well enough to realize she was on the verge of an explosion – then went into the kitchen, selected a packaged pie from the larder, removed the wrapping, and put it in the microwave. 'Feel like talking about it?'

'About what?'

Tom laid two places at the table. 'Well, if the boss just told me I should take off for a month's R and R, I'd be grinning from ear to ear.'

'Maybe I'll do that, when the idea sinks in. So what are you at? Still the ambassador?'

'And how.' The machine pinged and he served. 'There's enough for two.'

'I said I'm not hungry. Are you off tonight?'

Tom ate, hungrily. 'I am going to the opera tonight. Full bib and tucker.'

'What is it?'

'*Eugene Onegin*. And I don't even like Tchaikovsky.'

'Bring me a programme.' Jessica went into the bedroom, took off her dressing gown, and got into bed. He followed her a few minutes later.

'I have an idea. Why not spend the month here in the flat, redecorating it? It needs it.'

'Why don't you have a heart attack, or something constructive?'

'You look just like what I need for dessert.' He began to undress, but before she could think of an adequate reply the phone rang.

'I'm on my way.'

'No,' Jessica said. 'I'll come to you.'

'Ah ... that might not be a good idea.'

Jessica knew that since Andie's old partner, Chloe, had been retired following her encounter with a bushmaster during their Amazonian adventure, she had accumulated a new flatmate. As this was not a member of the force, she had never met her. 'Got you,' she said. 'Well then, you'll have to come here.'

'Right. Time?'

Jessica looked over the phone at Tom. 'What time are you off?'

'Seven.'

'Half past seven,' Jessica said. 'We'll have supper. *À deux*.'

28

'I'll be there.'

Jessica put down the phone, returned Tom's look.

'Don't tell me,' he said. 'You know what that bitch needs?'

'Just don't tell *me*.'

'She needs someone to take her aside, take down her knickers, give her six of the best, and then shag her till she squeals.'

'If you were thinking of having a rest,' Jessica said, 'do it in the lounge.'

'I thought we were going to get together.'

'Well, you were wrong.'

Andrea was twenty-nine years old, tall and slender. Off duty she went in for short skirts, which displayed her exceptionally long legs. But the rest of her measured up, and the classically, slightly aquiline features were framed with straight auburn hair, which, again when off duty, she wore loose and past her shoulders. 'You don't look good,' she remarked.

'I don't feel good.' Jessica gave her a glass of red wine.

'Trouble at the mill? Or in bed?'

'Both.'

Andrea sat down and crossed her knees. 'Tell me about it.'

'Oh, Tom's gone off in a huff. I wasn't in the mood this afternoon. And I'm away for a month.'

'A month! Great stuff. Where are we going?'

'It's not a job. Anyway, aren't you one of

29

those who don't want to work with me any-more?'

'JJ!' Andie looked so distraught Jessica kissed her.

'Sorry. I'm feeling bitchy.'

'I would follow you anywhere, any time,' Andrea said.

Jessica refilled both their glasses. 'There's not going to be anywhere, any time. I've got the push.'

Slowly Andrea put down her glass. 'You? From the force? You have got to be kidding me.'

'Not from the force. From the unit. I'm to take a month off and then go into records. As an inspector. Can you believe it?'

'I can believe the inspector bit. You should have been one long ago. But the unit? You're the best we have. You mean Adams has finally flipped his lid?'

'He was very logical.' Jessica outlined what the commander had said to her.

'What a load of bullshit,' Andrea remarked. 'What this country needs is a lot more people like you, not one less. We're being overtaken by a flock of wets. You're not seriously going into records?'

'You'll read about it in the *Gazette*. That is, when I come back from this month's vaca-tion. And please don't remind me that I have just had four months' vacation.'

'You have had four months of hell. What did the papers say? The sexual plaything of a deranged murderer. Brrr. It makes my skin

30

crawl even to think about it.'

'Then don't think about it, before you end a beautiful friendship.'

'You're not going to tell me you *enjoyed* it?'

'Actually, you know, I did, once I got used to it. Being on that boat, I mean. And then the island. And I was never a sexual slave, in the way that you mean. Lomas was impotent.'

'Say again?'

'You're the first person I have ever told that, and I don't really want it spread about. He was a sadly mixed-up character who had it in for me because my evidence had sent him down all those years ago. But you know what? He thought he hated me, but after all that time dreaming about me, about what he was going to do to me, he had actually fallen in love with me. It was all pretty tragic.'

'But the moment you got the opportunity you shot him.'

'I did not shoot him. I shot the man who shot him. And two of his companions. That's why I'm in this mess.'

'I just can't see you in records.'

'Neither can I.'

Andrea frowned. 'You're not going to do something stupid.'

'I'm thinking about it.'

'Oh, JJ, you can't! The force is your life. Anyway, what would you do? I mean, you're ... well...'

'I am thirty-seven years old, unmarried, and, it appears, totally lacking in any skills save for the ability to shoot people dead.'

31

'And if you quit, you'll lose your pension.'

'Yes,' Jessica said grimly. 'Let's eat.'

'I'm not really sure you should be alone,' Andrea said after the meal.

'I'm not going to be alone for very long. Tom's opera ends at eleven.'

'Oh. But you said you weren't speaking.'

'So what's new? There is only the one bed.'

Andrea made a face. 'Well ... you know where to find me.'

'You on duty tomorrow?'

'I'm on report. I'll be in touch to let you know where I'm going and with whom. Well...' They kissed. 'Have a nice vacation.'

Tom actually didn't come in until after midnight, by which time Jessica was determinedly asleep. Next morning she stayed in bed until after he'd left. Then she got up, showered and dressed ... and realized she had nothing to do. Usually, when she had no assignment and was not required to report at the Yard, she would go down to the gym, work out, and then visit the range for gun practice. But what was the point if she was going to spend the rest of her professional life sitting behind a desk? She opened her top drawer, and gazed at the automatic pistol lying there. It was a Skorpion 7.65 M-61 machine-pistol; fully loaded with twenty cartridges the little blowback weighed only three kilos and fitted neatly into the shoulder bag she wore on duty, or in a shoulder holster. With its extendable butt it could be accurate at close to a

32

hundred yards. They were old friends, but now she had to wonder if she would ever use it again.

She breakfasted, then took the tube down to the West End to a travel agency she knew, collected some brochures, and took them home to study. Tom didn't come home for lunch – as they had hardly spoken since last evening she had no idea whether he was still on assignment with his ambassador – so she was able to spread her material over the dining table. The problem was that nearly all holidays were designed for two people; there were singles, but she got the impression that these were designed for the under twenty-fives – a nearly forty would stick out like a sore thumb, even supposing the commander had been right and she didn't look it. Going alone on a 'normal' holiday not only involved a supplement for a single room but promised a good deal of loneliness. In any event, the really interesting ones, such as to China or India, were way out of her price range.

She found herself staring at the wall. Obviously, to quit her job, at her stage of life and career, would be madness. Unless ... She pinched her lip. There should be an opening for a position in security, somewhere, with her qualifications. Except that, as the commander had indicated, not every firm requiring a high-powered security expert would necessarily go for a CV which included such pieces of information as 'have killed upwards of twenty men in the line of duty'. She

33

actually had no idea how many people had been in that helicopter, or if they had all been men.

She collected the brochures, put them in a drawer, made herself a cup of tea and sipped it, still staring at the wall. There was so much to remember. The Alicante bomb, which should have ended her career, and her life, there and then; it had been the merest chance whim that, being off duty, she had decided to take a walk on the beach instead of going down to breakfast, moments before the entire hotel had collapsed, burying well over a hundred people, including her client of the moment, and her two colleagues of the moment too.

Yet that catastrophe had launched her on the second, spectacular phase of her career. Because she was the only person who could identify the bomber, having seen him seconds before the blast as she had returned towards the hotel, she had been seconded to the SAS unit despatched to find him in his Turkish lair. Because she had matched the men when push had come to shove, she had suddenly found herself the most famous policewoman in England. Now ... She supposed she could be a legend.

The phone rang. Lazily, Jessica picked it up, gave the number. 'Would I be speaking with Detective-Sergeant Jessica Jones?'

Jessica frowned. The English was perfect, but the voice had a faintly foreign tang. More importantly, it was not a voice she had ever

34

heard before, and in the telephone book she was listed as plain Jones, J., with not a hint of her profession, rank, or indeed sex. 'I'm afraid you have the wrong number.'

'Oh, Miss Jones, please forgive me. I do not blame you for being cautious. However, *should* you be the lady I am seeking, I should like to invite you out to lunch.'

'Can you tell me why the lady you are seeking should accept such an invitation from a complete stranger?'

'Firstly, because I admire you so very much. Secondly, and far more importantly, I wish to discuss a business matter with you, which could be of enormous value to you.'

'I'm sorry,' Jessica said. 'I'm not in business.' And mentally slapped her wrist for having betrayed herself. But he had known who she was, anyway.

'But you are, Miss Jones. Are you not in the business of smiting the unrighteous?'

'I'm not all that much into religious attitudes, either,' Jessica pointed out. 'How did you get this number? There are well over a hundred J. Joneses in the book. Perhaps you should try some of them.'

'I was given your number by a friend, who felt sure you would be interested in my proposition.'

'I need to know his name.'

'She specifically asked me not to divulge that. I do promise you that she has only your best interests at heart.'

Andie? Andie had never betrayed a confidence in her life. But who else could it be? Oh, the witch!

'Well, I'm afraid I can look after my own best interests, Mr ... I didn't catch your name.'

'Until we have met, and talked, I would prefer to be known as Smith. I do beg you to accept my invitation, Miss Jones. There is nothing sinister or, shall I say, underhanded in the proposal I am going to put to you. What I am going to offer you is a very large sum of money to carry out a small task for me.'

Jessica couldn't help being intrigued. 'As Detective-Sergeant Jones?'

'No. I do not feel that would be appropriate. The job I have in mind can easily be accomplished in your spare time. And you have a lot of spare time coming up, do you not?'

Oh, Andie, Jessica thought. I am going to break your fucking beautiful neck.

'All I am asking you to do,' the voice went on, 'is have lunch with me, in the most public of places. I think The Ivy would be best. Over lunch, I shall put my proposition to you. If it appeals to you, we will have a deal and will then discuss the details. If it does not appeal to you, then you have simply to walk away. What can be wrong with that?'

Everything is wrong with that, Jessica thought. Beginning with Andrea revealing to some foreigner information given her in the utmost confidence, and ending with the

36

obvious fact that what he wanted her to do was outside of normal police activities. But her instincts told her the man needed to be investigated, and his proposal. Besides, she had only lunched at The Ivy twice in her life, and both the previous occasions had been in the line of duty when she had been unable to do justice to her meal.

'All right,' she said. 'I accept.'

'Then shall we say one o'clock?'

'And I ask for Smith?'

'Yes. John Smith.'

Two

Mr Smith

Point one, Jessica thought: my would-be client has no imagination, and not all that much knowledge of England; she wondered just how many John Smiths there were in Great Britain, or indeed, how many of them were likely to be lunching in The Ivy at any one time.

But point number two was more immediately important. She punched numbers. 'Hi.'

'Where are you?'

'JJ! Brilliant! I'm home.'

'Well, don't go out. I'll be there in half an hour.'

'Ah, well, you see...'

'Oh, send *her* out. We need to be alone.'

'Oh! Well ... I'll see what I can do.'

'Half an hour,' Jessica reminded her.

She took a taxi, as she regarded the business as urgent. She had only visited Andrea on a few occasions, and never since Chloe Allbright's forced retirement. But she was prepared to keep an open mind about her replacement – on a policewoman's salary it was obviously essential to share expenses wherever possible.

She reached for the bell, and the street door opened. The woman who emerged was extremely average, apart from an oversized bust. Jessica remembered that Chloe had also been very well upholstered. 'You the Jones woman?'

'So they say.'

'She's waiting for you. Third floor.'

'I know the way.' Jessica went inside, climbed the stairs.

Andrea stood in the doorway. 'Josie wasn't rude, I hope.'

'I have a suspicion that we are never going to be close friends. Where did you find her?'

'She answered the advert. Well, quite a few people did. But she seemed to fit the bill.'

'Lucky you.' Jessica went into the lounge.

Andrea followed. 'What's up?'

Jessica faced her. 'I want to know who your friend is, and why you repeated to him what I told you in confidence.'

38

Andrea sat down, frowning at the unusual brusqueness in Jessica's voice. 'My friend?'

'He calls himself Smith, right?'

'I know lots of Smiths. But I haven't seen any of them recently. As for talking to anyone about you ... about us ... I wouldn't do that, JJ. You know that.'

'I thought I did. All right. This character telephoned me about an hour ago. He knew exactly who I was and what I did for a living. He knew that I have just been given a month's leave. And he wants me to spend some of that leave doing something for him.'

'Doing what?'

'He hasn't told me yet. He's going to do that tomorrow, when we lunch at The Ivy.'

'That at least sounds as if he's up-market.'

'How did he get all that information?'

'Haven't a clue. You mean you actually thought it was me?'

'I'm sorry. I just knew that you were the only person I had confided in.'

'Except for Tom.'

'I haven't told Tom, yet. Anyway this Smith used the word "she".'

'So we have a rotten egg. Or at least a gossipy one. Will you do anything about it?'

'Let's see what friend Smith has on his mind first.'

'Mr Smith,' the maître d' said. 'He's at his table. If you will come this way, madam.'

Jessica followed him into the restaurant. She was wearing one of her best dresses, in

39

pale green with high heels but no hat; her hair was brushed in smooth perfection down to her shoulders.

'Miss Jones!' Smith stood up. 'Do you know, you are absolutely nothing like what I expected.'

Whereas you are exactly as I expected, Jessica thought: Middle European and heavy. 'Do I take that as a compliment?' she asked. 'Or are you disappointed?'

'It is a compliment. I had expected, well...'

'Some big, raw-boned, uniformed officer?'

'Well, your reputation does suggest a woman of action. Now I am enchanted. But please sit down. An aperitif?'

'Thank you.' Jessica sat opposite him across the table.

Smith nodded to the waiter. 'I am so happy to have met you at last.' He also sat down.

'Should we have met before?'

'Oh, indeed. I feel that we should have met years ago. When I was younger.' Champagne cocktails were placed in front of them. But he can hardly mean to seduce me in a crowded restaurant, Jessica reflected.

'Shall we order?' Smith invited. They did so, and discussed the weather until the main course arrived. Then he said, 'I understand that you serve in what is known as the Protection Unit of the Special Branch. Or you did up to two days ago.'

'You must have a very good friend at Scotland Yard.'

'Well, one tries to have friends everywhere,

doesn't one? What intrigues me is that your rank is that of detective-sergeant. Does that mean you are also a detective?'

'I have been trained in CID procedure, yes.'

'So you are an expert at finding things, or people.'

'I have some experience of it. Is that what you want, someone found? Wouldn't you do better with a private detective?'

'Is there a private detective in the world, outside of fiction, of course, who is your equal?'

'At being a detective? A few thousand, I would say.'

'I do not agree with you. Do you like this wine?'

'It's very nice, thank you.'

'Do you drink a lot of wine?'

'At the right times, yes. But the stuff I drink isn't often in this class.'

'I think you are a connoisseur. I saw you give an appreciative sniff before drinking.'

'Let's say that I can tell the difference between a *grand cru* and a *vin du pays*.'

'How would you like to have a bottle of *grand cru*, for lunch and for dinner, every day for the rest of your life?'

'It could become boring. Are you a wine merchant, Mr Smith?'

'Only in the sense that I buy a lot of it. What I was suggesting was the lifestyle you will be able to enjoy when you have completed the task I require of you.'

'Aren't you driving just a little fast for such

41

a crowded road, Mr Smith? Your requirements and my future lifestyle have not yet gelled.'

'I am sure they will. To put it simply, I wish you to recover my son for me.'

Jessica all but choked on a piece of lamb, washed it down with a gulp of wine. 'Would you explain that?'

'I am told it is an everyday tragedy of domestic life. But you see, I do not regard myself as an everyday representative of domestic life. My wife has left me, taking with her our only son. I want him back.'

'I'm so sorry. But the custody of a child of a broken home is a matter for the courts.'

'The courts, your English courts, have no jurisdiction in this matter. My wife has left the country and returned to her family. With my son.'

'And where does her family live?'

'In Nigeria.'

'Ah. Your wife is Nigerian?'

'My wife is the daughter of a Touareg chieftain and a French mother.'

'That sounds exciting. And you are?'

'I was born in Switzerland. But I have British nationality.'

'And a British name.'

'Well, Miss Jones, I am sure you have deduced that Smith is not my real name. But that can wait on the progress of our negotiations.'

'To tell you the truth, Mr Smith, I don't see what we have to negotiate about. As you say, what has happened to you is a misfortune which sadly overtakes too many families, especially when there is a mixed ethnic and therefore cultural background. May I ask, how old is your son?'

'He is six years old.'

'Hm. That's a tricky one. Unless you can provide incontrovertible proof that his mother is a danger to him, or cruel to him, or can prove that she is unable to afford to bring him up in the manner you would consider appropriate, the courts will almost certainly award custody to her rather than the father. What you need is a good divorce lawyer ... I'm assuming that you do mean to divorce your wife?'

'I have not yet considered the matter.'

'Well, I don't know your domestic situation. Obviously your wife had a reason, at least in her opinion, for leaving you, and most wives, doing that, would wish to take their child ... You said there is only one.'

'Yes.'

'Right. Well, as I was saying, what you need to do is place the matter in the hands of the best divorce lawyer you can find here in England. He will be able to find you a top lawyer in Lagos, and, well ... You'll have to hope for the best. I'm sorry to be negative, after such a lovely lunch.'

'But you are not hopeful.'

'I'm afraid I can't be. Unless, as I say, you have proof that the boy's life is in danger, or at least in danger of being unacceptably

43

downgraded.'

'You think very clearly and lucidly. I like that. Will you take coffee?'

'Thank you.'

'And brandy?'

'No, thank you. The day still has rather a long way to run.'

'You know,' Smith said, after ordering. 'I like everything about you, Miss Jones. Your incisiveness, your self-control, and then, of course, your reputation. I look forward to working with you.'

'I've just explained that I have nothing to offer.'

'But you do. You have the courage, the determination, the clear-headedness, and the skill, to bring my son back to me.'

Jessica watched the cups being placed in front of them and filled, the tray placed between them. The waiter withdrew. 'I hope I didn't hear what I thought I did,' she remarked.

'Miss Jones, I will pay you one million pounds for the safe return of my son to me.'

Jessica had been slowly raising her cup. Now she gasped, sipped, burned her lip, and spilled coffee on the tablecloth.

'Oh, my dear,' Smith said. 'I am so terribly sorry. Have you hurt yourself?'

'Not seriously,' Jessica muttered.

Waiters hurried forward with napkins, a fresh tablecloth, and more coffee. The delay gave Jessica time to regain some of her composure. But not all. 'Would you say that again?' she asked. 'I promise not to spill any more coffee.'

'One million pounds, Miss Jones. Paid into untraceable bank accounts. Tax-free, and in complete confidence. Why, when you come back from your vacation you can even resume working for the Metropolitan Police, knowing that you are financially invulnerable.'

Jessica was trying desperately to think, to get things straight in her mind. But it was difficult. She wished she hadn't enjoyed that wine so much she had drunk half the bottle. 'You value your son at a million pounds?'

'Do you have children, Miss Jones?'

'Unfortunately, no.'

'But if you did have a child, and he was stolen from you, would you not pay every penny you possessed to get him back?'

Jessica stared at him. 'I don't have a million pounds.'

'But I do. And I want my son back.'

Just for a moment the urbanity disappeared, and was replaced by an expression of almost animal intensity. Jessica swallowed. 'Wouldn't it make sense to offer your wife that money to come back to you? Or at least share your son's custody?'

Matthieu smiled. 'If I can afford a million pounds, my wife has access to a hundred times that sum.'

'Oh. Well, you people seem to be entirely out of my class. So...'

'What is money, Miss Jones? Pieces of paper

45

in a wallet, coins in a bag, entries in a ledger, files in a computer. Can you eat any of those? More importantly, can any of those stand at your shoulder and defend you when you are in danger, or of themselves succour you when you are hurt?'

'It's a point of view.'

'You, Miss Jones, are in a class of your own when it comes to things that matter. Affairs of life and death.'

'I'm a reluctant performer, Mr Smith. But spell out exactly what it is you would like me to do. Without prejudice.'

'I would like you to visit my wife's home, and return with my son.'

'Just like that. From what you have said, the lady may object to letting him go.'

'That is why I am employing you.'

Jessica held up her finger. 'Uh-uh. You are not employing me, as General Alexander Haig would say, now sadly overexposed at this moment in time.'

'But you are interested. One million pounds, Miss Jones.'

'Stop confusing me. I would like you to answer one or two questions.'

'If I can.'

'Right. Number one. Why can't you, at least in the first instance, employ a lawyer to call upon your wife and find out where she stands? She may have left you in a huff and now be prepared to think things over. Surely you can't lose by this.'

'She did not leave me in a huff, as you put

46

it. This was a carefully premeditated move. She is at present living with her family, because where she is her family is virtually above the law. But should there be any suggestion that the law, in the person of a lawyer, is entering our dispute, she will leave her home and go elsewhere. At the moment, I know where she is. If she disappears from there our task may be insoluble.'

'I'd like to come back to this above-the-law business, if I may. But question number two. Why can't you go to her yourself?'

'Because the moment I set foot in her father's house, I would be killed.'

'You seem determined to ruin my digestion,' Jessica pointed out. 'So let's move on to number three. Just what did you quarrel about, to make her so anti?'

'I would prefer not to discuss that until you have agreed to work for me.'

'That's not too unreasonable, I suppose. So let me get this straight. You wish me to go to this place where your wife is living, call on her, try to persuade her to bring your son back, and...'

'If you do that, Miss Jones, you may well wind up dead yourself. I wish you to visit my wife, yes. But under no circumstances must she discover that you are working for me.'

'Then why should she receive me?'

'Again, I will tell you that when you are on my team. But she will, providing she does not suspect you come from me. You will have an opportunity to look over the house and the

47

situation, and make your plans.'

'To kidnap your son. You do realize that you are asking me, a police officer, to break the law?'

'There is no law where you will be going.'

'Where I am concerned, there is law everywhere. Certainly ethical laws.'

'I can produce proof why my son must be freed from that woman.'

'Show me.'

'You will have to come to my home.'

'Ah. But if you have such proof, then you have a legal case.'

'I have told you that these people do not deal in legalities.'

'You are starting to sound as if this son of yours could be the heir to something big.'

Smith's face seemed to close.

'I would have to know what I am getting into,' Jessica said.

'When you have agreed to get into it. Will you dine with me tomorrow night? My chauffeur will collect you. I have your address.'

Jessica gazed at him. This man is either dangerously aggrieved, she thought, or part of something very sinister. And I have got to be mad even to be considering his offer. But ... one million pounds? That was crazy even to think about.

On the other hand, simply because he was either dangerous or sinister, or both, he was worth investigating as a police officer. What she should do, of course, was take the whole business to Adams tomorrow morning and

48

let him handle it. But he would kiss her off. She had absolutely no proof that this conversation had ever taken place, no proof of this man's identity, no proof that he was actually a father, and, incidentally, no proof that he actually did have a million to spare.

But surely she could find out all of those things without actually committing herself?

'All right, Mr Smith,' she said. 'I'll dine with you. Without prejudice.'

'Hi.'

'You free?'

'Oh, sure. Nobody's coming to London right now.'

'Do you have any leave coming up?'

'I have ten days still due. You're not inviting me to vacation with you? Wowee! I accept.'

'I'm inviting you to work with me, one last time.'

'Like I said, wowee! I accept.'

'Then if you can get rid of your friend Josie this evening, I'll come round and talk to you.'

'So have you made any plans?' Tom asked as he dressed for dinner. The ambassador was, as usual, intent on living it up. He eyed Jessica's most expensive black underwear. 'It looks as if you have some for tonight.'

'Maybe.' Jessica put on a white shirt, took out her dark blue trouser suit.

'I think you need to tell me about it.'

'Well, I don't.'

'You are not on duty,' he pointed out. 'But

49

that suit is especially cut to contain a shoulder holster.'

Jessica put on the pants. 'It's nice to know you take such an interest in my clothes.'

'So what's up?'

Jessica opened her top drawer, took out her shoulder holster, and strapped it on. Then she put on the jacket. None of the straps showed in front, even when the jacket was opened, and as Tom had remarked, the left shoulder and armpit were so cut as to entirely conceal the bulk of the holster. She now checked her Skorpion to make sure it was fully loaded, then placed it in the holster and buttoned the jacket.

'As you're not on duty,' Tom said, 'you do realize that you're breaking the law by carrying a concealed weapon, or indeed by carrying a weapon at all.'

'Are you going to arrest me?'

'I just think I am entitled to know what's going on.'

'I have been invited out to dinner by a gentleman I don't altogether trust; that's all.'

'And if he tries to get his hand in your knickers, you intend to blow his whatsit off? Isn't that going over the top?'

'I'll tell you about it some time. There's the phone. Have fun with your ambassador.' She picked up the street phone.

'Miss Jones?'

'I'll be right down.'

Predictably, it was a Rolls. Jessica wondered if Tom was looking down on her. More

50

importantly, she hoped Andrea was in position. She carefully hesitated on the pavement before getting into the car; it was just growing dark, so anyone who knew her by sight would have no trouble identifying her.

'Is it far?' she asked.

'Farnham, madam. It will take about an hour. Would you like some music?'

'That would be nice.'

'Classical or modern?'

'I think classical.'

He inserted a CD and she was shrouded in Chopin. At least it was lively enough to keep her awake. She knew the chauffeur was watching her in his mirror, so she couldn't look through the rear window to see if Andrea was behind them, but there was a lot of traffic, and even, as they drove at a very steady speed, overtakers from time to time.

'Have you been with Mr Smith long?' she asked, fishing for a name in reply.

'Not very, madam. I come with the car.'

'You mean he hired you for this evening?'

'No, madam. He hired me for six months.'

'Ah.'

So Mr Smith was a transient. But if he had actually hired the car for six months, he was not being transient on her account. And the house, if a rental, was clearly pricey. They drove through an electrically controlled gateway from which high walls led away to each side; Jessica could only hope that they were not topped with broken glass, although Andrea would undoubtedly be wearing

51

adequate clothing as well as gloves. And as far as she could make out, there were no dogs, which fitted in with Smith's impermanence, at least at this address. Additionally there were several very climbable trees just outside the walls, and the distance from them to the front door she estimated at not more than fifty yards, well within the range of a high-powered infra-red camera.

At the doors there were a butler and a couple of footmen, and a tray of champagne, and Smith himself, beaming at her from the entrance to a very well-furnished drawing-room. 'Miss Jones. JJ. May I call you JJ?'

'That's reserved for my friends and colleagues.'

'But we are going to be both friends and colleagues, are we not? Smith and Jones! What could be better? Welcome to my home. At the moment, my lonely home.' He sat beside her on a settee. 'Have you considered my offer?'

'I'm waiting for it to be substantiated.'

'Of course. Straight to business. I like that. Very good. Now, I have taken the liberty of opening four accounts for you.'

'You're jumping the gun again.'

'In the event that you agree to work for me, I wish there to be no delay.'

'And if I do not agree to work for you?'

'I can always reclaim the money. Now, the four accounts are, respectively, in Nassau, the Caymans, Geneva, and Guernsey. They are in the names of, respectively, Amanda Black,

52

Brigitte Green, Charlotte White and Deirdre Brown. I have the mandates here for you to sign, and once you have done that, they will be delivered by courier to the two banks in Europe first thing tomorrow morning. The two on the other side of the Atlantic may take another twenty-four hours. Each account contains a quarter of a million pounds. You are welcome to start using the accounts as from tomorrow. I'm sure you're familiar with the requirements of the modern banking system. On that table there are four envelopes. In each there is the necessary information for each account, that is, account number, sorting code, date of birth, mother's maiden name, etc.'

'You must be a very trusting man, Mr Smith. What's to stop me closing all these accounts, putting the money in an account of my own, and giving you two fingers? I'm sure you'd have more sense than to come, or send someone, after me with a gun.'

Smith smiled. 'That quick brain again. You would shoot such an emissary before he could shoot you, would you not? I am a trusting man, and I am sure that you would not do such a thing as attempt to swindle me, but as you have suggested, I am also a sensible one. There is a caveat.'

'I thought there might be.'

'It is simply that on each account, only withdrawals of up to ten thousand pounds are permitted in any one day. The respective managers have been informed that while you

53

are an heiress, you are of a wayward and extravagant disposition, and this is your father's way of protecting you from yourself. So you see, if you were to telephone each bank every day you would be able to withdraw forty thousand pounds a day. That is to say, you would require twenty-five days to remove the entire amount, and the mission you are going to carry out for me will be over in far less time.'

'There you go again. The figures sound fine, Mr Smith, but I still need a good reason for sticking my neck out and risking the ruin of my career.'

'Even if some would say that it is already ruined? No matter. I have promised you proof. My wife's father is a very wealthy man, as I have told you. I talk in millions; he talks in billions. Unfortunately, he hates the western powers; thus he uses much of his wealth to finance various terrorist organizations.'

'Are you talking about Al Qaeda?'

Smith shrugged. 'You know more about these things than I do, I am sure.'

'Did you know this when you married his daughter?'

'No. Claudine uses her share of the family wealth to jet-set around the world. I met her on the beach at Phuket. She was – she is – a strikingly beautiful woman. I fell in love at first sight.'

'And is your current separation a result of your discovering her father's activities?'

'Not in so many words. I was of course

54

shocked, horrified, when I discovered it. But I do not believe the sins of the parents should be visited on the children. It took me some time to realize that she was his daughter more than my wife.'

'Tough. But if you'll forgive me, as a *dear* friend of mine would say, those are perceptions and attitudes. Your perceptions and attitudes. I still haven't seen anything to prove what you say.'

'You are a very hard-headed woman. I like that.' He got up, went to a roll-top desk against the far wall, opened it, and took out a sheet of paper. 'This is Claudine's farewell note.'

Jessica scanned it.

> You have failed me. You have failed the boy. You have failed his ancestors. And you have failed the Lord. I will leave you now. Follow me, and die. Seek the boy, now or ever, and die. When he grows to manhood, all those that oppose the Lord will die. Kanem will come with me. I will not touch your money. I will leave you to die in loneliness. Claudine.

'She sounds fairly agitated. Can you prove she wrote this?'

'Here.' From the desk he took several more sheets of paper. These were mundane notes on various household matters, even what looked like a laundry list, but the handwriting was undoubtedly the same.

'Who is this Kanem?'

'Her servant.' Smith's mouth twisted. 'I had thought he was *my* servant.'

'And who is this "Lord" she refers to?'

'It is a term for her grandfather. The family greatly respects him.'

Jessica had no doubt that he was lying. 'So it would appear.'

'So?'

Jessica considered at a rate of knots. If this Claudine's family was mixed up with Al Qaeda, or any other international terrorist group, it was something the department would wish her at least to investigate, supposing they believed her ... which at the moment they wouldn't. On the other hand, the risks appeared monumental, especially as she would be entirely without any back-up. Unless... 'There are a couple more questions, I'm afraid.'

'I thought there might be. But shall we discuss them over dinner?'

The meal was almost as good as that at The Ivy, the wine close to being superior, the table a long glitter of silver and crystal, the service – apart from the butler there were two waiters – immaculate.

'Now tell me what you wish to know,' Smith invited.

'Just three things, now. You have described Claudine's father as being worth billions. What is her grandfather, this "Lord", worth?'

'He is actually the man with the money. But

his son has the spending of it.'

'And may I ask, what is the source of your wealth?'

He shrugged. 'Why should I be coy about it? Claudine came to me with a very substantial dowry, which I was able to invest and multiply.'

'And she has decided not to take it back. She can't be all bad.'

'You have never met her.'

'But if I do as you wish, you tell me that I am going to. Suppose I get into her house, and can't get out?'

Smith spread his hands on the table. 'I picked you for this task, JJ, because I estimate, judging by your record, as for example, the destruction of Korman or the raid on the headquarters of Ramon Cuesta, you are perhaps the only person in the world who could successfully gain access to my son and bring him out. But I do understand the risks; that is why I am prepared to pay you so well.'

'I'm glad of that. But on both those two businesses you mention, I had considerable back-up.'

'Yes. Unfortunately, I do not think a man would be allowed into my wife's company.'

'But a woman would.'

He regarded her for several seconds. 'Is there a woman who would risk it? And who would be of any value to you?'

'I think I can find one.'

'Would she be trustworthy?'

'Yes. I will also need access to arms. We

cannot carry our own on international flights or across borders without risking being stopped.'

'Of course. You understand that if my son is harmed in any way, your credit will immediately evaporate?'

'I understand that. And your wife, and any servants or bodyguards who may be around?'

'I accept that you must protect yourself, JJ. I will give you an address in Kano where you may obtain what you require. Now listen very carefully. My grandfather-in-law controls a religious sect. Thus the "Lord". Such is the way of the world, and especially the female half of it, that he obtains acolytes from every walk of life, including the so-called North Atlantic Community. These essentially innocent people have no idea what it is all about. They believe they are joining a vast movement dedicated to world peace.' Another visit to the desk and he gave her a small booklet. 'You should read this. You, and your aide, will visit Kano as would-be converts to this sect. People do this all the time. You will be required to pay an entrance fee of a thousand dollars each, and to guarantee a continuing yearly subscription of five hundred dollars. This is of course irrelevant in your case, although I will provide you with two thousand dollars in cash should you be required to pay your entrance fee before gaining access to my wife.'

'But we will gain access?'

58

'Oh, indeed. All would-be acolytes have to be vetted before admission. My wife used to take part in this, as regards female applicants, before our marriage. Now that she has returned she will undoubtedly be doing so again. Now, tomorrow I will arrange your flights to Kano. All I require is the name of your associate. As it is highly unlikely that anyone in northern Nigeria will ever have heard of you, you will use your own names. In any event, you will be on holiday, not duty, and that will save any delay while false passports are arranged. So, will you give me the name?'

'I don't think that would be much good until I discover whether she's willing to stick her neck out. I'll let you have it tomorrow. Now tell me how we get back out with some religious sect on our tails?'

'There is an international airport at Kano. You will fly in on a scheduled flight, and when your business is completed, you will fly out, but by private jet, which will be waiting for you.'

'The last time I worked to such an arrangement I had a very unpleasant experience.'

'In Bolivia, of course. But you were betrayed. And, of course, you shot your way out. How many people did you kill?'

'I have absolutely no idea. It's not an episode I care to remember.'

'Well, this time there will be no betrayal. I want my son.'

'Of course. Because he is his grandfather's

heir, right?'

'That is one reason, certainly.'

'What about afterwards? The rest of his life. And yours.'

'I will have to protect him. Perhaps I will invite you to be my chief bodyguard.'

'First things first. That was a lovely dinner, Mr Smith.' She pushed back her chair. 'I hate to gobble and go, but I have a lot to think about.'

'Would you not like a snort? I have only the very best.'

'Mr Smith, please. I am a police officer.'

'Well, then, would you not prefer to do your thinking here? I would be very gratified were you to spend the night.'

'Ah ... no. I am sleeping with somebody else tonight.'

'What a shame. But may I take it that you accept my proposition?'

'I will let you know when I call you tomorrow.'

'But you will sign the mandates?'

Jessica considered, briefly. 'Why not?' She did so, using the four different names as indicated. 'Will your car take me home, or shall I call a taxi?'

'My car will take you home, of course.'

'Well, then, will you see me out?' He walked her to the door. The outside lights were on, and on the porch they were bathed in brilliance. Jessica stood with her back to the waiting Rolls, and held Smith's hands, to his obvious pleasure. This meant that he was facing past the car at the trees lining the property's wall. 'I have enjoyed meeting you, and I have enjoyed dinner,' she said, putting years of practice at docile dissembling into use. 'I do hope to be able to call you tomorrow and say yes.'

'I shall look forward to that, JJ.'

She had held him long enough. She squeezed his fingers and then got into the car.

Jessica switched on the reading light and flicked through the booklet on the drive home. It seemed fairly innocuous and extremely hackneyed, talked of universal love and brotherhood, an end to violence, the rule of the Lord, and somewhere described as the Centre of the Universe, which was not identified. The only interesting piece of information was that it claimed that the Followers of the Lord numbered ten million. If they had each paid a thousand dollars to join up, and were each paying five hundred dollars a year in membership fees, she could understand that he was not short of a bob or two. What was thought-provoking, however, was that she doubted there were ten million people in Africa capable of maintaining that level of subscription, so maybe he did have acolytes scattered all over the place. Quite apart from 'Smith's' problem, that might be worth investigating.

As it was only eleven when she got in, Tom was not yet home. She said goodbye to the chauffeur, went up to the flat, used her mobile. 'You home yet?'

'A couple of blocks. I had to park some distance away, and then wait for you to leave. And guess what? You were tailed.'

'Say again?'

'There was a car lurking in the shadows. Which pulled out and followed you back to London. He didn't stay too close, so I guess he had some kind of up-market GPS system. Anyway, I let him get on with it, as I didn't want him to spot me. You had any trouble?'

'Not so far. How did you get on?'

'I think I got a couple of good shots. Not that that tree was a very stable platform. Shall I come round? I'm dying to know how it went.'

'Tom may be home at any moment. We'll get together tomorrow.'

'We can't do it here. Wednesday is Josie's day off. There's no way she's going to get out of bed until noon.'

'Okay. The coffee shop on the corner, ten o'clock.'

She put down the phone, and saw that Tom hadn't drawn the blinds before going out. She went to the window, casually looked down, and saw a movement on the street. It was just a flicker, only picked up by her highly trained eyes, and then was gone. As she was not given to imagining things, she had no doubt there had been someone watching her flat, or else why disappear so urgently the moment she appeared at the window? She reckoned Mr Smith was keeping an eye on his investment

... or someone was keeping an eye on Mr Smith.

After the usual exchange with Tom – fortunately, coping with the ambassador was keeping him too tired to be interested in partnership rights – she met Andrea and brought her up to date. The photographs were better than she had expected. 'Wowee,' Andrea said. 'I'm in. How much do I get?'

'I think we should split it down the middle, as we'll be taking the same risk.'

'Give me a line on that.'

'Well, these people have links to terrorist organizations, and they appear to have an Arab background...'

'So if we were men, and they captured us trying to make off with their future king or whatever, they'd probably cut off our prospects. But as we're women, we don't have any prospects.'

'You'd be surprised. In some parts of Africa they practise female circumcision.'

'You have got to be kidding me.'

'Look it up. In any event, I'm sure they'd find *some* bits of us to remove.'

Andrea put both hands over her breasts. 'But you're still going. For the money?'

'It's attractive. But there's more to it now. The whole thing stinks. I reckon an awful lot of what Smith has told me is a lie, or at least a distortion of the truth, apart from where his wife can be found. I think he knows she is going to react badly to us descending on her doorstep and trying to snatch her child. And he knows we are not going to lie down and be trampled on; my record indicates that. He hasn't seen yours yet. So he reckons there is a good chance of her stopping a bullet, or in any event, the whole business in which she is involved being blown wide open, without him being remotely involved.'

'But what about his son? For whom he is paying a million pounds?'

'I don't think he gives a damn about his son. He'd like him to go up with his mother. And if we don't come back, the money reverts to him.'

'There's a thought. Supposing we *do* come back, and he has already reclaimed it?'

'Wouldn't work. Because if we come back, we'll have the boy with us, and be in a position to blow *his* little game, whatever it is, apart. Even six-year-old kids can be lucid.'

'Um. Listen, if this thing is as big as you seem to think it is, shouldn't we bring in the department? Go to Adams?'

'That was my first reaction. But he would not believe us, Andie. We have absolutely no proof that anything I have told you isn't just a nightmare. We don't even know Smith's real name, although I hope you're going to be able to pencil that in. If it really is big, when we come back we'll have the proof to bring the department in. On our terms.'

'And of course there's always the money.'

'That too. So, are you still in? I don't think I can swing it without you.'

'Oh, I'm in. If I have to die screaming, I'd like to be next to you.'

'Good girl. How soon can you arrange a week's leave? We won't need more than that.'

'I'll do that this afternoon.'

'They'll quibble at the lack of notice.'

'I'll tell them you've invited me to go on holiday with you. Well, you have, haven't you?' She giggled. 'They'll think we're off on an affair.'

'Hope springs eternal. Okay. Make your leave from the weekend; Smith still has to arrange our flights. You go to the Yard and arrange it. But also find out what you can about Smith. Try Bill Storey. He has the hots for you. If you let him feel your ass he'll do anything for you. We want an ID on that picture, and we want it today. We also want anything known on some place called the Centre of the Universe.'

'Oh, I know where that is,' Andrea said. 'It's in Delphi, in Greece. A piece of stone sticking up out of the ground at the Shrine of Apollo.'

'I don't think we're talking about the same place. See what you can turn up, and come back to me.'

Jessica returned to the flat. It was past noon, and Smith had said that the mandates, at least for the two European banks, would be delivered first thing this morning. It was time to test both his honesty and his efficiency. She decided to try Guernsey first.

'European District Bank. Good morning.

65

May I help you?'

'Good morning. I'd like to make a credit transfer, please.'

'I'll just put you through.'

There were a series of clicks, then another woman said, 'Good morning. Your name, please?'

Jessica had the appropriate envelope open in front of her. 'Deirdre Brown.'

'Deirdre Brown.' Click click. 'Oh, yes, Miss Brown.' The voice had changed. 'Your mandate came in an hour ago.'

'I wish to make a transfer into the account of a friend of mine.'

'Of course, Miss Brown. Will you give me the account number and the sorting code, please? Of your account.'

Jessica read off the figures.

'Thank you. May I have the date of your birth, please?'

'December 16th, 1970.' If he had accurately summed up her character, Smith was being quite generous with her age.

'And your mother's maiden name?'

'Birch.'

'Would you give me the account number, please?'

Jessica did so.

'And the first and third figures of your code number.'

Jessica checked the paper. 'Four and eight.'

'Thank you. What amount would you like to transfer?'

'Firstly, will you give me the balance?'

66

'Two hundred and fifty thousand and thirty-four pounds. We calculate interest on a daily basis on large balances.'

Jessica had forgotten about interest. Even at the low rates currently in operation the four accounts would be generating something like twenty-five thousand a year.

'Thank you. I'd like to transfer five hundred pounds to the account of Miss Jessica Jones.' She gave the name and address of her bank, the account number, and the sorting code.

'Very good, Miss Brown.'

'When will that be done?'

'This afternoon, Miss Brown.'

'Thank you.' Jessica did the same with the bank in Geneva, with the same satisfactory result. So the money was there and available. She was strongly tempted to start moving the whole ten thousand from each account, but she had nowhere to move it to, at the moment, save her own account, and just in case things went wrong she wanted to keep her nose clean as long as possible. As she had told Andrea, when they returned with the boy they would hold all the trump cards, at least long enough to extract all the money and create their own bank accounts.

She wondered if Andrea's suggestion had been more accurate than she had been prepared to admit. To someone who had never had more than her salary to live on, the idea of possessing half a million pounds of her own was certainly mind-consuming. So was she on her way to becoming a bent cop?

She refused to admit that, either. There *was* something going on which needed investigation. And she *would* be ignored if she went to Adams, certainly at this moment in her career.

And she had a strong desire to cock a snook at the department, prove to them that she was too good at her job to be cast aside like a worn-out glove. She felt that was childish, but also that it could well be true.

She telephoned the number Smith had given her. 'Good morning, JJ. I hope it is a good morning?'

'It's a point of view. My partner will be Miss Andrea Hutchins.'

Smith apparently wrote it down. 'Very good. Your flight leaves Heathrow at noon on Sunday. You will be flying Lufthansa via Frankfurt. Your tickets and all other necessary information will be delivered to your flat by my chauffeur tomorrow afternoon. You should now make no further attempt to contact me until you return to England with my son.'

'Suppose there is something in these instructions I don't understand, or can't handle?'

'JJ, I picked you for this assignment because your record indicates that there is nothing you are not capable of understanding, and no situation you are incapable of handling. Have a good journey and I hope to hear from you in a few days' time.'

The phone went dead. Well, bugger you,

68

Jessica thought. She rang her bank, ascertained that two five-hundred-pound deposits had been paid into her account, and had herself put through to the manager.

'Why, Miss Jones, how good to hear from you. Is there a problem?'

'Not really. It's just that I have recently sold some property I've inherited.'

'How very nice for you.'

'Thank you. What I would like to do is open a separate account into which the money can be paid until I can sort things out. I have to go away on assignment, you see.'

'Of course. I understand.' He knew she was in the Protection Unit. 'I'll arrange that for you.'

'I'll need the number and code.'

'Of course. My secretary will come back to you first thing tomorrow, and send over a mandate.'

'Thank you ever so much. The first payments will arrive tomorrow afternoon, and I hope to be in touch in a week or so. I also need some foreign currency. Could you tell me the currency used in Nigeria?'

'Ah ... the naira.'

'Say again?'

'The naira. It's made up of one hundred kobo.'

'Are you sure you're not pulling my leg?'

'That's what they use, Miss Jones.'

'But I suppose they also take credit cards?'

'In the big cities, I would say.'

'Right. Well, could you let me have a

69

hundred pounds worth of ... naira, is it? Tomorrow morning, if possible.'

'Certainly. I'll have it delivered by messenger. To the Yard?'

'To my flat.'

'Will do.'

As promised, next morning at nine the secretary called with the necessary figure, and the messenger soon followed with the cash, which looked suspiciously like monopoly money. That afternoon Jessica did the round of the banks again, making four transfers of ten thousand. In each case she had the same conversation. 'I understand Daddy has made a rule that I can only have ten thousand of my inheritance a day.'

'I'm afraid that is so, Miss Brown,' said the woman in Guernsey.

'That's okay. No problem. It's just that I have to go away for a week. Do you think I could make a standing order for you to transfer ten thousand a day until further notice, or until the money runs out?'

'Well, I'm not sure that is what your father intended.'

'But if I didn't have to go away, I'd make the transfers myself, right?'

'Well, I suppose so. I should think that would be all right, Miss Brown.'

'Thank you.' She wondered if 'Smith' had thought of that. But even if he was planning to close the facility the moment she was out of the country, she reckoned she'd still pick up at least a hundred and twenty grand.

It was just coming up to noon, and Tom was obviously not coming in for lunch. She surveyed the larder, opted for a tin of soup and some biscuits, emptied the soup into a saucepan, switched on the hotplate, and wandered to the window to look down.

And saw a man on the far side of the street.

Three

Kano

Jessica stepped back, turned off the stove. She had no intention of being hounded by 'Smith's' underlings. But after her experience of being kidnapped a few months ago, in broad daylight and entirely because, being off duty, she had been totally relaxed, she was no longer disposed to take risks.

She went into the bedroom, took out the Skorpion, tucked it into the back of her waistband, pulled on a jacket to conceal it, and the street bell rang.

She picked up the phone, hoping it was Andrea. 'Yes?'

It was a man. 'Detective-Sergeant Jones? I'd like to speak with you, please.'

'If you have the right address, you are doing that.'

'I meant face to face.'

71

Jessica let the phone hang from its cord and went back to the window; the man was still there. So there were two of them, at least, and at noon on a Thursday the street was entirely deserted. In all probability, so was the building.

She went back to the phone, which was asking, somewhat plaintively, 'Are you there, Miss Jones?'

'I'm here. But I don't think it would be a good idea for us to talk right now. Come back this evening.'

'This is very important, Miss Jones. It could be a matter of life or death. Your life or death.'

The accent was American, Park Avenue rather than Canal Street. That was interesting.

'Trust me,' the man requested. 'I'm a cop like you. Well, in a manner of speaking.'

Which was more interesting yet, if true. 'So tell me what you know about Mr Smith.'

'It is Mr Smith I wish to talk about. I think we may have a mutual interest.'

'Okay,' Jessica decided. 'Come up. One of you.'

She released the street door, unlocked the flat door, and stood against the wall behind it. She drew the Skorpion and held it in her right hand, resting on her shoulder. She listened to feet on the stairs; if there were more than one set the other man was tip-toeing.

There was a brief rap. 'It's open.'

The door swung in, and the man stepped

into the flat. 'Miss Jones?'

Jessica drew a deep breath, and used all her force to close the door. The man received it on the shoulder and staggered sideways. The door slammed and Jessica levelled the gun, now held in both hands, at his head.

He had fallen against the wall. Now he straightened, holding his arm. 'Jesus Christ,' he gasped. 'Do you always open the door like that?'

'Is there another way?' Jessica flicked the latch shut. 'Take off your jacket.'

He gazed at her. He was actually quite a pleasant-looking man, tall and well built without being heavy, and had rounded features, with a wide mouth and lazy brown eyes. His hair was also brown, thick and wavy. She put him down as in his early forties.

But she was still not disposed to take risks. 'The jacket. Nice and slow.'

He removed the jacket; there was no holster.

'Now turn round.'

He obeyed. 'If you're looking for a weapon, I was told I couldn't wear one in England.'

'You'd be surprised how many people are ignorant of the law. Okay, let's have a badge.'

'We don't actually carry badges.'

'CIA? You must have some form of identity.'

'In my jacket pocket.'

'So take it out. Remembering always that shooting people is my hobby.'

'I believe you.' He extracted the ID wallet, opened it for her.

73

'Agent Jackson Smollett. So have a seat, Agent Smollett. Would you like a cup of tea?'

'I sure need something. You wouldn't happen to have a cold beer?'

'There should be some in the fridge. Help yourself.'

He did so, pulled the ring, turned back to her. 'You aiming to keep pointing that thing at me?'

'It's a habit. Don't worry, it only goes off when I squeeze the trigger.' She sat in a straight chair, waved the pistol at the settee. 'So tell me about Smith.'

'I was hoping that you were going to tell me.'

'I asked you first, and I have the gun.'

'Good point. Right. You are Detective-Sergeant Jessica Jones, and you are a member of the Scotland Yard Special Branch.'

'What I would really like,' Jessica said, 'is for you to tell me something that I don't already know.'

'Right. You are investigating Matthieu.'

'Who?'

Smollett gave her an old-fashioned look. 'You don't know his name?'

'If we're talking about Smith, no. Because I am not investigating him. He invited me out to lunch.'

'You mean dinner.'

'That too.'

'You mean you already knew him?'

'I had never heard of him until five days ago.'

'But you went out to lunch with him, and then to dinner at his house. What was it? Love at first sight?'

'We seem to have our numbers crossed,' Jessica pointed out. 'This is my flat, I am the one with the gun, and I am the one who is asking the questions. If that is unacceptable to you, there's the door.'

'Hold it. I thought we were on the same side.'

'Convince me.'

He drew a deep breath. 'If I fill you in on Matthieu, will you tell me what your angle is?'

'I might.'

'It's a long story.'

'I have no plans for this afternoon.'

'Can I smoke?'

'No.'

'Right. Does the name Coleby mean anything to you?'

Jessica frowned. 'There was some kind of celebrity whiz-kid by that name. A few years back.'

'Edwin Coleby. Spoke Latin when he was four. Understood calculus at five. Spoke Greek at six. Could multiply twelve figures each way in his head. Was reputed to have memorized the entire Encyclopaedia Britannica by the age of fourteen. Claimed by some to be the greatest brain the world has ever seen.'

Jessica nodded. 'I remember. And then, like so many raving geniuses, he died young.

About six years ago. Something about a fire.'

'He didn't die, Miss Jones. He was pushed. But there was a fire.'

'Say again?'

'He went into hospital for a minor operation on his toes at the De Groot Clinic in Chicago, and never came out. Neither did a lot of other people. While he was on the table, the whole two upper floors of the clinic exploded.'

'Holy shit!' Jessica commented. 'How many went?'

'No one ever worked that out. The blast was so severe, the heat generated so great, that quite a few of the bodies were incinerated. That includes both Coleby and De Groot himself. Probably the greatest brain, and certainly the greatest transplant surgeon in the world, just like that.'

'If all the bodies were incinerated, how can you be sure?'

'Forensics were able to prove that the operation was in progress when the explosion took place, and that it took place in the theatre.'

'Wait just a moment. You are saying that Coleby went into hospital for a minor operation, and this was carried out by Adrian De Groot himself? The world's greatest transplant surgeon? What was he having? A complete set of new toes?'

'There are several aspects of the case that remain unclear.'

'But you don't think it was a leaking gas

76

main.'

'No, Miss Jones. Like I said, the bodies in the theatre were entirely incinerated. We can't even be sure exactly how many there were; the best estimate is about six. But our forensic people found traces of melted lead in the remains. There was no lead used in the theatre. Again, best estimates are that at least some of the victims were shot.'

'By someone else who was present, who then set up the explosive. So who was he trying to kill? Coleby, or De Groot?'

'No one has any idea. Neither man had any known enemies. Both were exceptionally well known, in, shall I say, clean and above-board walks of life.'

'But someone got in there and blew them both up. Rough. How does this relate to Mr Smith? Or Matthieu? Or whoever?'

'Well, as you can imagine, the investigation was very thorough. Everyone in the hospital was interviewed, all patients checked out, all comings and goings recorded, everyone accounted for, with one exception. Or rather, three exceptions. Two men and a woman left the clinic shortly before the explosion. Quite a few people did that, but all exits were recorded, and these people were either checked out and found to be clean, or came forward with the same result. All except these three people. One of the men signed them out as Mr John Smith.'

Jessica put down the gun and made herself a

77

cup of tea. 'Do you know how many John Smiths there are in the world?'

'Sure,' Smollett acknowledged. 'But we had a little more. The woman, who was apparently his wife, or so he said, was on a hospital trolley, having apparently just undergone minor surgery, and the two orderlies who saw them out are convinced that she was pregnant.'

'How many months?'

'They couldn't be sure, but they reckoned about six.'

'They reckoned? Surely her exact condition was in the clinic's records?'

'No, it was not. Again the entry is simply, Mrs Smith, Mr De Groot's patient, minor operation. There is no mention of her being pregnant. Nor is there any mention of what this "minor" operation was for. Just that she was De Groot's private patient.'

Jessica sat down again. She thought of the woman who had written that so chilling note to her husband. If Smith-Matthieu *was* her husband. 'So, relate this to our Mr Smith.'

'Well, tracing her turned out to be an impossible job. Obviously the name was false. All we had to work on was that pregnancy. But was it five, six, or seven months?'

'So which did it turn out to be?'

'I have no idea, Miss Jones. We never found her. We reckon she, they, left the country immediately after the explosion.'

Jessica put down her teacup. 'Forgive me for wondering just what we are talking about, why we are talking about it.'

'We did not give up, Miss Jones. We never do. We were tracing what we knew of the explosive, seeing if there were any links to any terrorist organization; no dice there. And no one, no group, has ever claimed responsibility, which is itself odd. We were tracking all births which took place four to two months after the explosion, until we had to conclude, as I said, that she had left the country. We were hunting for motives, even for any relationship between De Groot and Coleby, all without getting anywhere. But eventually we got our break.'

'I'm fascinated.' Actually, she was.

'We had people going through every newspaper for the past ten years, just looking for any acquaintances of either Coleby or De Groot who might provide an answer. And last year one of our researchers turned up a photograph in a British paper, taken six months before the explosion, of two men. One was De Groot. The other was a Mr Henri Matthieu.'

'But presumably this photograph was taken in England, if it was a British paper.'

'It was still a lead. It was the only lead we have ever got.'

'Let me get you another beer. So who is Henri Matthieu?'

'Swiss-born, English-naturalized millionaire and international playboy.'

'Who once had his photo taken with Adrian De Groot. That's evidence?'

79

'We were able to discover that Matthieu and his pregnant wife, name of Claudine, were in the States in the spring of 1998. That is, the time of the explosion. Don't tell me that is just too circumstantial to stand up. We know it. But we thought it might be a good idea to put him under surveillance, which has been my team's job for the past couple of months. With absolutely nothing to report, until two nights ago he entertains a glamorous blonde to dinner.'

'You're so kind.'

'My pleasure, Miss Jones. Well, routine. We followed you home, got your name and address, did some research, and what do you know? Said blonde turns out to be a high-powered Special Branch operative. So, that's my story.'

'Not quite. You say you have been keeping Matthieu under constant surveillance. Round the clock. So tell me what time I arrived there.'

'We have to eat, and do one or two other things. My man wasn't there when you arrived. But he was there when you left.'

So he hadn't seen Andrea taking up position. But he was clearly the man she had seen following the Rolls. 'May I also assume that you have investigated Matthieu's immediate background? Like, you know his wife has left him?'

'I know she's away right now. With the kid. One of my people saw them leave.'

'Did Matthieu see them off?'

'Not from the house, as I recall. He had left earlier in the day to go up to town.'

'And your man didn't follow him?'

'He had some trouble with his car. While he was calling for a replacement, he says he saw Mrs Matthieu and the kid get into a taxi, and they didn't come back. You say she's left him. How do you know that?'

'He told me so, over dinner.'

'And this is important?'

'It could be. If you are right about him being the bomber, then she must have been the pregnant woman. So at the very least she was an accomplice. Now they seem to have split up.'

'Say, that is a point. You say he told you where she went?'

'No,' Jessica said, looking into his eyes. 'If he knew where she has gone, he wouldn't have needed me.'

'I'm not with you.'

'Mr Matthieu got hold of me because, as you so kindly mentioned, I am a well-known police officer who has the reputation of being good at finding people. He wanted me to find his wife.'

'You mean he is employing Scotland Yard.'

'No. He is employing me. Or he would like to. In a private capacity.'

'That's interesting. So, presumably he gave you some ideas on how to find the lady?'

'I do not propose to find her, Mr Smollett. I am a serving police officer. I do not accept outside employment.'

He stared at her.

'So I'm afraid I cannot help you.'

'Listen, lady. I have just given you a lot of classified information.'

'I felt that you were being careless. But as I said, I am a serving police officer, and I will respect your confidence. Now, I hate to be rude, but I am expecting someone to tea, so...'

'You know,' Smollett said, 'the department never forgets a friend. Likewise, it never forgets an enemy.'

Jessica picked up the pistol, and stood up. 'You could say snap.'

Smollett rose in turn, picked up his jacket, and the street bell rang.

Jessica answered the phone. 'Hi,' Andrea said.

'Come right up.'

'You know there's a guy still watching your flat?'

'That's not a problem anymore. The doors are open.' She replaced the phone. 'It's been a pleasure, Mr Smollett. If you don't mind, I won't shake your hand. You might just be a black belt or something, in which case I would have to break your arm.'

Smollett put on his jacket. 'You think you're pretty hot stuff.'

'Mr Smollett; karate is a sport. It is a very good sport, although in the wrong hands it can be dangerous. I was trained, by the SAS, of whom you may have heard, to put people out of action, sometimes for a long time, sometimes forever. It's not a sport to me.'

He snorted and turned to the door as it opened.

'Well, hello there,' Andrea said.

'Why don't you fuck yourself,' Smollett said, and went down the stairs.

'I do like polite men.' Andrea closed the door. 'Is that the end or the beginning of a beautiful friendship?'

'It never existed. Tea?'

'You bet. Have I got news for you.'

'I have a little for you, too.' Jessica poured. 'You go first.'

'Well, this guy Smith is really named Matthieu.'

'I know. Friend Smollett, he who just left, told me that.'

'Oh.' Andrea looked crestfallen.

'But I'm sure you have more than that.'

'Ah. Yes. About his wife.'

'Give.'

'Well, she's the daughter of a man named Kwarism, who lives in a place called Kano.'

'I know that too. That's where we're going. Sunday night.'

'Oh. Right. I suppose you know about her grandfather too.'

'I know she has a grandfather.'

'Ah.' Andrea brightened. 'Does the name Ukuba mean anything to you?'

Jessica frowned. 'It rings a little bell.'

'He's a kind of guru, but in a pretty big way. He toured the world about ten years ago, airing his views that the only thing wrong was excessive civilization and technology. I don't suppose that's very original, but he was at least prepared to practise what he preached. The papers gave him a lot of space when he took an entire floor at the Royal Oak, had the furniture and fittings moved out, and slept on the floor in the middle of his followers. Apparently he made quite a few converts.'

'About ten million, at the last count,' Jessica said thoughtfully.

'Is that a fact? Well, people go to see him to get rid of all their angst, and presumably feel better for it.'

'That's our cover, seeking refuge from our angst.'

'Oh. I'm rather fond of my angst. All of it. Anyway, the bottom line is, there is apparently no record of the sect ever having any links to terrorism or indeed any political significance.'

'Save that there are those ten million people scattered around the world who obey this Ukuba's every word. And this bloke lives in Kano?'

'No, no. No one quite knows where he lives, but it's supposed to be Chad.'

'I hope you are going to be a little more specific than that. Chad is getting on for five hundred thousand square miles. That is like Germany and France lumped together with something left over.'

'But there's a lake. Also named Chad. Latest information is that he lives on an

84

island in this lake.'

Jessica took an atlas from her bookcase, studied it. 'Could be. As far as I can make out, Lake Chad is between Nigeria and the country of Chad, not to mention Cameroon.'

'You reckon this is important?'

'I don't reckon anything at the moment except that to live in a place which may or may not belong to any one of three countries can be very useful for someone who is up to no good. My brain is spinning. Listen.' She sat down and gave Andrea the gist of what Smollett had said.

'Are all these things related?'

'They usually are. I believe the CIA have got the right man, at least on the ground. So, Matthieu and his wife and a sidekick blew up the De Groot Clinic. Why?'

'To kill Coleby, or De Groot, or both.'

'I would say De Groot, as we do know that he and Matthieu had met only a couple of months earlier.'

'But why kill Coleby as well?'

'Maybe he was just unlucky to be there.'

'The bomb was planted in the theatre where Coleby was. That's a whole lot of bad luck.'

'Okay. So it was meant for them both. But why? Where's the connection?'

'I suppose we could track it down.'

'By putting in a few days of serious research. Only we don't have the days. But there is something else, which does not seem to have occurred to the CIA, because they're all men. Would any woman, several months pregnant with her first and, so far as I know, only child, take part in a bombing, in which she was actually in the building moments before the explosion, unless she had a compelling reason for being there?'

'Like what?'

'I haven't a clue. Unless she was the CO. But even that seems to have been taking an unnecessary risk. I reckon if we can find out her reason for being there, we're home.'

'You mean you're going ahead?'

'Have you lost interest in half a million?'

'No. But if this woman is a bomber...'

'She won't know who we are.'

'You reckon? You trust this Matthieu? It seems to me there's a lot going on that he hasn't told you.'

'Right. And for that reason there is a hell of a lot going on that we have to find out. People don't blow people up without a reason unless they're out-and-out terrorists. Equally, most terrorist organizations aren't slow in claiming responsibility, but no one ever did. Smith – or Matthieu, rather – suggested that there might be links to Al Qaeda, but you tell me there are no such links. Smollett never suggested it either, and I am sure the CIA would have covered every possibility. And as you said, there are no known political affiliations. The only certain link is to this Ukuba character.'

'Who preaches nothing but universal peace.'

'That makes me suspicious for a start. But

86

this Claudine will have the answers. I think having a chat with her could be very enlightening.'

'And suppose it's a set-up? A trap.'

'A trap for whom?'

'Well ... us.'

'Why on earth should Matthieu attempt to lay a trap for us? We're policewomen, of no value to anyone. He could only stir up trouble for himself.'

'Um.' Andrea hunched her shoulders. 'Except that we're acting off the cuff.'

'So nothing in life is certain. Are you in or not?'

'I've never seen you so, well ... agitated.'

'I am agitated. I'm agitated about my job, my love life, my future...'

'And you want to go out and take on the world.'

'And collect enough money to give Adams two fingers. So, yes or no?'

'Oh, I'll come. I reckon you need a nursemaid. But listen, if we're not on duty, can I wear janglies?'

'Wear what you like. Just look like a hippy with angst.'

'So what are your plans?' Tom asked over dinner.

'Do I gather that the ambassador isn't going out tonight?'

'He has caught a cold and thinks it's flu. He's cancelled all engagements for the next week, so...'

87

'I leave on Sunday.'

'Well, that gives us a couple of days. And once he goes I'm due for some leave. I could come with you.'

Shit, she thought. 'I'm sorry. I'm already booked.'

'You mean you're in a tour? Paying a supplement?'

'No. I have a travelling companion.'

'Oh, yes. Am I allowed to know her name?'

'Who said it's a her?'

'Look, are you deliberately trying to break up the happy home?'

'I was just testing. This is an old school friend.'

'Who you haven't seen for ten years.'

'Eh?'

'I know all your friends from that time.'

'Well, I bumped into Annie a few days ago, when I was planning this vacation. And I mentioned it to her, and she said she'd like to come along.'

Tom gazed at her. 'You're lying.'

'Oh? In that case...'

He was instantly contrite. 'I'm sorry, I'm sorry, I'm sorry. I don't want you going off in a huff. You do your own thing. But, as I'm free tonight, I thought maybe we could do something together. Just for a change.'

Jessica considered. But she really was very fond of him. And she had no idea when she would have sex again. If ever.

As promised, the next afternoon the Rolls

arrived, fortunately after Tom had left for the Yard, following a fond farewell; the ambassador had made a sudden recovery and was planning a trip to the Outer Hebrides, complete with bodyguards. 'You'll keep in touch.'

'If I can.'

'For God's sake, you're going on a tour, not to darkest Africa.'

'Ah ... of course.'

'You never did tell me where.'

'Ah ... Moscow. And then St Petersburg.'

'Sounds like fun. When do I see you again?'

'It's only a week's tour. Back next Sunday.'

The chauffeur gravely presented the parcel. 'Mr Smith said you would be expecting this, Miss Jones.'

'I was, thank you.'

'He asked me to give you a message. He wishes you good fortune and says he hopes to hear from you in a few days' time.'

'Again, thank him for me and tell him I'll be in touch.'

He left, and she placed the parcel on the dining table and cut the string. Inside were two British Airways first-class return tickets to Frankfurt, the return date being a week Sunday, and two first-class Lufthansa return tickets to Kano, this return date also being in a week's time. There was a note attached.

These return dates are necessary or you will certainly not be allowed into Nigeria. When you land in Kano, you

89

are booked in to the Majestic Hotel; your accommodation, for two, is paid for a week. If you decide to leave before the week is up, just do it. When you have checked in, you should go in the first instance to the shop of Elihu Masud. He is my agent and will give you the necessary information as regards the private jet which will bring you back. Masud will also provide you with firearms. This note should be memorized and burned.

There was also a cardboard wallet containing two thousand dollars. If Smollett hadn't called, she thought, she could almost feel that everything was on the up. But just what *was* going on? Matthieu had hired her because someone at the Yard had told him that she was free for at least a month and had a reputation as a killer. She didn't feel very proud about that, even if she had only ever fired a gun in self-defence; she considered that the people who really should feel guilty were those, like Commander Adams, who sent her on missions where they knew 'executive action' might be necessary because they knew she was the best they had ... and who were happy to drop her like a hot brick when questions began to be asked.

But there was no point in again working herself up into a fuss over that. Matthieu was the one who now mattered. He had hired her for those assets she was known to possess.

Therefore he expected her to use them. Against his wife? And why? Because he was afraid she would shop him over the bombing of the clinic? That seemed the most obvious answer. But it was also the most superficial. Of one thing she was certain: the business about getting his son back was pure pie in the sky; in her judgement, Matthieu did not care whether his son lived or died.

Again she wondered if she knew what she was doing. A million pounds had been such a pull, but that had been before she had known she had become mixed up with a mass murderer. Now the money had been taken over by the instincts of a policewoman. There was something very big roaming around out there: ten million people, a whole lot of money, and a whole lot of death. And she had, inadvertently, got herself in the middle of it. If she didn't see it through, and bring both Matthieu and his wife to justice, she'd never forgive herself.

And the million was still there!

She spent the next couple of days getting ready for her trip, having the required shots and obtaining her visa. She and Andrea met for lunch each day to compare notes and remind each other of items they might have forgotten. She had expected some further unwanted contact from the CIA, but there was none, and as far as she could tell, the watcher had been withdrawn.

Andrea was waiting for her at the check-in

desk. They both wore jeans and shirts and trainers and carried backpacks in an effort to look as much like tourists as possible. And Andrea was sporting a huge pair of jangly earrings, as she had threatened. Jessica had stuck to studs.

'Do we overnight in Frankfurt?' Andrea asked.

Jessica checked the tickets. 'No. We have a few hours to spare, though.'

Andrea looked disappointed, but relaxed over a gin and tonic once they were airborne.

'So how is Josie?' Jessica asked.

'Fed up that she's not coming with me, and you are.'

'Think of the welcome you'll get when you go home.'

Andrea made a face.

They had several hours to kill at Frankfurt, and after lunching – naturally on frankfurters – they left the airport and took a taxi into the city, strolled around and looked up at the forty-seven-metre-high Eschenheimer Tor, then wandered around St Bartholomew's Cathedral before finding a park to sit in the sun.

'Wouldn't it be lovely if we were actually on holiday,' Andrea said, 'with nothing to do but sightsee, eat, drink, and–'

'Down, girl,' Jessica recommended.

'Don't you ever get the urge ... well...'

'I get lots of urges. But I never let them get in the way of the job.'

'I do envy your self-discipline. Your single-mindedness.'

'And I'm counting on yours.' But she had to be kept happy, so Jessica squeezed her hand. 'Listen, if the urge ever overwhelms me, you'll be the first to know. Now let's get back to the airport.'

They took off into darkness, and were fed an excellent dinner. They had finished eating, and were contemplating visiting the loo before going to sleep, when two brandies arrived on their trays.

'We didn't order these,' Jessica told the hostess.

'They are the compliments of that gentleman.'

Andrea was in the aisle seat. Jessica leaned past her, and the gentleman raised his own glass. There were actually two men seated together. She had noticed them when they had been taking their seats. One was short and stout; he had the window seat and was invisible. The other, who was now smiling at her, was considerably larger, had massive shoulders and long legs, lank fair hair, and big, friendly features.

'What do you reckon?' she asked Andrea.

'It'll help us sleep.'

'I wasn't thinking of the brandy. Brace yourself.'

Because the large man was rising from his seat and coming towards them. 'I heard you speaking English,' he said. 'So how're things?'

He leaned on the back of the seat to look

93

down on them, brandy balloon in hand, thus putting Andrea's hair in imminent danger of an unusual shampoo.

'Up to this moment,' Jessica said, 'things have been fine. Thank you for the drinks.'

'I'm Giles.' He paused, expectantly.

'That's interesting. I've never known anyone named Giles before.'

'And you are ... Let me guess. Claudine.'

For the first time Jessica really studied his face. He didn't look like a villain ... but then villains seldom did. 'Do I look that French?'

'No, no. I just picked a beautiful name for a beautiful lady. Are you French?'

'Sadly, no.'

'Can't win 'em all, eh? And your friend?'

'If you'll take that glass away,' Andrea said, 'I might tell you.'

Giles drained it, and placed it on the tray.

'It's Andrea. And she's Jessica.'

'Oh, I like those. And you're on holiday, eh? Lagos? I must say, I wouldn't altogether recommend it for two gorgeous women on their own.'

'We're getting off in Kano,' Andrea said.

Shit, Jessica thought. Correctly.

'Why, so am I. We.'

'I imagine you're on business,' Jessica said.

'In a manner of speaking. But we'd be happy to keep an eye on you girls. Kano is even less safe for white women than Lagos.'

'I'm sure we'll manage.'

'No, no. I insist.'

'You would really be wasting your time.

94

We're lesbians.'

Giles jerked upright. So did Andrea.

'But anyway,' Jessica said, 'thanks for the drinks.'

Giles returned to his seat.

'Wow,' Andrea commented.

'You never know your luck,' Jessica said. 'But he needs keeping an eye on.'

'He's a creep.'

'Undoubtedly. But he called me Claudine.'

'So?'

'Claudine is the name of Matthieu's wife, remember?'

'Oh, shit! You reckon he's on to us?'

'On to us as what; that's the question.'

'It could be sheer coincidence.'

Jessica gave her an old-fashioned look.

She awoke at four, to gaze through her window at a brilliant dawn. She presumed they were over the Sahara, and however bright it was up here it was still utterly dark down there. And she was awake. That was a nuisance, because she knew she was going to brood, and now that they were actually launched she needed to think only of the next step – and the next step could only be calculated when it was encountered.

But it was disturbing how lonely, exposed, she felt, even with Andrea snoring gently beside her. Throughout her career she had operated with the umbrella of the force above her. Even with her kidnapping, however horrendous some of her experiences, she had never doubted that all the while the force was looking for her, closing in on her, determined to carry out both rescue and retribution. That she had rescued herself, by her own courage and determination, did not alter the fact that the force had always been behind her.

This time, she and Andrea had no one to turn to save themselves. Andie, of course, had complete confidence in her. Well, for that very reason she had complete confidence in Andie; together they had survived too many tricky situations. But it was still a heavy responsibility to be the brains as well as the driving force.

'Good morning everyone.' The senior hostess smiled at them. 'Time for breakfast. We'll be down in an hour.'

Andrea sat up with a grunt, and the hostess stood above them. 'Look!' She leaned across them. 'Isn't that tremendous?'

The sun was just beginning to reach the land beneath them, and there were no clouds. They were flying over the most lunar of landscapes, coloured an inhospitable light brick. To the far south there was a line of darkness, like a distant sea. Presumably that was forest.

'It always makes my blood tingle.' The trolley had arrived and she disbursed food and coffee.

'Just imagine coming down in it,' Jessica agreed. 'Where would Lake Chad be?'

The hostess thumbed eastward. 'Maybe four hundred miles away. Mind you, it's not

96

much to look at right now. This is the very end of the dry season, you see, and the lake is just one great bog. But it's due to start raining any day, and then it spreads pretty quickly.'

It occurred to Jessica that of all the many environmental sacrileges of which twenty-first century civilization was guilty, dumping an international airport within even five hundred miles of Kano had to rank with the worst. Certainly it was comparable with any she had been to in remote areas of the world. Their porter assured them that Kano handled some eighty flights a day, and looking at the signpost outside the terminal building, with its impressive list of destinations that ended in New Zealand, she could well believe it. Yet it left her with a feeling of depression.

Perhaps, she thought, it had something to do with P.C. Wren, one of her favourite novelists as a girl. John Geste's tragic wanderings across the Sahara had finally brought him here, as Lawrence and de Beaujolais had passed through it on their way to the coast and the mystery of the Blue Water sapphire. She expected the Americans, Hank and Buddy, to be standing outside the customs hall, and she was disappointed at not being greeted by an escort of mail-clad lancers, their faces concealed behind flowing white robes. Perhaps that was still to come: Matthieu had said his wife was half Touareg, supposing anything he had said was the least true.

There were certainly enough haiks, the all-enveloping white robes of the desert Arab women, and for a very good reason: by the time they reached their taxi, a Mercedes that had seen many better days, the soughing wind had already driven a layer of fine red dust into their faces, their hair, although they were both wearing headscarves, and into the open necks of their shirts. And the city itself seemed to be shrouded in a driving, brick-coloured cloud.

'Jesus,' Andrea commented. 'Does it get any hotter?'

'It's only eight o'clock in the morning,' Jessica pointed out. 'The sun has hardly warmed up yet.'

'What are those pyramids for?' Andrea asked, pointing. 'Tombs?'

Jessica had bought a guidebook at Heathrow. 'Those are ground nuts.'

'Say again?'

'What you know as peanuts.'

'All of them?'

'Every last one. It's a staple crop round here.'

'And people eat that many?'

'Probably. But they are also a source of cooking oil and things like that.'

'A nation existing on peanuts. Wowee!'

'You have hotel?' asked their driver, no Arab this, but clearly a Hausa, tall and aggressive, whose left hand seemed attached to his horn by an invisible wire.

'The Majestic,' Jessica told him, watching

Giles and friend getting into another taxi, and fervently hoping they weren't going the same way. She also registered that, oddly, Giles walked with the aid of a stick. In a man that big she supposed that was possibly necessary ... but he had not appeared to need it on board the plane. It was also a very odd stick, tapering from a thick base almost like the hilt of a sword. Perhaps, she thought, it really is a swordstick.

'The Majestic is good,' the driver said.

Andrea took off her scarf and regarded it in disgust. 'How do I look?'

'You look fine. Your hair is virtually the same colour as the dust. How do *I* look?'

'Like a tint job gone wrong.'

'Thank you for those few kind words. Tell me,' Jessica asked the driver. 'Do you know where a Mr Kwarism lives?'

The driver guffawed. 'Oh, yes, madam. Everyone knows where Mr Kwarism lives. You going there?'

'We're going to the hotel, I hope.'

The driver's amusement bubbled over the steering wheel and out of the window to include various passers-by. He allowed his horn to lead him through the Town of Strangers and under a low gateway into the city itself, scattered like a child's mud village around the Founder's Rock, where the red dust streets ended disconcertingly in European 'Give Way' signs, and the crumbled wall, thick, dark, loop-holed, suggested a perpetually beleaguered city, while the bicycle riding

99

Fula, their magnificent robes always about to become entangled in their rear wheels, constantly tinkling their bells, seemed to be outriders for the Sahara caravans which imagination suggested could at any moment appear over the northern horizon, and which – so Jessica's guidebook assured her – still accounted for most of Kano's prosperity. There was, inevitably, a high-rise business section, but that seemed an even greater excrescence than the airport, although oddly enough the railway station seemed entirely appropriate, perhaps because it had so obviously been there a long time, no doubt built by the British in the colonial days. Kano had to be romantic, but it was also unattractive and dirty, quite apart from the dust, its drabness relieved only by the white-walled, green-domed mosque, effortlessly beautiful in a way no Christian church could suggest.

The Mercedes negotiated a succession of narrow streets and emerged into a square, one side of which was occupied by a huge, multi-windowed façade, which at street level presented an awning and two men at last wearing cuirasses and armed with swords. One of these stepped forward to open the door.

'Jesus!' Andrea muttered. 'Are we for the chop, already?'

'Welcome to the Majestic,' the man said. 'You will have a nice day.'

'Good to know he's so positive,' Jessica remarked. She got out, paid the driver, and had a distinct feeling she was being robbed. Their backpacks had already been unloaded from the boot by the other major-domo, and they were escorted through a curtained doorway, which seemed to be keeping out most of the dust and flies, and into a cool and elegant lobby.

The clerk behind the reception desk looked at their jeans and trainers, and then at their packs, and then looked doubtful. 'May I help you ladies?' he inquired.

'We have a reservation,' Jessica explained.

'Indeed, madam? What name would that be?'

'Jones.'

'Ah, Miss Jones.' He brightened. 'Yes, indeed. If you will sign here.'

Jessica signed. 'What time is lunch?'

'Lunch is served from half past twelve until two. But...' He peered over the desk. 'Ladies are not permitted in the dining room without sleeves and in pants.'

'I should think so too,' Jessica agreed. 'No one would eat a thing.'

'I take it you did bring a dress?' Jessica asked as they went up in the lift.

'Yes, but it doesn't have sleeves.'

'Did you bring a cardigan?'

'I didn't think it would be necessary.'

'I brought one. You can borrow it.'

'What, for lunch? In this heat?'

'In case you hadn't noticed, the hotel is air-conditioned.' Although she couldn't blame

Andrea; while the temperature was a relief after the street, it was by no means cool. She tipped the porter and surveyed the room. It was actually quite well furnished, and very clean.

'Those look good.' Andrea stood above the twin beds, which were pushed together. 'I'm for a nap. I didn't sleep very well. I never do on planes.'

'You could've fooled me. We have to get on.'

'Well, then, I simply have to have a shower and get rid of some of this dust. Brrr. It's even inside my bra.'

'That's a good idea,' Jessica said. She waited for Andrea to emerge, towelling herself vigorously. 'What's that smell?'

'Chlorine. The water absolutely stinks of it. And I had to wash my hair.'

'Me too.' Jessica stood beneath the shower, which was by no means free flowing, but it did get rid of the dust. 'Now,' she said, when she joined Andrea, also towelling away at her hair, 'put on a dress, and we'll have lunch as soon as we come back.'

'Come back from where?'

'Mr Masud. Hopefully with some hardware.' She watched Andrea adjusting her dress with a sinking heart; she had forgotten her weakness for short skirts.

'Mr Masud?' the reception clerk asked. 'You know this man?' His name, apparently, was Achmed.

'Shouldn't we?'

102

The clerk scratched his nose. 'Many people do not wish to.'

'You're probably right. But we'll chance it. Where do we go?'

The clerk produced a map. 'Here is the hotel. You go so, and then so, and then so and so, and then so, and there it is.'

'I think you had better mark it on the map.'

He did so. 'The area is not good.'

'Even at ten o'clock in the morning?'

'At any time. And...' He peered over the desk at Andrea's legs? 'Not good,' he said again.

'Right. So listen. We are going to visit Mr Masud, and then come straight back here. If we are not in for lunch, call the cops. You with me?'

He rolled his eyes. 'You wish the police?'

'Only if we're not back for lunch. Or if I call you.'

'He may not have a phone.'

'But I do.' Jessica opened her shoulder bag and showed him her mobile.

'Ah, the cordless telephone. I have heard of this.'

'But you don't have one?'

'There are not many in Kano.'

'Then there's hope for you yet. Remember. Lunch.'

'What did he mean, "not good"? Was he criticizing my legs?' Andrea asked as they went outside, hastily putting on their dark glasses. With their still wet hair bound up in their scarves they looked entirely anonymous.

103

But she was clearly miffed.

'No one could possibly criticize your legs,' Jessica assured her. 'I think he meant that we're probably in danger of having our bottoms pinched.'

'How do we handle that?'

'We giggle girlishly. We're not here to draw any attention to ourselves by breaking arms and legs.'

Actually, they were not molested, although they attracted a lot of attention. 'All those eyes,' Andrea muttered. 'If we could see the rest of them, it wouldn't be so bad.'

'I'll bet they're thinking, all those legs. If we could see the rest of *them* it'd be just great.'

Soon they accumulated an escort of small boys. 'You want crack, missy? I got some here. Only one pound.'

'How old are you?' Jessica demanded.

'I is eight, missy.'

'Jesus,' Andrea muttered. 'And we think we have problems.'

'You want a man, missy? I know a good place.'

'Then I suggest you go there. Hallelujah.'

The sign was in both Arabic and English. Masud and Company, General Merchants. Inside was at least cooler than the street and less crowded, but distinctly more noisome. 'What *is* that?' Andrea asked.

'Mostly fruit and veg that have passed their sell-by date.' Jessica gazed at a young woman with a ring through her nose. 'Mr Masud at home?'

104

'I am here.' A short, stout, mainly Arab man, she estimated, equipped with both beard and moustache, hurried from the back of the store. 'Miss Jones! I have had the e-mail.' He gazed at Jessica's bust, then turned his attention to Andrea's legs. 'And this is...?'

'Miss Hutchins.'

'It is my pleasure. Oh, yes, my pleasure. You come.' He led them deeper into the cavern, past stacked sacks of indescribable contents, while the stench of rotting vegetation grew, and arrived at a desk. 'You sit.' There was one chair, but he produced an empty box for Andrea; this meant that her knees were higher than her hips, which seemed to please him. Hastily she stretched her legs. He had a swivel chair behind his desk, which squealed in an appeal for oil every time he moved. 'You have had a pleasant journey?'

'Different,' Jessica said.

'So. You will wish to leave again, perhaps in a hurry.'

'Perhaps.'

'The aircraft will be here tomorrow, and will wait for you. It has not the range to fly directly back to London, but will refuel in Algiers. This has been arranged, and will not be a problem...'

'We'll go along with that. How do we contact the pilot?'

'You simply go to the airport, and ask for Captain Broome.'

'You mean he's English?'

'No, Miss Jones. He is Australian.'

'Takes all sorts, I suppose.'

'What happens if we are in a hurry?' Andrea asked. 'Or it's the middle of the night?'

'You have the cordless telephone?'

'Yes.'

'Then I will give you his number.' He wrote it down. 'He is awaiting your call, any hour of the day or night.'

'Can't complain about that.'

'So, is there anything else?'

'You were going to supply us with weapons.'

'You think this is necessary?'

'This is always necessary, in our line of business.'

'Very well.' He got up, the chair protesting more than ever, went to a wall safe. This he opened, and took out two little parcels of oiled cloth. These he laid on the desk and opened. 'Ingram Mac 10 automatic pistols. Very good.'

Jessica and Andrea each picked up one of the tiny machine-pistols. They knew the guns, which were very popular with British drug gangs, and were also used by Secret Service agents charged with protecting the president because they were so small they were very hard to detect. But firing at a rate of a thousand rounds a minute from a twenty-shot magazine, they could be lethal at close range. 'These are great,' Jessica said. 'Just what the doctor ordered. Where did you get them?'

'I have my sources. Who is this doctor?'

'Just a manner of speaking. Well, thanks a

106

million, Mr Masud. I don't suppose you'll want to see us again.' She stood up.

'You will pay for the guns now? They are one thousand dollars each.'

'Mr Masud, let's stay friends. I know, and you know, that Mr Matthieu has already paid you for these guns. Or if he has not, then I suggest that you bill him. Good morning.'

They ran the gauntlet of the crowds and the small boys and regained the hotel. 'Whoosh,' Andrea said. 'I feel like another shower.'

It was a quarter to one. 'I think we should eat first,' Jessica decided. 'Then we can pay a call on Mrs Matthieu this afternoon.'

'What's our plan?' Andrea asked as they ate their stewed lamb. The hotel dining room was only half full.

'This is a reconnaissance. We meet the lady, tell her we've come to join her grandfather's sect, need to go to the loo so we can have a look around, discover if possible where the boy is, and tell her we'll report for duty tomorrow morning. Then we'll come back here and make plans. If it's an easy business, we'll spring the boy tonight. If it isn't, we may have to go along with the mumbo-jumbo for a day or two while we work things out.'

'You make it sound so simple.'

'The best plans always are. But don't forget we're also here to find out what we can about that bomb, and the reason for it.'

'I'll leave that to you,' Andrea suggested. 'But haven't we got to have a reason for

107

wanting to become a follower? Apart from just angst?'

'Broken marriages.'

'Together? At the same time?'

Jessica gave a wicked smile. 'That's it. We're old friends, right? Now our marriages have broken down, we've sort of come back together, and have discovered that we rather hanker for each other. This bothers us, so we're trying to find a cure.'

Andrea gazed at her. 'Is that what we want?'

'That's our story.'

'But suppose we get sucked into this thing, and they do manage to cure us of ... well, liking each other?'

'Life is full of risks. Look, these people are obviously fakes. They can't possibly influence us.'

Andrea considered for some minutes. Then she asked, 'What's the name of my husband?'

'What was the name of your last boyfriend?'

'I've never actually had a boyfriend. Not since I turned twenty.'

'Well, then, let's go for Bob.'

They finished their meal and went up to their room. 'Now can I have a nap?' Andrea asked. 'In this part of the world people have siestas, right?'

'Actually, that seems like a good idea. But we must be on our way at four.'

'That gives us an hour. I'll shower when I get up.' She stripped off and got into bed. Jessica was about to do the same when there was a rap on the door. 'Tell him we don't want any,' Andrea said, drowsily.

'Who is it?' Jessica called.

'Police, Miss Jones.'

Four

The Lord

'Oh, my God!' Andrea sat up.

'Lie down!' Jessica said. 'Pull the sheet to your throat. That way you look like innocence personified.'

'I *am* innocence personified,' Andrea muttered, obeying.

'Miss Jones?' the voice said again.

Jessica hastily put on her jeans and added a shirt. 'Just coming,' she called. There was no time for shoes; the man sounded about ready to force an entrance. She buttoned the shirt, unlocked the door. 'I'm afraid we were just about to siesta. You know, have a nap.'

Then she looked at the man. He wore a long blue robe decorated with gold thread, and a matching round hat, but was unarmed save for a swagger stick. He was about six foot six, she reckoned, his skin the purest ebony, his features carved from granite by a master sculptor. His dark eyes seemed to take in the entire room in a single glance, and if they lingered for a second longer on Andrea than

109

anywhere else, she didn't feel she could blame him for that: Andrea was slowly sitting up as if mesmerized – fortunately she had the presence of mind to retain hold of the sheet at her throat.

His gaze came back to Jessica, and rested. 'Miss Jones,' he said. 'Forgive this intrusion. I had no idea you would be resting. Shall I go away and come back in half an hour, after you have dressed?' His English was flawless.

'Perhaps if you would tell me the reason for this visit. Have we committed some crime? And how did you know my name?'

'Your name was given to me as part of a routine check of hotel registers. And I simply had to find out if it was really you.'

'Me?'

'The famous detective-sergeant. The name in the register was Jessica.'

'What on earth makes you think I am a detective-sergeant? In which police force?'

'You are too modest, Sergeant. I was on a course in London, three years ago, and you were pointed out to me. We never actually met, but I have never forgotten you.'

'Well, you'd better come in, Inspector...?'

He entered the room and closed the door. 'Douglas Kahu.'

'Right. This is Andrea Hutchins.'

Andrea had been slowly sliding back down the bed again. Now she managed a strangled 'Hello.'

'My pleasure,' Inspector Kahu said. 'And are you also a policewoman?'

'She is a detective-constable,' Jessica said. 'Won't you sit down, sir?'

'Thank you.' The inspector lowered himself into a chair.

'So this is a social call?' she asked, hopefully.

'Not entirely, although I hope it may become so. But I must ask you the reason for your visit to Nigeria. We have not been informed of it.'

'Well, you see, it's not official. We're on holiday.'

'Two most attractive young women, on their own, in a place like Kano?'

Not another MCP, Jessica thought. 'Believe me, Inspector, we can take care of ourselves.'

'I am sure you can. But it is unusual. And possibly dangerous. It is my business to keep the peace. You are potential disturbers of that peace.'

'In that case, we'll leave again. Just give us another day or so to look around, then we'll be out of your hair.'

'I do not wish to drive you out, Sergeant. I just wish to make you fully aware of the situation, and perhaps to advise you. Such as, for instance, of the unwisdom of visiting Mahmood Kwarism.'

Andrea's earrings jangled. Jessica kept her cool. 'Who?'

'Please, Miss Jones. We are in the same profession. We are colleagues. And I admire you greatly. Should we not therefore be frank with each other? You inquired as to the

111

address of Kwarism from Achmed at the desk this morning, almost immediately after checking in.'

'Ah ... yes, I did.' She took a stab in the dark. 'Before we decided to come here, I was discussing the country, and in particular Kano, with a friend who knows it, and he said we must try to have a look at Kwarism's house.'

'Why? It is a very ordinary house.'

'He didn't say why. But I put it on my list.'

Inspector Kahu regarded her for some seconds. Then he said, 'My advice would be to take it off your list. Did your friend also recommend that you visit Elihu Masud?'

Shit, Jessica thought. I am going to ring that Achmed's neck. 'He had shopped there, and recommended that we try it, yes.' She could tell by his expression that he did not believe a word of what she was saying, but she had to brazen it out. 'Why, do you also regard him as ... What do you regard Mr Kwarism as, anyway?'

'I will just say that he is on our files.'

'Isn't he a very wealthy man?'

'That is always a good reason to keep a file on someone. May I ask if you purchased anything at Mr Masud's?'

Jessica restrained an urge to glance at her shoulder bag. 'No, we didn't. He didn't have anything that interested us.'

'I am glad of that. But I would recommend that you have as little as possible to do with this friend of yours when you get home.

112

Masud deals in drugs.'

'Oh. Right. I will take your advice.'

'Miss Jones, Miss Hutchins, I do not wish to spoil your holiday. I just wish to make sure that you enjoy yourselves while you are here. Would you permit me to assist you to do that?'

'Well, that would be very nice.'

'Well, then, will you dine with me tonight?'

'Ah...' Jessica looked at Andrea, who was again prone, only her nose, eyes and hair showing.

But now the rest of her face emerged. 'Yes, please. We'd like that.'

'Excellent.' He stood up. 'I will show you the town after dark. Shall we say eight o'clock in the lobby?'

'We'll be there,' Jessica said. She closed the door behind him, and turned to face the beds. 'Well?'

'Wowee! I need the loo.' Andrea got out of bed and disappeared.

Jessica waited for her to return. 'You do realize that he knows we're not really on holiday?'

'So? We'll be out of here in a couple of days.'

'And suppose he contacts Scotland Yard asking for information?'

'They can only express surprise that we've chosen to holiday in Nigeria. Our business is to get the job done and get back to London with the goods on Matthieu, and his wife, and her father, if possible. Meanwhile, what's wrong with having dinner with a

113

gorgeous man?'

'*What* did you say?'

'Well...' Andrea blushed. 'He is, isn't he?'

'Get dressed,' Jessica told her. 'Let's be about our business.'

Achmed willingly showed them Kwarism's house on the map. 'Thank you,' Jessica said. 'Now let me give you a word of advice. We're having dinner with Inspector Kahu tonight, and if he tells us that you told him where we are going this afternoon, I am personally going to wring your neck.'

He goggled at her; he was a large man. But he couldn't meet her gaze.

They followed the map, running the same gauntlet as before, and arrived before a tall, windowless red house, the façade of which was pargeted in symmetrical black designs, while from the roof the dog's-ears gutters leaned forward like medieval sentries about to deliver a bucket-full of boiling oil. The square itself was packed with people, donkeys and dogs, and was supervised by two blue-clad policemen, their waists bound with wide red sashes, and red tassels hanging from their blue fezzes.

'Shit!' Andrea muttered. 'Do you think they'll report to base?'

'Why should they? *They* don't know who we are.'

'Do you think Inspector Kahu wears a uniform like that when he's on duty? He'd look tremendous. Even better than in that

114

jibbah or whatever.'

'I have an idea he *was* on duty just now,' Jessica said, and rang the bell.

A man opened the hatch. 'You have business?'

'We have come to see Mrs Matthieu.'

'Mrs Matthieu is not here.'

'Oh, what a shame. If you'll tell us when she'll be back, we'll call again.'

'Mrs Matthieu...'

'Show the ladies in, Osman,' said a quiet voice.

There was a clanking of bolts, and the door swung in. Jessica glanced at Andrea, whose right hand rested on the catch for her shoulder bag, inches away from the machine-pistol. Then she stepped through the half-open door, blinking in the sudden gloom. The room was low-ceilinged and lit by a single electric lamp. A jalousied inner window looked into a courtyard, in the centre of which there was what appeared to be a large walled pool, apparently reached by a ramp, across which stretched an iron gate. Beside the wall grew a red-barked acacia, its yellow leaves starting to droop as the sun dipped behind the high roof of the rest of the building, which was in the shape of a square, with verandahs on the upper floors. It was even larger than it had appeared from outside.

Standing in an inner doorway was a man, tall and thin, with a hooked nose and thick beard. He wore a deep red jibbah, and although his face was exposed Jessica had no doubt that he was a Touareg; his skin was pale and his dark eyes were never quiet for a moment, but darted to and fro, enveloping both the women. 'I am Mahmood Kwarism. You have come to see my daughter?' His voice was as deep as his eyes.

'We were told to do this by a friend in London.'

'Why do you wish to see her?'

'We wish to become followers of the Lord.'

Kwarism's eyes at last came to rest on hers. 'I do not understand you. What is your name?'

'Jessica Jones. This is my friend, Andrea Hutchins. We have both suffered much misfortune recently. We were told that Mrs Matthieu would be able to help us.'

'It is customary to write, to make arrangements.'

'Oh. We were told that Mrs Matthieu would interview us, and if we were found suitable...'

Kwarism stroked his beard. 'Your friend was misinformed, Miss Jones. The followers cannot be joined ... How do you say in England? On the spur of the moment? Nor can such a step be undertaken lightly. For one thing there is the expense...'

'One thousand dollars in cash.' Jessica opened her bag and took out the envelope with the money. 'My friend has one too.'

Kwarism did not take the notes. 'You are certainly anxious to become a follower. And you know a great deal about us. You are right in supposing that my daughter usually inter-

116

views the female applicants. But she is not here. If you are serious about becoming a novitiate, you will have to go to her.'

'That seems reasonable. Where do we go?'

'I will arrange it. Come.'

Jessica glanced at Andrea, and they followed him through the doorway into a much larger room, also looking out on the centre courtyard and sumptuously furnished from the divans to the carpets on the floor. Seated on one of the divans was the man Giles and his companion, drinking coffee, which was brewing on a table in the corner, and which, Jessica deduced, was responsible for the peculiar smell pervading the house. 'Shit!' Andrea muttered under her breath.

Jessica felt the same way as Giles said, 'Well, what do you know? The two bimbos from the plane!'

'I see you know each other,' Kwarism remarked.

'Only in a manner of speaking,' Jessica said. 'Don't tell me they're joining your sect?'

'And why the hell not?' Giles demanded.

'Please, Mr Golightly. Swearing is not permitted in the Fellowship of the Lord. And we are not a sect, Miss Jones. We are a religion.'

'I do apologize.'

'But lessies are allowed, eh?' Giles inquired.

'I do not understand you. What is this "lessie"?'

'It's a word we use for women who prefer sleeping with women rather than men.'

117

'We told him that to get rid of him,' Andrea said. 'He was being a nuisance.'

'Ah. But it is of no importance. In the Fellowship of the Lord all thoughts of the flesh are forbidden.'

'Is that a fact?' Giles commented, looking at Andrea's legs.

The servant who had let them into the house presented a tray with steaming cups of coffee.

'Sip it carefully,' Kwarism recommended. 'It is very strong.'

'You can say that again,' Andrea said, having sipped.

'Now, if you are still serious, Miss Jones, Miss Hutchins, I will accept your money.' They handed it over and Kwarism went to a roll-top desk in the corner, placed the money in a drawer, and returned with four large yellow capsules. 'You must each take one of these.'

'Why?' Giles asked, suspiciously.

'It is to combat malaria.'

'I thought they had it under control in Nigeria. Anyway, there's not a lot of water around.'

'It is virtually extinct in Kano, certainly. But where you are going, who can say? Abdullah.'

The servant presented a tray on which there were four glasses of water.

'If you will, ladies. And gentlemen.'

Again Jessica and Andrea exchanged glances; the tablets were nothing like the mepacreme they had been given in London.

But there was nothing for it. They had to play along with this strange multimillionaire until they had Claudine in their sights. Jessica put the capsule in her mouth and washed it down. It left a faintly bitter taste.

'Ugh!' Giles remarked. 'You're sure you don't mean to poison us?'

'It is best to be protected,' Kwarism said urbanely. 'Now, it is necessary for you to change your clothes.'

'We have a change at the hotel,' Jessica said. 'When do we leave?'

'In half an hour, Miss Jones.'

'Half an hour?' Andrea queried.

'We have a long way to go. But in any event, I do not suppose any of your clothes will be suitable. We have the necessary garments here.'

'But ... when are we coming back?'

'Who can say? After you have been inducted into the Fellowship.'

Andrea stared at Jessica in consternation, as Kwarism observed, 'There is a problem with this?'

Jessica had already determined that it would be to their advantage not to let him know that there was a police inspector interested in their activities. 'Our hotel may worry if we do not return this evening.'

'I will have a message sent to the hotel to inform them that you have decided to go on a safari, as you say, and that they are to hold your belongings until you return or until you send for them. Will that be satisfactory?'

'You think of everything.'

'Well, then, go with Serene.'

A young woman had appeared in an inner doorway. Small and slight, black-haired and black-eyed, she had attractively diminutive features. She wore a white haik, but her hair and face were exposed. Andrea and Jessica followed her from the room and up a flight of stairs into a dark corridor, off which opened several doors. Serene gestured to one of these. 'In here, please.'

Her English was disconcertingly good. Jessica and Andrea could only exchange more glances, but Jessica reckoned they were both thinking the same thing: that they were being kidnapped, with a minimum of fuss and effort. But if this was the only way they could get to Claudine Matthieu...

Inside the room there was a table, two chairs, and a bed. There was also an open window, looking out on to one of the verandahs, and beyond, the courtyard and the pool. Andrea moved to the window, and gasped. 'My God! That's a crocodile!'

Jessica went to her side, gazed at the huge reptile, which had emerged from the pool and was lying on the ramp, regarding the gate speculatively. She gave a little shudder. Both she and Andrea remembered the large caiman they had encountered in South America, but this monster made the alligators seem like puppets.

'There are three of them,' Serene said. 'They are Mr Kwarism's pets. Do not be afraid; they cannot get out unless the gate is opened. Now come. We must make haste.'

Almost reluctantly they left the window. 'I feel quite shook up,' Andrea muttered.

'As the lady says, they're down there and we're up here,' Jessica pointed out. But she felt quite shook up as well.

Lying on the bed were two voluminous white robes and two undergarments which suggested pictures Jessica had seen of the Spartan chiton. 'It almost looks as if we were expected,' she commented.

'Everything is known.' Serene remarked, enigmatically. 'Undress please.'

'How much?' Andrea asked.

'There is nothing worn beneath the haik save for the shirt. It is not transparent.'

'But we are not used to it,' Jessica pointed out. 'So if it is all the same to you, we'll keep our underwear.'

'If you wish. But you will be uncomfortable.'

'We'll take our chances.' They took off their dresses, watched with interest by the girl.

'You are very beautiful,' she commented. 'What is that you are wearing?'

'It is called a brassiere.'

'What is its purpose?'

'Basically to give a good shape. Stops the breasts from sagging.'

'Your breasts do not sag. They are lovely breasts.'

'You haven't seen them without the bra.'

'They would be beautiful in any circumstances.'

'Seems to me you have made a conquest,' Andrea remarked.

'This lady is far more beautiful than I,' Jessica suggested.

Serene looked at Andrea. 'She is not so beautiful as you. But she has nice legs.' Which was a considerable understatement, Jessica thought when Andrea was down to her knickers. 'Our women do not reveal their legs, any more than they reveal their breasts,' Serene added a trifle censoriously. 'Now, I will show you how to wear the haik.'

'You're sure they're clean?' Andrea asked. 'No bugs?'

'Of course they are clean, Miss Hutchins. They are freshly laundered. Now do as I show you.' This wasn't difficult, although it necessitated the constant use of one hand to grasp the inner folds of the garment to keep it in place.

'But this is wool,' Jessica protested. 'You mean we must wear wool, in this heat?'

'It is not always hot,' Serene pointed out. 'The nights can be very cold.'

'It certainly doesn't go with our shoes,' Andrea remarked.

'But you will not be wearing shoes, Miss Hutchins.' Delicately she raised the hem of her haik to her ankles. 'I am not wearing shoes.'

They hadn't noticed that before. Andrea gazed at Jessica with her mouth open, and Jessica shrugged.

122

'And the yashmak.'

'Is this necessary?' Jessica asked.

'Out of doors, yes. It is the law.'

'Muslim law. But we are not Muslims. Do the followers have to become Muslims?'

'It is not a Muslim law,' Serene explained patiently. 'It is a custom, which is best obeyed.' She fitted the little face masks over their mouths and noses, secured them on the back of their necks, under the haik, the top fold of which enveloped their heads.

'How do we breathe?' Andrea asked, the linen flattening itself against her nostrils.

'You should breathe slowly and evenly. You will get used to it.'

'I hope you're right.'

'This mask is a bit tricky with our glasses,' Jessica remarked.

'But you should not wear such things,' Serene said. 'Your eyes will become used to the light. Now we must go.' Jessica picked up her shoulder bag. 'No, no,' Serene said. 'You must enter the Centre of the Universe unencumbered by worldly trappings. Indeed, I must ask you for your wristwatches and your rings. And your earrings,' she added.

'Oh, shit!' Andrea remarked.

'But our bags accompany us everywhere,' Jessica objected, unstrapping her watch and taking off her studs. 'We'd feel naked without them. Everything is in here: our money, our passports, our tickets, our mobiles...'

'Your belongings will be perfectly safe here until you return.'

123

'No way,' Andrea said. 'Just forget it. Shoes are one thing. But where I go, my bag goes. Where my bag stays, I stay.'

'It is not possible,' Serene said.

Andrea looked at Jessica. 'Will you excuse us for a moment?' Jessica asked. 'You can wait outside.'

'We must hurry,' Serene said. But she stepped outside and closed the door.

'If we are separated from our guns and mobiles we're dead ducks,' Andrea said.

'We don't know that,' Jessica argued. 'These people don't know who we are.'

'So how come this Serene addressed me as Miss Hutchins? We weren't introduced.'

'She must have been listening from outside the room. Look, they are treating us with the utmost courtesy. And what is the alternative? We came here to get hold of Claudine Matthieu and son, if that is possible. Or at least enough evidence to link her to the Chicago bombing and thus justify our being here. But she isn't here. The only way we are going to get hold of her is by going to where she is. If we quit now, all we can do is hop the next plane back to England, give Matthieu back his money, and pray that no one finds out about this little caper.'

'Oh, JJ. You know I'd follow you anywhere. I just wanted to be sure you know what we're getting into.'

'Actually, I don't. But we came here to get into it. And don't forget that we have an ace up our sleeve. In a few hours' time friend

124

Kahu is going to start wondering what's happened to us, and if he gets curious enough, that beastly Achmed is going to tell him where we went this afternoon. Let's join the gang.'

Kwarism's Mercedes station wagon was very large, very highly polished, and very new. To Jessica's surprise he drove himself, although he seemed as attached to his horn as their taxi driver of that morning. Was it only that morning?

Serene sat in the front beside him; she was appearing less and less like a servant than an integral part of his set-up. Giles Golightly and his friend, whose name appeared to be Lennon, sat in the next row – Giles accompanied by his stick, which was apparently considered by Kwarism to be necessary – and Jessica and Andrea were at the back.

The temptation to worry about the situation was enormous. But that would be pointless. They were now playing it entirely by ear. At least, she was. Andrea, she knew, would follow her in blind faith up to the last moment ... whenever that might be. What she now had to do was concentrate very hard on their surroundings and where they were going. Which, in the first instance, was the airport. But not to the terminals. Kwarism went down a slip road to reach a secluded parking apron where there waited a helicopter.

'That must have set the Followers of the

Lord back a bob or two,' Giles remarked.

'The Lord lacks for nothing, Mr Golightly. Why should he? Will you please get out.' The pilots, who appeared to be Caucasian, were already on the flight deck, looking down at them. 'Will you go first, Mr Golightly? It is a matter of weight distribution,' Kwarism explained.

Giles went up the ladder, and checked. 'Who the shit is this?'

'Mr Golightly, please. This is a poor old beggar who has requested assistance in reaching his home. I could not refuse him. Charity is an important tenet of the Lord's rule. He will sit at the back.'

'Of course, my son,' said the old man, and judging by the length of white beard that escaped his burnous he had to be very old indeed.

'You mean he speaks English?' Giles sounded more offended than ever.

'Do not let it concern you. He will not take offence.' Kwarism gave Serene a hand up. She went to the rear to sit beside the old man. Lennon went forward to sit beside Golightly. 'Now you ladies. I will wish you a pleasant journey.'

'You mean you're not coming with us?' Jessica asked.

'My duties detain me in Kano. But you will be well looked after. These pilots have worked for me for some time.' He slammed the doors, and within seconds they were whirring above the city, from the air even more

126

suggestive of the work of an imaginative child at low water.

'Now this is quite civilized,' Lennon remarked. 'Don't you agree, Giles? I really thought we were going to be stuck in one of those local trains for a couple of days.'

'Shut up.' Giles closed his eyes.

Jessica looked down at the empty, dusty country beneath them; they were flying east, the now drooping sun behind them. The landscape was hypnotic. For a while they followed a railway track over a brick-red plain, undulating as they passed over it although from a distance it gave the impression of being flat. There were a couple of roads and quite a few tracks but little traffic, and there were scattered trees and a great deal of scrub, dotted with large anthills, constructed like miniature forts and, she estimated, several feet in height. There was little water to be seen, and almost as few people, except for the occasional village, each with its small herd of cattle, which even from the air could be described as scrawny. But soon these visible evidences of humanity disappeared and they flew over semi-desert, in which the lonely acacia represented vegetation and the red dust rolled beneath them like a blood-coloured sea.

As the afternoon advanced the temperature dropped, but it remained very hot in the aircraft. 'Does anyone have any idea how long this trip takes?' Lennon asked, plaintively. He turned in his seat. 'Hey, you. Young lady.

When do we set down?'

Serene ignored him. 'She's asleep,' Jessica said.

'Well, wake her up.'

Jessica turned, and the old man smiled at her. 'You are going to seek the Lord?'

Every head turned to look at him. 'Isn't he supposed to address you as memsahib or something?' Golightly asked.

'I don't think he means to,' Jessica said. 'Yes, we are looking for the Lord.'

'The Lord is good.'

'He'd better be,' Lennon said.

'He will make a new man of you, my son. He will say you must give up your innermost thoughts to him. He will release your mind.'

'Do we want our minds released?' Andrea whispered.

'What I really want is something to drink,' Golightly said. 'Come to think of it, something to eat wouldn't be too bad either. We had an early lunch.'

'Food will be there when you land. What is a few hours of hunger? But if you are truly in need, I have some sweetmeats here which will make you feel better.' The old man produced a round box, opened it, and handed it to Jessica. 'Have one.'

'It looks like Turkish Delight.'

'That it is not. But you will certainly find it delightful. I would be honoured if you would partake with me. See?' He placed one of the soft sweets in his mouth.

'They do look rather good.' Andrea tasted one.

'Yes,' Jessica agreed. The men also each took a sweet.

'And you, my child,' the old man invited Serene. Serene, who apparently had not been asleep after all, accepted one. 'Now we shall all feel better,' the old man said. 'Tell me, Miss Jones, have you ever heard of borbor?'

'I don't think so.'

'It has several ingredients, but the main component is the juice of the plant you would know as calotropis procera. Borbor is a white liquid extracted from the bark. Do you know, Miss Jones, it is used by the women of the desert to destroy their enemies.'

'Eh?' Lennon cried.

'Oh, yes, indeed, Mr Lennon. A single drop of undiluted borbor in the eye, for example, will blind a man instantly. Or a woman, of course. Taken internally, the drug consumes the brain, takes away the will, makes the subject a mindless lump of clay.'

'Oh, my God,' Golightly gasped. 'I've swallowed it!'

'There is nothing to be afraid of, Mr Golightly. The mixture you are digesting will do you no permanent harm; it has been carefully prepared. And the Lord needs your brain in order to reshape it into a proper appreciation of what life is about. He will restore it to you in due course; you may be sure of that. No doubt the drug is already having a soothing effect upon you, removing your fears, your

129

ingrained suspicions, making you more willing to trust me, to confide in me, to surrender yourself to me.'

Jessica realized he was right. She seemed to have no weight above the neck. She knew she should do something, but suddenly it no longer seemed important. With a gigantic effort she attempted to resist the swirling clouds that were rising from the base of her brain, gazed into the smiling eyes that gloomed at her. She summoned a gigantic effort, turned in her seat and reached back to grasp the old man's beard, and tug it. 'JJ!' Andrea cried, whether in criticism or desperation it was difficult to tell.

'Now, Miss Jones,' the old man said. 'Why did you do that?'

'I wish to look upon the face of the Lord,' she gasped.

Ukuba smiled. As Jessica had guessed, his beard was false, but his face was certainly old enough to have owned one of that length and colour. His skin was pale, his forehead high. He had a large, straight nose, separating two enormous dark eyes. His features were a mass of lines, and his flesh sagged away from his cheekbones, but the eyes were alert and amused. 'You are strong-willed and perceptive, Miss Jones. Yes, I am the Lord.'

Jessica got her breathing under control. 'You wouldn't consider the title just a little blasphemous? Whether you call him Allah, or Jehovah, or God.'

130

'I do not ape the creator, Miss Jones. The word "lord", *dominus*, means one who has power and authority. I dominate those around me, Miss Jones.'

'I didn't mean to be rude when we came on board, Mr Ukuba,' Golightly said, anxiously. 'I didn't know who you were. I hope I didn't hurt your feelings.'

'Now, Mr Golightly, how could you possibly hurt my feelings? Do the thoughts of the ant, crawling over the floor at your feet, ever trouble you?' Golightly gulped as he flushed. 'Now, we shall be flying for some time yet. Why do you not all try to get some sleep.'

Jessica stared into Serene's eyes, waves of drowsiness threatening her mind. She did not dare look at Andrea, whose eyes were in any event fast shut. She knew that something was very wrong even if she could not determine what. More important was the realization that even if she could deduce the situation, decide whether the drug was given to all acolytes or whether it was intended specifically to destroy her and Andrea's ability to defend themselves – in which case they *had* been betrayed – there was nothing she could do about it until she recovered.

Suddenly she was awake, her mind clear and more free from tension and anxiety than at any time in the previous couple of years. Still the rotor blades whirred overhead, but the sun had gone and she looked down into darkness, as it was dark in the cabin save for a faint light emanating from behind the

131

closed flight deck door. But they were descending, and now she saw lights beneath them. She turned in her seat to look at Ukuba. 'Have we arrived?'

'No, no, Miss Jones. There is still some way to go. But the machine must be fuelled.'

There were only a few lights, but these clearly marked a landing pad, and once down the helicopter was immediately surrounded by people. 'Say, can we get out?' Golightly asked.

'I do not think that is necessary,' Ukuba said. 'It will not take long.'

'You mean you're gonna fuel this crate with us on board?' Lennon asked. 'The FAA wouldn't go for that.'

'The FAA has no jurisdiction here, Mr Lennon. This is my private depot. Few people even know it exists.'

It was certainly a very slick operation. They were airborne again in less than half an hour, flying now into pitch-blackness. 'We are close to the lake,' Ukuba said out of the gloom when they had flown for another hour. 'It is the fourth largest lake in the world. At its fullest extent it covers an area of approximately eight thousand square miles. It is now at its lowest because we are at the end of the dry season. Any day now the weather will break, and in a few weeks' time, perhaps before you are ready to leave us and resume your place in the world, Miss Jones, the level will have risen by six metres or more. Mind you, it is true to say that the lake is shrinking. Two centuries ago there were great cities on the banks of Chad. Now they are huddled heaps of ruins, ten kilometres from the nearest water. Even Maidugari, which is the capital city of the Chad province of Bornu – it is some distance to the southeast of us now – used to be close to the lake. It is the desiccation, Miss Jones. But then, once upon a time, as I am sure you know, all of North Africa was fertile beyond imagination, and indeed, perhaps from Kano to the Tibesti Mountains, on the borders of the Sudan, was one vast inland sea. There are beautiful lakes at the foot of the Tibesti, Miss Jones, their waters a kaleidoscope of colour from the salts and minerals they contain. But they too are shrinking.

'What caused such a change? What causes it to go on changing? Because it is doing that, you know, Miss Jones, slowly turning northern Nigeria, as it has already turned northern Chad, into desert. Was it a climatic upheaval? Or was it endless eons of man himself, chopping down trees for firewood, turning the good soil into sand by his abominably careless and repetitive cultivation? One could envisage the dust bowl of the United States becoming a similar Sahara were the Americans not wealthy enough and technologically advanced enough to keep the water flowing. But for all their efforts, the world is drying out. Is that not a terrifying thought, Miss Jones? This vast ball, which the scientists tell

133

us contains far more water than land, has been drying since time began, and is at last being overtaken by man's wastefulness. I look forward, perhaps ten thousand years, perhaps only a thousand, to a time when the Atlantic itself will be no larger than Chad.'

'You're a cheerful soul, Mr Ukuba.' Andrea had also woken up.

'I'm starving,' Lennon complained.

'We shall soon be at my home, Mr Lennon, and then you will have your fill, I promise you.'

Jessica looked down into the darkness. There was not a gleam of light to be seen, no indication that there was any living creature within a thousand miles, and certainly no clue how, supposing they did manage to get hold of Claudine Matthieu and her child, they were going to regain Kano, unless they could hijack this helicopter, and that was going to be difficult without their weapons.

Ukuba was gazing at her, and it occurred to her that even mind-reading might not be beyond this unusual old man. She wondered how long it might be before the effects of the borbor wore off. 'Why did you choose to make your home in such a wilderness?' she asked.

'I live there now because it gives me, and my guests, the inestimable boon of complete privacy, Miss Jones. But in the beginning my family was forced to it. We have lived in Chad for a very long time. How old would you say I am?'

134

'Eighty?'

Ukuba smiled. 'You do me a slight injustice, although you are close. But yet, only a couple of generations before I was born, Miss Jones, this country was the Kingdom of Bornu. At its greatest, some hundreds of years ago, it dominated West Africa. By the time I was born, it had been attacked by the slave general Rabah. You have heard of him?'

'I think so.'

'He marched west from Egypt in 1880. My family looked upon him as a saviour. For I, and Serene here, are descended from the first of all the Ukubas, in a direct line. Did you know Serene is my great-granddaughter?'

'She never told me,' Jessica murmured.

'So who *was* the first Ukuba?' Golightly had also apparently woken up, and had been listening to the conversation.

'Ukuba commanded the first Fula armies ever to march into West Africa, Mr Golightly. More than a thousand years ago. You could say that we were the Goths of Nigeria. But sadly the Fula never really established themselves in Bornu. We did not conquer it until the turn of the nineteenth century of the Christian era, only to be in turn driven out by the Faki Mohammed el-Amin el-Kanemi. My family fled to the remoteness of Lake Chad to preserve the purity of our blood no less than our independence. And then came Rabah with his army, three thousand of the best fighting men in Africa, fleeing the fall of his leader, Zobeir Pasha, at the hands of your

135

General Gordon, Miss Jones. In thirteen years he fought his way across Africa, a prodigious feat of arms. He would have made Pizarro seem insignificant, but for one thing. Pizarro was conquering a world which could not match his technology. Rabah was fleeing from the monstrous effects of a superior technology, only to find that same technology waiting for him. Fifty years earlier his would have been a name to conjure with, like Shaka the Zulu, or Lobengula, or our own Idris. Instead he met the Germans, pushing up through the Cameroons, and the French pushing south through the Sahara, and behind them the British, spreading north from the coast, all armed with their machine-guns and their repeating rifles.'

'According to the history books,' Jessica suggested, 'Rabah was a bit of a thug.'

'English history books, Miss Jones. He saved my family, although certainly he was a dark and cruel man. Alas, when he was cut down by French bullets, we again had to flee to Chad. But by then we had money, and so my father decided that if I was ever going to amount to anything I must adopt the ways of the Europeans. What is it your classical desert chieftain never omits, Miss Jones? His three years at Oxford University. My father was very classical, although he himself had never left Bornu. He sent me to England to study under a tutor, with Balliol as my destination. We have arrived.' He pointed out of the window. 'The Centre of the Universe.'

136

Five

The Punishment

The moon had risen, and they could see broad stretches of water interspersed with huge beds of reeds. And now there appeared several islands, denoted by thick clumps of trees. They were approaching the largest of these, on which there was not only a small wood but a pasture dotted with cattle, beyond which were several acres of cultivated land, and at last, close to where the reed beds started again, a village of what looked like extremely primitive huts.

'My God!' Golightly commented. 'I thought the chopper meant that things were looking up.'

'The helicopter is necessary because there is no other way in or out of the Centre of the Universe,' Ukuba explained. 'At least in the dry season. But even when the rains come, few boats can penetrate the reed beds. And even if one does reach the mainland, what has been accomplished? It is two hundred miles to Ngura, which is the nearest railhead. You will observe, Miss Jones, that while I detest everything about the modern age, I have no intention of being left behind by the most

137

obviously useful aspects of its technology. Now we must prepare to land. Will you refasten your seatbelts.'

The helicopter settled, the blades stopped rotating, and a vast silence drifted through the cabin, which ended when the door was opened by the whistle of the wind, twice as strong as in Kano, scything through the reeds, setting the trees swaying to and fro.

'The harmattan,' Ukuba explained. 'It is with us always, until the rains start. You will get used to it.'

Steps were put in place, and a European face appeared in the doorway. The owner was a muscular young man, with a complexion the colour of the desert and wearing a khaki bush jacket over khaki shorts, khaki stockings, and a bush hat. He had pushed his goggles up on his forehead, and smiled at them with blue eyes. 'Let me give you ladies a hand,' he suggested.

'My chief pilot, Captain Anderson,' Ukuba said.

'South African?'

'What used to be known as Rhodesian, Miss Jones. I don't much care for the new version.'

How did he know my name? Jessica wondered; there had been no introductions at Kano airport. She gave him her hand as she stepped down, and he did the same for Andrea. Both of them had to clutch their haiks to avoid having them blown away. Golightly and Lennon followed. Serene joined

138

them, and Ukuba was the last. He remained on the steps, and raised his arms. 'The Lord is good.'

From the huts, and the wood, had come perhaps forty people, who now knelt and touched their foreheads in the dust. It was impossible to tell either their sexes or their nationalities, not only because of the darkness but because they were all dressed identically, in rough white blouses and pants; their feet were bare. Jessica could see no children, although as it had to be about nine o'clock they could well be in bed, but she had a peculiar prickling feeling at the nape of her neck: her quarries, child and mother, had to be within a few feet of her.

'They seem pleased to see you,' Golightly remarked.

'These are the Inner Court of the Followers of the Lord,' Ukuba said. 'Most of them, at any rate. We have several novitiates always in residence.' He clapped his hands, and the heads raised. 'Zobeir!' One of the tallest of the Followers stood up and came towards them. Like his leader he was beardless, thus aggressively demonstrating that he no longer accepted the Muslim faith. In other respects he was entirely Arab, with a large, slightly hooked nose and glooming eyes, and a spare physique. 'You may remember that Rabah's leader under the Mahdi was Zobeir Pasha. The first Zobeir was the most infamous slave trader in all history, Miss Jones. Far more beastly than people like your own John

Hawkins. My Zobeir is a descendant of his; he is my assistant, my right-hand man.'

Zobeir bowed to them all. 'Welcome to the Centre of the Universe.'

'It's our pleasure, I hope,' Jessica said.

She watched the Followers, having greeted their lord, melt away back to their huts or into the wood, and wondered if they had any weapons. She could not help suspecting that this was some gigantic scam; she thought there might well be a gun or two lying about. Besides, how could anyone live in a place as remote as this without some protection, if only from wild animals?

'This is Mr Giles Golightly, and Mr Peter Lennon,' Ukuba was saying. 'You will remember that we were expecting them.'

'Oh, yes, indeed, my lord. And these ladies are Miss Jones and friend?'

Oh, shit, Jessica thought, and cursed the borbor, which was still leaving her feeling too relaxed to be afraid. But she had to be afraid, if they were expected.

'Indeed,' Ukuba said. 'You have heard from my son?'

'His report awaits you, my lord.'

'You mentioned something about food when we landed,' Lennon said.

'Zobeir will see to your wants,' Ukuba said.

'You don't eat?' Golightly asked.

'Alas, my son, when you reach my age, so many of the pleasures of the flesh must be forgone, or at least treated with caution. One picks amongst them, anxious to preserve

140

one's strength for the more important tasks. I take my meals alone. But I will soon be with you again.'

Jessica glanced at Andrea, but she was clearly still under the full influence of the borbor, and was smiling pleasantly. She was certainly unaware of the danger they were in.

'Come.' Zobeir led them away from the helicopter and across the baked mud of the compound to the largest of the grass huts, clearly an assembly point, for before the opening which served as a doorway there hung an iron triangle. The ground felt quite pleasant on Jessica's bare feet, although she could not help wondering when the bugs were going to make their presence felt.

Within the hut the gloom was relieved by two guttering oil lamps, but the sudden cessation of the whistling wind was breathtaking, while, as she had feared, immediately they were assaulted by a swarm of mosquitoes that had them stamping and slapping, but which ignored their feet in favour of their arms and faces. As their eyes became accustomed to the dim light they discovered that the hut was devoid of furniture apart from a pile of blankets in a corner, but it was larger than Jessica had supposed, and the rear of the building was lost in darkness.

'Well, really,' Golightly complained. 'I paid a thousand dollars for this?'

'Here in the Centre of the Universe,' Zobeir said, 'we are concerned only with the mind, not the body. But we know the body must be

141

strong, to feed the mind. Pray be seated.'

'On the ground?'

Zobeir sat down, drawing up his knees and crossing his legs. 'The earth is the source of all things, for good and for evil, in this world.'

'Well, having come so far, I suppose.' Golightly sat down, slapping his face as he did so, and gazed at the splodge of blood on his hand. 'You're sure it's us who're supposed to be eating? I'll tell you, Mr Zobeir, I have no objection to camping out, but I'm damned if I'm going to let these things take me apart.'

'They will soon become tired of you, and you will become used to them. As you have taken the antidote to their poison before leaving Kano they cannot harm you. Ladies?'

'How do we do this?' Andrea muttered.

'With difficulty,' Jessica replied.

Actually, thanks to the innumerable folds of material, it was easier than it had first appeared, although Jessica was very glad that they had retained their knickers.

Zobeir clapped his hands, and two of the Followers entered, carrying between them a large earthenware tureen. Jessica decided that they were women, and probably African, but the long-haired and definite girl who followed, carrying a jug, gazed at her with blue eyes. The tureen was placed in front of Zobeir, the pitcher next to it, and the three women withdrew, shuffling softly through the dust.

'They forgot the plates,' Lennon said.

'And the cutlery,' Golightly added.

'We use our fingers.'

142

'You mean we all dig from the same bowl?' Lennon cried. 'Without even washing our hands? You must be out of your tiny mind.'

'Well, I could eat a horse,' Andrea said. 'But it isn't a horse, is it, Mr Zobeir?'

'It is couscous, really. But as we are un-restrained by outmoded beliefs, the meat is beef rather than lamb. We have our own breed of cattle in Chad. Very tasty. And the stock is porridge made from guinea corn, with some vegetables added.' He scooped out three fingers of the stew, deposited it in his mouth. 'If you gentlemen prefer not to eat, the decision is yours. Alas, we have nothing else, except this drink.'

'I'm for eating,' Andrea said, trying to follow his example. Most of the food reached her mouth, but a lot fell on her haik as well.

Jessica did no better, watched with quiet amusement by the Arab. Now he passed the jug to her. 'Try some. I'm sure you will enjoy it. It is merise, a liquor made from the date palm. Or there is sour milk.'

'I'm for the date wine,' Jessica decided. She was still trying to think, to anticipate what the fact that their identities, or at least their names, were apparently known might mean. But if Kwarism was in touch with Zobeir, presumably by mobile phone, as there was no evidence of any electricity on the island to support a radio, he would have given their names. Perhaps she was worrying needlessly. In any event, there was nothing she could do but wait and see how things turned out. The

143

drink, which could easily have been a too-recent Muscadet with half a bottle of scotch thrown in for good measure, to a certain extent made her less aware of the mosquitoes.

Andrea also took a swig, and rolled her eyes.

'Give me some of that.' Golightly wiped the neck of the jar with his sleeve, and drank deeply. 'God Almighty.' He handed the jug to Lennon, raised his eyes to heaven, and dipped his fingers into the pot. 'It's not bad. Or maybe I'm just too hungry to care. Okay, Mr Zobeir, tell us what happens next.'

'You will not be bored, Mr Golightly. There is always much to be done. The Followers of the Lord all have their part to play in the Centre of the Universe. Whether it is the care of the cattle or the tilling of the soil. And then there is much discussion. This occupies our evenings.'

'No meditation?' Jessica asked.

'No meditation, Miss Jones. The Followers are a group, not an accumulation of individuals. We believe in discussing, everything.'

'Sounds like fun,' Golightly said. 'Well, you can put me down for the cows, Mr Zobeir. My dad is a farmer when he's not doing something else. He has seventeen of them. I've always enjoyed milking cows.' He eyed Jessica, speculatively. 'I love pulling tits.'

'All in good time, Mr Golightly. But first, as novitiates, you must become part of the spirit of the community. This requires that you must share everything you possess.'

144

'Here we go. But Harry Walton did say that even to think about this place gave him goose pimples. Nice goose pimples.'

'Of course, Mr Walton is your sponsor. But now you will appreciate why Mr Kwarism insisted that you leave your valuables in Kano. You would have been unhappy had you arrived here to have your money and personal possessions shared amongst the rest of us.'

'Unhappy! You sound like a British politician.'

'But what are possessions? It is the sharing of oneself, of the mind, that is the most important function of the Followers of the Lord. Even our domestic arrangements are subjected to this rule. For example, you may have observed that there are twenty-four houses in our village. This one is the eating-house, and beside it stands the cookhouse. There are twelve houses for those of our people who have decided to couple.'

'I'm surprised you recognize marriage,' Jessica remarked.

'We recognize our own ceremony, with its own laws, Miss Jones. Because the female of our species can bear only one offspring at a time, as a rule, mating between the human animals must be a matter of much seriousness, and some permanence.'

'I couldn't have put that better myself.'

'What about the other ten houses?' Andrea asked.

'They belong to the bachelors of our community, whether male or female. You will

145

share one of them, Mr Golightly, with three of our male Followers. As will Mr Lennon.'

'I share a house like this with three guys?'

'A much smaller house, of course,' Zobeir pointed out.

'What time did you say the chopper went back to Kano?'

'*That's* what's been bothering me,' Lennon said, with the air of a man just beginning to understand Einstein's theory. 'If you believe in marriage, and, er, all that sort of thing, how come there aren't any kids knocking about the place? Most African villages are crawling with kids.'

'No doubt the Lord will be happy to explain that, and anything else that may be troubling you.' Zobeir stood up as Ukuba entered.

'You have enjoyed your meal?'

'I didn't think I would,' Golightly said. 'But I am quite replete. On the other hand, the more Zobeir tells me about this paradise of yours, the less I like it.'

'You are naturally conservative, Mr Golightly, and therefore instinctively dislike social conditions to which you are not accustomed. Give us time.'

'Yeah. I'd like a word in private.'

'We are in private, Mr Golightly. There can be no secrets in the Centre of the Universe.'

Golightly flicked a dead mosquito from his wrist. 'If that's how you want to play it. The fact is, Mr Ukuba...'

'You must address me as "Lord" here in the Centre of the Universe, my son.'

146

'Oh, very well, my lord, I just wanted to say that in my opinion this set-up of yours is one big fraud designed to fleece rich guys like me of our money. So I want out. You send Mr Lennon and me back to Kano, and we'll call it quits. You can keep the deposit, but you're sure as hell not going to get any more.'

Ukuba smiled. 'I am afraid that the borbor seems to be still working, making you feel disoriented. By tomorrow morning you will be fully refreshed, and fully in command of all your faculties as well.'

Golightly stood up, a trifle uncertainly, as he had had several gulps of the date wine. He leaned on his stick. 'Now you look here...'

Ukuba clapped his hands and two large Followers came into the hut. 'These are my grandsons, Fodio and Kanem.'

Jessica's head jerked, but Kanem did not appear to notice: if she was staring at him, he was staring at Andrea. He was good-looking in a spare, aquiline fashion, as was Fodio, who certainly looked like his brother. But they were both clearly very fit and very powerful.

'Mr Golightly appears to be confused,' Ukuba said. 'I think he is drunk. Would you remove him, and place him in ... hut number six, I think. Tell the young men to keep him there until he is recovered. I think tomorrow morning would be best.'

'You lay a finger on me and I'll knock your fucking blocks off,' Golightly snapped. 'Up, Pete.'

147

'Well, now, look here, Mr Ukuba...' Lennon also got up.

'Physical violence is strictly forbidden in the Centre of the Universe,' Ukuba remarked. 'Except when my will is defied. Remove them.'

The men stepped forward, and Golightly raised his stick. Apart from being a big man, he was also clearly fit and able to take care of himself. Normally. But the drug in his system made him appear to be moving in slow motion. Fodio ducked under the swinging arm and hit him in the stomach. Golightly gasped, and doubled, and Kanem stepped behind him and struck him on the nape of his neck with the edge of his hand. Golightly continued on his way with no further sound, save for that of his body hitting the earth.

'Oh, my God!' Lennon cried.

Andrea uncoiled her feet, and Jessica put a hand on her arm. While their combined skills might well be able to handle these two toughs, there were quite a few other toughs waiting to take them on if Ukuba summoned them, and what she had seen happen to Golightly made her unwilling to risk anything physical until she was quite sure the drug had left her system. She had not yet seen any sign of a weapon, or any means of leaving the island, save by the helicopter. Equally, they had not yet glimpsed their quarry.

'I hope you did not hit him too hard,' Ukuba commented.

Fodio knelt beside the unconscious man,

148

put two fingers on his neck. 'No,' he said, tersely.

'Then take him to his hut. Put Mr Lennon in number four. He is also to be confined until tomorrow morning.'

Fodio pulled Golightly into a sitting position, then got him to his feet, put his shoulder into the big man's stomach, and lifted him with only the slightest effort. 'Wowee!' Andrea commented.

'You may leave now, Mr Lennon,' Ukuba invited.

Lennon went out of the door, Kanem at his shoulder.

'I am truly sorry that happened, Miss Jones, Miss Hutchins,' Ukuba said. 'And that you had to witness it. But it is surprising how many people come here with pre-conceived ideas. You know, the concept that one can be freed from the prison of the over-civilized mind is a most attractive one. But so few people understand that to achieve that state such an over-civilized mind must first be emptied of those absurd pre-conceptions.'

'The in word is "brainwashing",' Jessica suggested. 'Are you thinking of doing that to us, too?'

Ukuba sighed. 'I would like to think that it could be possible, Miss Jones. But I suspect your mind is too highly trained to be susceptible.'

'I'm not with you. Why should my mind be more highly trained than Golightly's?'

'Simply because you are one of England's
149

best-known police officers, and he is not.' He smiled at Andrea. 'Are you also a police officer, Miss Hutchins?'

Andrea looked at Jessica.

'We have no idea what you are talking about,' Jessica said, feeling an utter fool even as she uttered the words. But she was also very angry. When she worked out which bastard had set them up...

'Oh, please, Sergeant. It is sergeant, is it not? At least do me the credit of not considering *me* a fool. I have known who you are almost from the moment you set foot in Kano.'

Jessica drew a deep breath. 'I am sure, my lord, that you, with your immense wisdom, understand that even police women, in fact, police women probably more than most, are subject to extreme mental pressures. My friend and I were told that we could obtain relief from those pressures by joining your Fellowship.'

'I am sure you would be able to do so,' Ukuba agreed. 'Were you genuinely in search of such relief. But you are the first would-be Followers ever to introduce weapons into our midst.'

'Weapons?'

'You will not deny that in the bags you left at my son's house there are two machine-pistols?'

'Shit!' Andrea muttered.

'We are police officers,' Jessica said. 'It is our business to be armed.'

150

'But those are neither regulation British weapons, nor did you bring them into the country with you. You purchased them from the man Masud.'

'Masud!' Jessica said, far more calmly than she actually felt.

'He is a Follower, you see, Miss Jones.'

'Shit!' Andrea said again.

Jessica wondered if Matthieu had known that. But there were so many imponderables that had suddenly sprung up around her. 'Ukuba,' she said, 'I am getting a distinct impression that we are not welcome here. So I suggest that you put us in your helicopter and send us back to Kano.'

'I am afraid that may not be possible.'

'I think there is something you should know,' Andrea said. 'One of the first things we did on landing this morning was make our number with the local police. He was a real nice guy, named Douglas Kahu. You may have heard the name. Well, he was so pleased to have us on his patch that he invited us out to dinner. And we accepted. He was supposed to pick us up at eight. I reckon that's about two hours ago. What do you think he's doing now?'

'He will have gone home,' said a quiet voice. 'Assuming that you have stood him up.'

Jessica stood up before she could stop herself. The voice had come from the darkness at the rear of the hut, which meant that the woman must have been there all the time, watching them, listening to them. Now she

151

came into the light, and Jessica suppressed a gasp. The only word to describe Claudine Matthieu was exquisite. She was very small, certainly no taller than Jessica herself, and even under a haik, clearly very slim. Her hair was black, brushed neatly past her shoulders, with a low fringe over the forehead. It was her features which were unforgettable. Also small, every contour fitted perfectly into the next. Her mouth was a superb rosebud, her eyes dark. Her nose, surprisingly for a half-Touareg, was small and could almost be described as snub. Her chin was pointed, her complexion pale but flawless. And her voice was entrancingly liquid.

She came up to them. 'My husband sent you.'

'Ah...' But she and Andrea were up the creek at this moment. 'Yes, he did.'

'To kill me.'

'To speak with you.'

Claudine regarded her for several moments. 'What about?'

'He misses his son. I hope the boy is well?'

'My son is very well. Misses him? Henri wants him back.'

'Well, he is his father. He feels that you could come to some arrangement.'

'For which purpose he sends two armed police women looking for me. You are either a fool, Miss Jones, or you take me for one. If he merely wishes to discuss the future of our son, why did he not come himself?'

'He said if he came himself you would

152

kill him.'

'And you believed him.'

'He sounded pretty sure.'

'He is a hysterical man,' Ukuba commented. 'I always knew this. As I have told you, Miss Jones, physical violence is not tolerated amongst the Followers unless specifically authorized by me. And certainly death by violence is abhorrent to me, and to my people.'

Jessica looked at Andrea, realizing that they might just have been thrown a lifeline, if they dared use it. But Andrea was looking thoroughly bemused. The decision would have to be hers alone.

'Henri knows that as well as anyone,' Claudine said. 'He did not send these people here to negotiate about Hercule. He sent them to kill me.'

'Why should he wish to do that, my child?'

'Because I left him. With Hercule. He is a vengeful man.'

'He certainly seems worse than I suspected. But to send women to carry out such a crime, and for them to have accepted such a commission ... They must be truly debased creatures. The question is, what is to be done with them?'

'JJ,' Andrea whispered.

Jessica squeezed her hand, and looked at the doorway of the hut. Fodio and Kanem had returned and were standing there. And Kanem was again staring at Andrea. But that made an already grim situation potentially a good deal worse.

'They should be executed,' Claudine said.

Andrea caught her breath.

'That is not acceptable,' her grandfather said.

'They must certainly be expelled from the Centre of the Universe,' Zobeir said.

'Yes,' Claudine agreed. 'Let them be put off the island.'

'To go where?' Kanem inquired.

Claudine shrugged. 'That is up to them. It is only about ten miles to the mainland on the Nigerian side.'

'You mean to make them walk?' Kanem asked.

'The lake is hardly more than four feet deep between here and Nigeria. If they encounter a deeper patch they will have to swim a little.'

'And the crocodiles?'

'Crocodiles sleep during the night. Well, most of them.'

'My lord,' Kanem said, 'what she is decreeing is as much a death sentence as if we strangled them here before you.'

Andrea's fingers were tight on Jessica's. But then, Jessica's were tight on hers. Just as if they were two frightened little girls instead of two of the most highly trained, and dangerous, women in the world. But it was coming up to crunch time, and there could be only one way out, even if she had no idea what might happen when she took the lid off of that Pandora's box.

'You are right,' Ukuba said. 'I had no idea

154

that you could be so vicious, Claudine. They must be punished, but they are only the tools of a wicked man. They must be expelled from the Centre of the Universe. And they must be punished for what they have tried to do. Have them confined overnight, and tomorrow, when the helicopter has returned from refuelling, have them taken into the desert, a hundred miles from shelter.'

'Two European women?' Kanem protested. 'That will be a more certain death than the crocodiles.'

'It will be the decision of their gods.' Claudine smiled.

'Well, that's it,' Jessica said. 'You condemn us to death for an unproven crime, Ukuba, yet you shelter and protect in your midst a woman who is a mass murderess. Is that simply because she is your flesh and blood?'

There was a moment's silence, while Claudine's face stiffened.

'I do not understand you,' Ukuba said.

'Then listen. My colleague and I were not sent here by Mr Matthieu. That was our cover story to gain admittance to your home. We came here to see your granddaughter, yes. But it has nothing to do with her son or the state of her marriage. We came here to arrest her for master-minding and taking part in the blowing up of the De Groot Clinic in Chicago in 1998.'

'You unutterable liar!' Claudine cried. 'Who put you up to this? My husband?'

'That is hardly likely, Mrs Matthieu, seeing

155

that he was also involved. The evidence was presented to my superiors at Scotland Yard by the Central Intelligence Agency, who are also on your track.' She took a deep breath. 'And indeed, are close behind us.'

Claudine stared at her for several seconds, and then looked at Kanem. It was a very quick look, but Kanem swallowed, and Jessica immediately deduced the truth. So Kanem had been the other man who had left the hospital with the 'Smiths' immediately before the explosion. She thought that piece of knowledge might come in very handy – at the right moment.

'The CIA?' Ukuba asked. 'Scotland Yard? Can these accusations be true, my child?'

'Of course they are not true,' Claudine snapped. 'It is all some trick concocted by Henri.'

Ukuba stared at her for several moments, while Jessica held her breath and squeezed Andrea's hand more tightly yet.

'I had never expected to hear you lie to me,' Ukuba said.

'I...' It was Claudine's turn to draw a deep breath. 'It was done for the boy. We could not trust those people to keep silent. It was too great a risk.'

'So you killed a hundred people? To kill one human being is an abomination in the sight of God.'

'It is of no account. None of them were believers.'

'How can you say such things? You have a
156

lust for blood and violence. You revealed it but a few moments ago, when you would have sent these women into the swamp. And to think that I have nurtured you as my own, cared for you, educated you ... Now you are hateful to me. I shall not look upon your face again.' He turned towards the door.

'You miserable old man!' Claudine shouted. 'Do you think any of the Followers give a damn for your outdated morality, your absurd laws? They are all only waiting for you to die so that Hercule can become the Lord. And when he does that...'

'Do with her what you will,' Ukuba said, and left the hut.

'Well,' Claudine said. 'Good riddance. Now we can do what needs to be done. Dealing with these two bitches, for a start.'

Andrea's fingers tightened, but Jessica was content to wait on events for the moment. Correctly.

'The Lord must be obeyed,' Zobeir said.

'Oh, don't you start. I meant what I said. When Ukuba is gone, I will rule the Followers of the Lord, in my son's name. My "father" will not interfere. Ukuba told him long ago that he lacked the mental capacity to be the Lord. When Hercule inherits, I will remember who were my friends, and who was against me.'

She looked from face to face. 'You are afraid,' she said contemptuously, 'of the wrath of an old man? Why do we not end it now? He will be alone in his hut. It could be done in seconds, and we will be free of his intolerable morality.'

'You are an evil woman,' Zobeir said. 'We will obey the Lord, and spare your worthless life. But we will not merely send you, or them, back to Nigeria. Your survival, as the Lord has said, must depend upon the will of your god.'

Claudine frowned at him, delicious features puckering. 'What do you mean?'

'Bind her arms.'

Kanem stepped forward.

'You would not dare,' Claudine snapped. 'You, Kanem? When I speak of...'

'Silence is golden,' Kanem said, 'for those who would survive.'

Claudine stared at him, and then gave a little snort.

She has just been promised her life, Jessica thought, by her faithful servant, who also appeared to be a relative. But where did that leave them?

The same question had occurred to Andrea. 'JJ,' she whispered. 'Can't we take these guys?'

There was still too much borbor in her system. And in Andrea's, she had no doubt. 'I think we have to wait awhile.'

By tomorrow morning the drug would have worn off; she had Ukuba's word for it. She was beginning to feel quite warm towards the old man.

Kanem had completed tying Claudine's wrists behind her back. She was breathing heavily and looked fit to spit, but she made no effort to defend herself.

'Now the ladies,' Zobeir said.

Kanem attended to Andrea, bringing a little gasp as, apparently inadvertently, he brushed her breast. Fodio did Jessica's, not brutally but she could tell very efficiently.

'You cannot send my son into the desert,' Claudine said. 'He is your future Lord. He would not survive.'

'Hercule will not go into the desert,' Zobeir said. 'He will remain here.'

'You would separate me from my son? You...'

'It is the best course,' Kanem said.

Again they exchanged meaningful glances, and again Claudine accepted his silent promise. Her shoulders sagged.

'Now summon Captain Anderson,' Zobeir said.

'Now?' Kanem was surprised.

'Now is always the best time.'

Kanem glanced at Claudine again, then left the hut.

'Why do you not sit down?' Zobeir invited.

'I think we'd rather stand,' Jessica said.

'As you wish. But you may be in for a tiring night. Ah, Captain.'

The Zimbabwean looked somewhat tousled. 'Trouble?'

'A matter that needs an instant resolution. You fuelled at Gwala on your way here?'

'That's right.'

'And thus you have sufficient fuel to return

there?'

'Sure. Plenty.'

'Do you have sufficient to make a detour?'

'If it's not too big a detour.'

'A matter of a hundred miles.'

'No problem.'

'Very good. I wish you to take these ladies one hundred miles north of here. That will be into the desert, will it not?'

'I reckon so. But...' For the first time Anderson seemed to notice that Jessica and Andrea had their hands tied behind their backs. 'What's up?'

'These two ladies have turned out to be Scotland Yard detectives, sent here to disrupt the Centre of the Universe.'

'You're kidding. These two pretty chicks?'

'Unfortunately it happens to be true. They have admitted it.'

'And you want them dropped off in the desert? It would be kinder to shoot them.'

'There can be no bloodshed in the Centre of the Universe, as you well know.'

'Yeah? Well...'

'You will also take the Lady.'

'Eh?' Anderson blinked at Claudine, and he realized that her wrists were also bound.

'It is the will of the Lord.'

'To dump her in the sand?' He scratched his head, and looked at Claudine. 'You go along with this idea, Lady?'

'It is the will of the Lord,' Claudine said, her voice now again soft.

'Well, stone the crows. Okay, Zobeir, I take

these chicks up north, and drop them there...'

'They must not be dropped in Chad. We do not wish any trouble with the government. Fly northwest and drop them in Niger. Then you can go on to Gwala and refuel, then return here.'

'Okay. I may need a hand. When we come down.'

'I will come with you,' Kanem said.

Jessica watched the bosom of Claudine's haik give a little flutter as she sighed with relief. Her future was secure.

'Then let's get this show on the road,' Anderson said. 'I was just thinking of going to bed.'

'Aren't you breaking the law in putting in all these hours?' Andrea asked. 'And you've been drinking.'

'Who's to know, sweetheart?'

'You're also about to become an accessory to murder,' Jessica pointed out.

'Who's to know about that either? I hate to say this, lady, but come the day after tomorrow you are just going to be a heap of bones. As you're wearing native dress, whoever finds you, if anyone ever does, is not going to have a clue who you are, or were.'

'God, but you are a *bastard*!' Andrea said.

'He will know,' Jessica said, looking at Kanem.

'But he'll be an accessory too, right?'

'Make haste,' Zobeir said.

'I must say goodbye to Hercule,' Claudine said. 'I cannot just disappear into the night.'

161

'That is the best way,' Zobeir said. 'We will tell him that you have been called away. He will get over it.'

Claudine stared at him so venomously that he actually looked disconcerted, but then the three of them were pushed out of the hut into the still bright night. The co-pilot had by now emerged, also looking somewhat tousled. 'What's up?'

'Get your gear,' Anderson told him. 'We're leaving now.'

'Shit! You know the time?'

'You can spend tomorrow in bed.'

The three women were pushed across the compound and up the steps to the helicopter, their arms held by the pilots to maintain their balance, only to fall against each other as they entered the cabin. Claudine made no comment; she seemed content to wait for Kanem to show his hand. 'JJ,' Andrea whispered as they slumped into their seats.

'I know,' Jessica said. 'Seems we chanced our arm a shade too far. I am most terribly sorry.'

'Forget it. I said when I went I'd like it to be beside you.' She looked at Kanem as he got in beside them. 'Tell me something: you just going to push us out, like the drug barons do?'

'Certainly I will not,' Kanem said. 'You will be set on the ground.' He fastened her seat belt, slowly and lovingly, using the opportunity again to stroke her breast. Andrea shivered.

162

Then he did the same to Jessica, but with less interest, to her relief. Lastly he turned to Claudine. 'When?' she asked.

'When we are away from here. Anderson will never disobey the Lord.' He strapped himself in beside her, immediately behind Andrea and Jessica. The engine started and the blades whirred. Jessica looked out of the window, down at Zobeir and Fodio, and also at several other Followers who had been disturbed by the noise and were emerging from their huts. Serene, who had been a silent spectator of the events in the hut, was there; Jessica wondered if Golightly was amongst them but could see no one of his size, so presumably he was still under restraint.

Then the watchers disappeared into the darkness as they rose above the trees and turned northeast. 'This is not at all comfortable,' Claudine remarked. 'Untie me.'

'We must not do that,' Kanem said. 'You know that Anderson has a remote camera sighted on the cabin.'

'So? If he comes back here, you can take care of him.'

'While we are flying? That could lead to a crash. You must be patient until we land. It will not be long. Would you like something to drink?'

'Yes.'

He produced a bottle and held it to her lips. Then he offered it to Andrea, who also drank greedily. Then he drank himself, and corked the bottle. 'What about my friend?' Andrea demanded.

'It would be a waste.'

'For God's sake...'

'Forget it,' Jessica told her.

Kanem grinned. 'You have courage. That is good. I will think of you, burning in the desert.'

They droned on, and Jessica lost track of time, but she supposed it was getting on for midnight. She wondered what Douglas Kahu was doing. Claudine was probably right in estimating that his initial reaction would have been annoyance at having been stood up. But she did not think he would have gone home without asking the reception clerk where they had gone. And once he knew that...

But what could he do? He had advised against visiting Kwarism, but he had not indicated that the police had anything more on the Touareg other than he was very wealthy and they were not sure he had come by his money legitimately. Certainly he could not go looking for them until tomorrow morning, or this morning she supposed it was by now. And then what? Kwarism had simply to tell him the truth: that they were would-be Followers of the Lord, and had gone off to join him on his island paradise. From what she remembered of Douglas Kahu, learning that they were two giddy women seeking some kind of personal salvation would put him right off wishing to have anything more to do with them.

'Setting down.' Anderson's voice came

through the speaker.

Jessica looked down; there was nothing to be seen but darkness. Yet the helicopter was definitely descending. She braced herself for what might be a crash, and suddenly a searchlight came on. It illuminated the land immediately beneath them, picking out some undulating sand dunes, and then a patch of boulders. As on the flight out – was it only twenty-four hours ago? – Jessica had a sensation of being an astronaut looking for a landing place on the moon. But within a few minutes Anderson seemed to find what he wanted, and the machine landed with a gentle bump. 'Okay, Kanem, do your stuff,' he said.

Kanem opened the door, and they listened to the soughing of the wind, although it was not as loud as when they had landed on the Centre of the Universe, probably, Jessica supposed, because there were no trees.

Kanem unfastened her seat belt, pulled her forward, and released her wrists. Now was the time to take him out, but for the moment her hands were quite numb, and before she could get them working he had grasped her shoulder and in a single movement threw her out of the doorway.

She plunged downwards, getting her hands up just in time to prevent her face from slamming into the ground, but it was actually quite soft, earth rather than sand. Even so, she had to roll over very rapidly to save herself from taking a mouthful of dust. She

165

lay on her back, looked up at the machine above her, the light gleaming out of the open door. 'Now you,' Kanem was saying.

'Are you mad?' Claudine snapped. 'We are partners. You are going to help me.'

'I would rather help the beautiful one,' Kanem said. 'She will be my woman.'

'What?' Andrea shouted. 'JJ!'

Jessica scrambled to her feet. There were no steps, but she thought she might be able to swing herself up, as long as Kanem was occupied. But Kanem had already forced Claudine to the doorway, and he had not untied her wrists. She gasped and panted, twisted and tried to kick him, but was handicapped by the folds of her haik. 'Bastard!' she shrieked. 'Crawling thing from the pit of hell! When I return...'

'But you are not going to return, Lady. And without you, there will be no evidence against me. Except from your husband, perhaps. But I can deal with him.' He pushed, and Claudine gave a shriek as she fell from the doorway.

Six

The Desert

Jessica, standing immediately beneath the doorway, could not get out of Claudine's way, but at least she was able to break her fall, even if inadvertently. They went down together, tumbling into the dust, and Claudine jerked her head up to avoid inhaling any of it. Then they were enveloped in a cloud of it as the rotors, which had been moving very slowly, picked up speed. Jessica thought she heard another shout from Andrea, and then the sound of the door slamming shut, and the roar as the machine lifted off.

The dust cloud increased in force and volume, and she had to grab as much of her haik as she could to hold across her face and protect her mouth and nose and eyes, but even so she could feel the grit against her teeth as well as penetrating it seemed every orifice in her body. Then it slowly subsided, although there was still a constant movement of dust in the wind, and the wind, she now realized, was bitingly cold. She sat up and gathered the haik around herself, at last appreciating the reason for it being made of wool, then looked at Claudine, who was

167

trying to get to her knees. 'Will you untie me, please,' Claudine requested.

'Well, I might just do that,' Jessica said. 'But first, I must tell you that you are under arrest. I should also warn you I am an expert in unarmed combat and will hurt you if you try anything I don't like.'

'For God's sake untie me,' Claudine said. Jessica untied her wrists. 'Thank you.' Claudine sat up, her back to the wind, and rubbed her hands together. 'That swine,' she muttered, and then raised her head. 'So I am under arrest. Do you have a warrant?'

'I'll get one, as soon as we reach somewhere civilized.'

'And when do you think that will be?'

'As soon as I can figure out where we are.'

'How are you going to do that? Have you ever been in a desert before?'

'Well, in a sort of desert. In Turkey.'

'You were on holiday?'

'No, I was on a job.'

'So you were fully equipped. You had food and water, you had a weapon, and you even had your GPS, I have no doubt.'

I also had the assistance of six very large, very strong, and very experienced members of the SAS, Jessica reflected.

'Anyway,' Claudine said. 'The Turkish desert, pouf. This is the Sahara.'

'And you know where we are.'

Claudine smiled. 'Give or take a hundred kilometres.'

'That sounds just great. So I think we'll play

it my way. Come sun-up we may be able to get some idea of our situation.'

'Your way will lead to death. If you wish to die, then do so. I will leave you here. But if you wish to live, then you will come with me. But we must leave now. When the sun rises it will not be possible to move.'

Jessica blinked in the darkness. 'How can you know where to go?'

'I look at the stars.'

I should be able to do that, Jessica thought.

Claudine stood up. 'So, are you coming, policewoman?'

'I can't go anywhere. I have no shoes.'

'Neither have I. But one can walk without shoes.'

'Can one? Why do you wish me to come with you, anyway? I have just arrested you.'

'That was in another world. This is a world of which you know nothing. I will take you with me for two reasons. In this world, two are better than one. And if I save your life, you can hardly seek to take mine. Or even lock me up. Come along.'

Jessica got up. She was faced with a situation which needed a lot of thought. But survival came first. '*Can* you save my life?'

'I do not know. But if I cannot, no one can. And if we die, we die together.' Jessica found that an oddly comforting thought.

They stumbled into the night. Jessica regularly tripped over unseen obstacles or lost her footing when she stepped into a hole; it was a miracle, she supposed, that she did not break anything. Soon her feet were aching, and she even thought they might be cut, but the SAS training she regularly undertook meant they were tougher than most. Claudine also fell from time to time, but she kept striding purposefully onwards, up small hillocks and down the other side, while the wind howled around them. The walking at least helped to keep them warm, and as yet Jessica was not aware of any hunger or severe thirst; she had had a very good supper. And whether it was still the borbor dulling her brain or sheer exhaustion, she felt remarkably relaxed. All manner of horrendous thoughts were roaming about the recesses of her brain, but for the moment they were kept at bay by the concentration required to put one foot in front of the other, pick herself up every time she fell down, and keep her eyes fixed on Claudine's back. A cold-blooded mass murderess, who would have had her executed, but who was now intent upon keeping her alive. For how long? she wondered.

The darkness ended with startling suddenness as the sun appeared, virtually without warning. Almost immediately the wind dropped, and with it the constantly swirling dust. Jessica had just tripped and fallen to her hands and knees for the umpteenth time, and she stayed there for some moments, looking around her. Again the moonscape, but the more terrifying in daylight and at ground level because it stretched forever in every

170

direction, without the slightest suggestion of a tree or a bush, much less any living creature. Just an endless, undulating, brown vista. And there was not a cloud in the sky to suggest any relief from the heat which was already surrounding her, or the glare that was already hurting her eyes. Sweat was rolling out of her hair and down her neck, and she could feel it on her body beneath the wool of her haik and tunic. Her bra was acutely uncomfortable and her feet had become one vast ache. She had an awareness of helplessness, of total defeat she had never before experienced, even when in the grip of the typhoon which had so nearly ended her life only a few months before. Claudine stopped walking and looked back. 'Why are you not coming?'

'Just thinking.' She struggled to her feet.

'We must walk for another hour,' Claudine explained. 'Before the sun gets too hot.'

'And what then?'

'We wait for it to get cool again.' She turned away and resumed her march, Jessica stumbling behind her. Her despair was overtaken by a sense of wonder, and of humility. Her entire life was spent in keeping fit, in practising her many skills; she existed in the total confidence provided by exceptional ability. Yet here she knew she was out of her depths. While the woman in front of her, certainly younger, and even smaller, on her husband's description a jet-setting hedonist for most of her life, had apparently not given a thought to the possibility that they might be about to die. She had been faced with a problem how to survive, and she was tackling it without a moment's hesitation. No doubt she had a strong motivation, the determination to regain her son, and almost certainly be revenged on Kanem as well, although how she was going to do that when she was now *persona non grata* in her grandfather's world was difficult to determine.

But what of her? Did she not have an equally compelling reason for returning to the Centre of the Universe? Andrea! Together they had experienced and accepted, and overcome, some pretty dicey situations in the past. And Andie, whatever her preferences, was capable of appreciating men – the right sort of men, such as Douglas Kahu. But she had been appalled at the situation Jessica had found herself in when she had been kidnapped. And now she was in an even worse situation herself. *Her* kidnapper had been an educated, cultivated man, driven half mad by what Jessica had become convinced was a flawed conviction for murder. Kanem was a savage, who was also as much of a mass murderer as Claudine ... or Matthieu.

The day had grown intensely hot without Jessica even being aware of it. She *was* aware that her legs felt like lumps of lead, that her eyes were narrow slits, that her tongue seemed stuck to the roof of her mouth, and that her head seemed to be opening and shutting like a drum. Now, without any warning, Claudine stopped walking, sat down, coiled her legs, and drew a fold of her haik entirely across her face. Jessica knelt beside her. 'Are you all right?'

Claudine's eyes appeared. 'Sit down and save your strength, Miss Jones. It may be four marches to the nearest water.'

'Say again?'

'I know where we must go, Miss Jones, but as I say, it may take four days.'

'You think we can survive for four days, without food, without water, and in this heat?'

'You must have courage, and determination, and faith ... in me, Miss Jones. Zobeir and Kanem suppose that we are certain to die. But they know nothing of the desert. The Kanembu, who are their people, are creatures of the forest. My father was a desert Arab, a Touareg, who taught me how to survive the sun and the sand. The Tubbu, the people of the Tibesti, sometimes make journeys of up to a week without tasting water. But we have to preserve the moisture in our bodies. So you must sit still. If possible, you must sleep. At dusk we will move on.'

'Supposing one simply has to pee?'

'Then do so. Once the water reaches your bladder, then it is no more use to your system. If we had any receptacle, you could drink it again. But as we do not, it is simply an unnecessary burden. Now, we must not talk anymore, Miss Jones.'

173

She disappeared once again beneath her robe, and was still, a small statue shrouded in a dusty cloth. Jessica sat beside her. The sand was hot enough to send waves of feeling surging through her body. She wound the folds of the haik loosely around her face, wishing she had gone in for yoga. Then she took off her bra, which seemed to be eating into her flesh. She massaged her feet and thought about Claudine for a while: there was so much to be discovered about this woman, so much to be explained. Then she thought about Andrea. The helicopter, even after a refuelling stop, would have regained the island by now. So, presuming Ukuba had not immediately banished her again, she would have been raped by now, at least once. On the other hand, she thought, if Ukuba *had* banished her again, it would have been back to Kano ... and the arms of Inspector Kahu. What a story she would have to tell him. But he wouldn't know where to look for Jessica...

Claudine shook her shoulder. Jessica's head jerked, and she tried to move, but her arms and legs seemed to have solidified. Claudine pulled the cloth away from her face, and she found that the sun was behind her, sinking into the sand as a blood-red ball. The heat was gone, too, from the air, but it remained trapped inside her clothes, a melange of sweat and dust and sand; at least there were no mosquito bites. Claudine helped her to her feet. 'The stiffness will wear off when you

174

walk, and we must travel far tonight, while we have our strength. There is a small sand sea to be crossed.'

'Where?'

Claudine pointed at Venus. 'We keep that on our right hand.' She set off with an almost military gait, and Jessica forced her legs to follow. Within a few minutes the hard ground had given way to sand. It was like walking along the seashore, much easier on the feet, but if one was left on the ground for more than a second it sank ankle deep. It was exhausting, but not a fraction so exhausting as just looking. The fading light made very little difference to their ability to see; the night was brilliant and the dunes were etched in perpetual waves, undulating into the distance, in front of them, behind them, and to either side of them. Claudine looked over her shoulder. 'It will be easier when we leave the sand sea. Perhaps tomorrow night, if we are lucky.'

Jessica placed one foot in front of the other. Tomorrow night was not a practical objective. The wind was rising now, whipping the sand into stinging spurts, and the temperature was dropping like a runaway elevator, plunging them into a cold more intense that the previous night. Or was it just that she was so much weaker? They walked and shivered and stumbled through the sand. Jessica even thought she slept from time to time, staring at Claudine's back. Then she was on her knees, her body turned to lead from the waist down. The wind accumulated the sand into drifts against her thighs. She watched Claudine walking away from her, into the brightness, for the moon had risen, and hovered above them like a frozen sun. Then she stopped, and turned, and came back. 'No, no, Miss Jones. We must keep walking until dawn.'

'Anything you say.' Jessica stood up, wondering why she cared.

Dawn came as suddenly as the previous day. Claudine sat down without a word, wrapped herself in her haik. Jessica made the mistake of attempting to lick her lips, found her tongue sticking to them. Even breathing was difficult, because of the dryness of her throat, and now rumbles of wind filled her belly, had her shivering and shuddering. Coherent thought was no longer possible. Her brain just drifted.

'Come.' Claudine dragged Jessica to her feet. It was sunset again, and cold. She had survived two days without water, without food. The sand was getting softer and deeper with every step. Again she had no idea of how far they had walked, until Claudine suddenly stopped. Jessica did not notice, and walked into her. Claudine made no sound, caught her, steadied her, made her stand still while she knelt and gazed at the ground. There was a moon again tonight, glistening out of a cloudless sky. And in front of them there was scuffed sand, stretching north, stretching south.

Jessica dropped to her knees. 'A caravan?'

The words sounded like an unintelligible blah.

'Many camels, certainly. Going north.'

'We'll follow them?'

Claudine shook her head. 'These are not fresh tracks, Miss Jones. You see, there are layers of sand across them. They could be two days old.'

'But if one caravan has passed this way, there will be others.'

'Maybe tomorrow, maybe next month. We cannot wait.'

'I tell you what. You go on, and I'll wait.'

Claudine stood above her, so close she could smell her sweat. 'You will die if you stay here, Miss Jones. No one should willingly die before it is time.'

'And you don't think my time may have arrived.'

'You will live many years yet.' Claudine stooped, held Jessica's face between her hands, and kissed her on the mouth. Incredibly, she still had saliva. It tasted like nectar.

'Tell me why.'

Claudine smiled. It was something Jessica thought she would never forget. 'We have much to do together.' They walked, and stumbled, and staggered through the sand. But now Jessica could think only of Claudine. Of that smile. And that kiss.

Jessica sat, her legs crossed, her arms folded, her head sagging. She no longer felt thirsty, in recognizable terms. Her mouth was filled with cotton wool, which, if left undisturbed by opening or speaking, was not positively unpleasant. The rest of her had no existence. Only her brain, hovering above its layer of cotton wool, was actively painful, actively unhappy with its situation.

'It will be easier today,' Claudine said. 'Look yonder.' Jessica raised her head. There was no change in the colours in front of them, but the texture was different, and the shape of the landscape had altered, too. It sloped upwards, and at no great distance erupted into outcroppings of rock, towering into the air, carved into grotesque shapes by the wind and the ever-eroding sand, hovering and cowering, seeming about to overbalance.

'Then what are we waiting for?'

'We still have a great distance to travel. Now be quiet.' Her mistress had spoken, and she obeyed. But this was real servitude, not psychological: without Claudine she had no being.

Another day, but today, surprisingly, she found it less easy to sit still, to sleep, even though before today she had never really understood the meaning of the word 'exhaustion'. Instead of resting, her brain raced. It occurred to her that she knew she was going to die this time, that she was not going to survive more than one more night. That Claudine would have to go on alone. She envisaged her as some sort of spirit, wander-

178

ing across the desert, carried by the wind, seeking death and destruction. Seeking vengeance. In the desert it was easy to believe in ghosts. 'Come,' Claudine said. It was still daylight, but the heat was fading. 'We will find the walking easier now.'

Jessica got to her feet. She reminded herself of a donkey. If she was a donkey, Claudine could ride her from time to time, taking the load off her feet. She thought it would be rather pleasant to spend the rest of her life clamped between those golden-brown thighs. But Claudine would be a cruel mistress, and she would make a poor donkey. So she was a bitch, tired but faithful, incapable of thinking for herself, obeying Claudine's voice, the only voice she knew.

Perhaps the going *was* easier. The sand thinned, but instead there were stones. It would be easier when she became used to kicking against things instead of extricating her feet – if she had time to become used to it. She was on her knees, and her knees hurt. Claudine stood above her. 'You must get up, Miss Jones.'

'Not this time. I've had it.'

Claudine knelt. This time she did not kiss her; she seemed able to evaluate accurately the condition of her responses. So she bit the lobe of Jessica's ear. Possibly, she thought, she bit it right off. But she did not even cry out. Claudine parted the haik, pulled at the tunic beneath, exposing Jessica's neck, and this time sank her teeth into the flesh of her

179

shoulder. Now the pain was considerable, and Jessica was angry. She struck at her, but Claudine caught her arms, as easily as if she were a child. 'Get up, Miss Jones.'

Jessica reached her feet, and started walking. As always, she kept her gaze fixed on the small of Claudine's back, on her buttocks, as they kept moving, rhythmically, beneath the white wool. Suddenly Claudine stopped, throwing out her arm. The moon was still bright but sinking into the horizon; they had walked most of the night. 'We must be careful,' Claudine said softly. 'There are people.'

For a moment the word meant nothing to Jessica, then she stumbled forward. Claudine caught her arm. 'In the desert, Miss Jones, no man knows his friends at a distance. Be patient. Just a little while longer.'

Now Jessica could hear sounds, lost in the shadows of the vast rocks in front of them. Then a voice spoke. *'Kallahani?'*

Claudine answered in French. 'It is peace.'

'Lo barko?'

'Our jeep is dead. In the sand sea. We have walked for three days.'

'Ndi durummi?'

'We have seen the sand, and the sky, and the wind. We have seen neither food, nor water, for three days.'

Now Jessica could see them. Three men armed with what looked suspiciously like Kalashnikovs; their faces were invisible behind the folds of their burnous. One of them now approached carrying a water skin. He peered at them, then offered it to Jessica. 'You first,' Jessica said.

'No, no, Miss Jones,' Claudine whispered. 'They can see that you are European. It is the yellow hair.' Jessica realized that she had pulled the haik from her head during the night. 'We will receive better treatment if they think you are a wealthy lady and I am your servant. But take just a little.'

Jessica rinsed her mouth, allowed some of the water to trickle down her throat. It was warm, and musty, but it tasted like vintage claret. She took another sip, then handed the skin to Claudine, who also drank and then returned it to the man. He beckoned them, led them between the rocks and into a ravine gouged by some long dry river. Here there was a fire, and then a tent, while further away several camels were hobbled together, stamping and snorting. Another, obviously older, man – although his face was also concealed – waited for them in front of the fire. Behind him there were two women, huddled close together, staring at the newcomers. 'This is not good,' Claudine whispered. 'These are not Tubbu. These are Touaregs.'

'Then are they not your people?'

'To them I am of mixed blood, and hateful. And those women are not Touareg.'

The older man came forward, peered into Jessica's face while she held the torn haik closer about her, and then pressed the palm of his hand against her knuckles. Then he

181

pointed to a large iron pot suspended over the fire. 'Couscous.'

'God,' Jessica said. 'He is offering us food!'

'You must eat only a little, or you will be sick.' Claudine helped her to sit down, stood behind her.

'My servant must eat also,' Jessica said in French. She reached behind her to grasp Claudine's haik and give it a suggestive tug.

Their host smiled, and nodded. Claudine sat down. Jessica took three fingers of the lamb stew, chewed, each movement of her jaws pure delicious agony, smiled at her host, and fell asleep.

Jessica awoke just after dawn, and already the stony wilderness was beginning to scorch, although the encampment in the gully was still shaded. She lay on the ground, some distance from the tent, and Claudine was beside her, also sleeping. Their hosts were seated around the couscous pot having their morning meal, while the women were engaged in stamping out the fire with their bare feet.

Now she was both hungry and thirsty, and every bone, every muscle in her body ached, while her feet were extremely painful. But the important thing was that she was alive, that she had survived just about the worst the desert had been able to throw at her. She felt an almost irrational sense of euphoria, combined with an urgent desire to take command of her life again, to follow her own agenda,

182

and brush all opposition aside.

The old man, seeing her eyes open, beckoned her. She got up, accepted a drink of water, attacked the food. In the daylight, she decided that they were a father and three sons. They wore green robes and had the 47s slung on their shoulders, while each man also carried a wicked-looking knife stuck in his sash. But they seemed friendly enough, and while two handsome unprotected women were essentially vulnerable, apart from their bodies, which had not been interfered with, they obviously had nothing worth stealing. She wondered why Claudine had been so instantly distrustful of them. They watched her in silence for a while, and then exchanged words between themselves.

Jessica wiped her mouth on her sleeve, allowed herself a gentle belch, hoping these were the right sort of Arabs. 'I think we need to have a chat,' she said in French. 'I will wake up my servant.'

'I am speaking French,' said one of the young men. 'And she sleeps well.'

Jessica hastily tried to remember if they had said anything incriminating the previous night in his hearing. But they had spoken English to each other, and behind the fold of his burnous there was no way of telling which one he was. In any event, she had to go along with Claudine's plan. 'Well, firstly, I wish to thank you all most sincerely for saving our lives.'

'It is the will of Allah,' the young man said.

'It is hard for us to know how you are in the sand sea, along with your servant. Have you no husband?'

She had to build on Claudine's explanation, and hope she could keep their story straight between them – and also hope to keep these men in their places, as it were. 'Yes, I have a husband. We were in a caravan, bound for Kano, but there was a storm, and we became separated. My husband will be searching for me. If you will take my servant and me to Kano, I know he will richly reward you.'

'We are going to Agadem.'

'Which is where, exactly?'

'North. It is a journey of several days yet.'

'Are we still in Niger?'

He nodded. 'If your husband has crossed the border, he will have difficulty in returning without another caravan. This will take time.'

The watching eyes had become mere slits; they were coming up to the crunch. 'My husband is looking for me now. He will not rest until he finds me. But we will go towards Nigeria. Towards Kano. I have said if you will help us, you will be well rewarded.'

'It is many, many days,' the young man said. 'And you are not strong. Agadem would be better. It is not far.'

'This place Agadem, it has an airport?'

'Sometimes.'

'Point taken. We will go south, to Kano. How far is it to the next water?'

The young man spoke with his father and brothers. Then he said, 'Two days on foot.

But we will give you a camel. And food and water.' The old man said something. 'And one of our rifles,' the young man added. 'That is good?'

'That is out of this world. *Beau Geste* was nothing like this. I have no money to pay you with.'

'It is nothing. We will show you the way to go, so you will no longer need your servant.'

'I sit corrected.' Now it had to be all bluff; they were coming into the open. She wished Claudine would wake up. Her hands were tucked inside her haik. Now she made a fist of her right hand, and pressed the wool outwards into a bulge; they would not be able to tell what she held there. 'I won't accept the rifle; I have no need of it. As for the woman, you would not like her. She is too thin, and she is lazy.'

The young man grinned. 'Thin, yes. We have looked, while she slept. But she is still young. She will grow plump. And she has a face a man can remember. We will accept her.'

Claudine's eyes were open, watching and listening. 'I think this young fellow is making you a proposition of marriage, in a roundabout fashion,' Jessica said in English.

'They would sell me, Miss Jones. They are slave traders, and I am beautiful.' It was a very simple statement of fact.

'So what do you think we should do? You're the local expert.'

Claudine sat up. 'If you wish to survive, you
185

have no option. You will not be able to continue on foot without me. A camel will take you where you wish to go.'

'And you?'

'I will become some sheikh's concubine. Or perhaps a dancer.'

'And Hercule?'

'I will escape and reach him, eventually.'

'And Kanem?'

'Oh, yes. And my husband. I will reach them also.'

'It seems to me that we should stick together,' Jessica decided. In fact she had no intention of letting Claudine out of her sight until she had sorted this entire business out – and come to a decision on the gratitude versus duty question. So she smiled at the men. 'I would willingly give you this woman in payment for your camel and your food and water, but it would be dishonest of me to do so.' She took her left hand from inside her haik and rested it on her crotch. 'She has the sickness.'

The young man gazed at Claudine. 'There is no evidence.'

'It is there.' Jessica moved her right hand beneath the haik so that the bulge, which might or might not be a revolver, became more prominent. 'So, if she is your price, it looks as if we will have to skip the camel and get on with it. Again, thank you for your assistance.'

The young man spoke with his father and brothers again, then all four got up and went

186

farther down the gully. The women continued their work, taking down the tent, occasionally glancing at Jessica. She moved over to sit beside Claudine.

'That was good of you, Miss Jones. But there is nothing to stop them taking what they wish. And from you too.'

'We'll put our trust in the rumoured disintegration of your down-belows, and their uncertainty as to just what I have in mind. Here they come.' She stood up, and Claudine stood behind her. She wondered if these people knew anything about unarmed combat, and then wondered just how capable she was of *any* combat. But she was riding a high.

'So be it,' the young man said. 'We must go to Agadem. But as it is written in the Koran, we shall leave you food and water.'

'In that case, I'll take back what I was thinking. And if I manage to lay hands on a healthy bit, I'll send you an e-mail.'

The women were loading the camels, cursing and shouting. The men bowed to Jessica, and mounted, also cursing and shouting to make the animals stand. The women walked, glancing at Jessica and Claudine as they passed, and disappeared up the gully.

'I suggest we finish our breakfast,' Jessica said, 'since they were kind enough to leave it for us. And then I suppose you'll say that we should doss down for the rest of the day.'

'We must make haste today, Miss Jones. They are going to come back. They only left

187

us the food to make sure we remain here for a while.'

'Why should they do that?'

'Because they mean to kill you.'

'If they intend that, why did they leave us at all? Or do you think they're scared of my supposed weapon? They have assault rifles.'

'They know that you are not armed, Miss Jones. They will have looked while you slept. But they wish to make sure that the rest of the caravan you spoke of is not close by.'

'Then how long before they reappear?'

'If we *are* alone, and without transport, they know we will only travel by night. They will give us time to go back to sleep. Two hours.'

'Then we've time to eat.' Claudine gazed at her for a moment, then sat down and helped her finish the couscous. 'Isn't that better? I could go on eating for the next few weeks and not feel full.'

'You are a strange woman. You have just survived an ordeal which would have killed most Caucasians. Yet you make jokes. Almost you sound happy.'

'I am happy because, having survived that ordeal, we are now back in my territory.'

Claudine looked left and right. 'You have been here before?'

'I meant dealing with men with guns.'

'You have done that before?'

'How many hot dinners have you had in your life? Now tell me, how does your complexion stand up to this climate? Mine feels pretty foul.'

188

'You are sunburned, yes. And there are bruises and sand marks. They will heal. You say you are used to dealing with men with guns. You mean to stay here?'

'I certainly don't mean to be harassed for the next few days.'

'But you have no gun of your own.'

'You and I have lots of other weapons, if we know how to use them. Let's get undressed.'

Claudine raised her eyebrows. 'You wish to have sex with me? Here? We are too dirty.'

'I'll say amen to that. I am thinking of all the B-Western movies I have ever seen.' She took off her haik and her tunic, laid them on the ground behind the fire, and proceeded to fill them with rounded stones, using a mini-boulder for the head, wrapped in the top of the haik. 'I have to confess that I have never actually had to survive an Apache attack, but I don't think our Touareg friends will be too familiar with them either.'

Claudine took off her haik and tunic – unlike Jessica she had no knickers – placed them on the ground and filled it with stones. 'What will we use for weapons?'

'When pushed, I can generally find something. Now, I figure that they will come from that rise over there, in order to shoot down on us. Me, anyway.'

Claudine looked her up and down. 'You don't think they will want to capture you alive? You have a very good figure.'

'You say the sweetest things. But I suspect

189

in their eyes I am too old to be worth a damn.'

'Even if you are right, they will not shoot you. They have no spare ammunition for those guns. I saw this. So they dare not waste what they have. One man will go up there to give them cover, but the other two will come down the gully itself to use their knives.'

'You'll make a cop yet. What about the fourth?'

'One must stay with the women, or they will run away.'

'Why should they do that?'

'Because they are slaves.'

'Oh. Right. Let's get up top.'

Claudine nodded, but instead of leading Jessica out of the gully, turned to the almost sheer slope behind them and went up it as if she were abseiling, her bare toes and fingers discovering cracks where apparently none existed, and then just as suddenly she halted, hanging above Jessica, arms and legs spread wide, while a rivulet of sweat coursed out of her hair, down her back to the cleft of her buttocks and dripped on to Jessica's upturned face. 'Four men,' she said. 'They will surely kill you if you try to fight them, Miss Jones. But if you were to go on and leave me...'

'One would suppose you *wanted* to spend the next year dancing. Remember what you said: if we go, we'll go together.'

Claudine disappeared over the lip, some twelve feet above the floor of the gully, and

190

Jessica began her ascent. It took considerably longer, and was extremely painful. Claudine knelt above her, waiting to grasp her arms and drag her to safety. She lay on her back on the burning ground, gasping for breath, while Claudine crouched over her. 'You are hurt. There is blood. Here.' She touched Jessica's breast, softly.

'I'll survive. I hope.'

'They are so big. I envy you.'

'Right now, I envy your small ones. Let's find some shelter.' Claudine led her to a boulder, from beneath which there protruded a stunted bush, situated some six feet from the lip. There she squatted, staring at Jessica. Little beads of sweat clouded her cheeks and forehead, pitting the soft sand dust which coated her skin. Jessica supposed she must look the same, although unlike Claudine she couldn't ignore the irritation, and kept wiping and scratching. 'Tell me why you blew up that clinic,' she said, 'if it was against the wishes of the Lord?'

Claudine shrugged. 'My son is more important than the Lord.'

'Is the Lord not your grandfather?'

'No, no. I am not of his blood. My father was killed by robbers, and my mother and I taken prisoner. We were rescued by Zobeir, who found us pleasing, and took us to the Centre of the Universe.'

'You mean you've been through this slave business before?'

'Of course.'

'So Zobeir took you and your mother as his own...'

'He took my mother. I was very young. But Ukuba did not approve. He married my mother to Kwarism, and commanded him to send me to France for an education. He wanted me for himself. He was younger then,' she added, ingenuously. 'And virile. But he could not make me pregnant, and he wished my child as his heir. He had no son of his own, you see.'

'I thought Kwarism was his son?'

'Kwarism is one of his adopted sons, the only one still living.'

'I'm in a fog. Where did Henri come into the picture?'

'Ukuba was determined that I should have a son, by the right father. So he went through all the eligible Followers...'

'That must have been quite a job. Aren't there ten million of them?'

'Oh, more than that. But he knew what he was looking for. So he chose Henri.'

'You mean there never was a beach in Phuket?'

'I do not understand you.'

'Just an aberration. So you married Henri on Ukuba's instructions.'

'Ukuba paid him ten million pounds to be my husband.'

'Looking at you, I'd say he got a bargain. And you got pregnant, and went into hospital for a minor op ... and blew the place up. You have to tell me why.'

192

'They have come back,' Claudine said.

Jessica heard nothing for several seconds, and then a stone moved, some feet away. She touched her lips with her forefinger, held Claudine's arm, and pressed it down. Claudine nodded, and made room for her to squeeze past and kneel at the corner of the boulder. She was not aware of any fear, or even apprehension. This was her job.

A man came up the slope from the desert below, his rifle thrust in front of him. His face was invisible behind the roll of woollen cloth, but he was clearly one of the three sons. He advanced slowly, carefully, yet with a sense of urgency; his brothers would not act until he was in position. He reached the lip, knelt, peered into the gully. Claudine's fingers ate into Jessica's arm. But the others would still be waiting, and watching.

The man raised his left hand above his head, moved it to and fro, lowered it again. Jessica counted to ten; the gully was at least fifty yards deep. She stood up, drawing a deep, dust-filled breath into her lungs. The last man she had killed had been someone she had hated. She had no reason to hate this man – except to survive – thus she had no desire to kill him. She walked quickly across the red-hot rocks, allowed her shadow to fall on the man's arm. The Arab's head jerked, and he rose to his feet, turning his head as he did so. Jessica had already sidestepped, placing herself between the man and the lip, and had anchored her feet, transferring every ounce of her hundred and twenty-five pounds of bone and highly trained muscle from her thighs up to her shoulder and thence along her right arm, swinging it down to chop the side of her hand into the Touareg's neck where it joined the shoulder.

The rifle slipped from the already inert fingers, struck the rocks with a clatter. The man's knees gave way, and he followed the gun to the ground with a dull thud. Jessica was already on her knees, ignoring the stinging pain in her hand, wrapping her fingers round the trigger guard as she looked over the edge. She saw the other two young men on their bellies, unaware of what had happened above them as they wormed their way towards the silent bundles of white cloth. Both had their rifles slung across their shoulders; as Claudine had said, they were going to rely on their knives. Jessica felt the woman beside her, knew she was investigating the dead man. She made no sound.

The first man reached Jessica's clothing, reared like a striking snake, his knife glinting in the sunbeam which reached the floor of the gully. Jessica stood up. 'Drop it!' She spoke English as she did not know the requisite French, but she had no doubt that she was speaking a universal language when backed with a gun. The leader turned, dropping his knife and pulling the rifle from his shoulder in the same instant. Jessica squeezed the trigger, and the green robe exploded into

194

crimson.

The second man fired, the bullets whining away into the sky. Jessica squeezed her trigger again, and nothing happened. Only then did she realize that her weapon had apparently not encountered grease or oil for a very long time. She dropped to the ground, trying to free the jammed trigger. 'Stay down!' she snapped at Claudine. But Claudine remained on her feet, a golden-brown fury, her midnight hair disturbed by the gentle breeze, the long blood-wet knife she had taken from the unconscious man's belt between the thumb and the first two fingers of her right hand. As the Arab turned his rifle towards her, a bubbling explosion of pure glee accompanied the whipping motion of her arm.

Blood-wet? Jessica looked at the man on the ground beside her. His throat had been cut.

Claudine peered over the edge. 'He is dying,' she said with satisfaction. 'And the other one is already dead. And this one is dead. This was superb.'

'Don't you believe in any of the Lord's principles?'

'Ukuba's world is impossible to achieve, Miss Jones, even were it desirable. It is but a dream which binds the Followers to him.'

'Now you tell me. Don't you think we should do something about the other bloke?'

'He will have heard the shots, but he will assume that they were all fired by his sons. He will be coming to us now, to find out what has happened.'

Jessica at last managed to free the trigger mechanism on the Kalashnikov. She wondered how old it was; the 47 had been replaced, a good thirty years ago, by the 74. 'I don't think much of the care they take of their weapons.'

'But you do not need a firearm. This man...' She stirred the corpse with her foot. 'I could not believe it, the way you hit him. You must teach me how to deliver such a blow.'

'You seem to be doing all right with a knife. Is that our friend?'

Claudine peered into the gully. 'It is the father.'

Jessica stood up, the rifle butt against her shoulder. 'Stop!'

The old man checked and looked up at the rocks.

'Tell him to unsling his rifle and throw it behind him.' Claudine gave the order and he obeyed. 'Now,' Jessica said, 'can you handle one of these things?'

Claudine nodded. 'My father taught me. When I was a little girl, every year for three months he would take me into the desert so that I could learn the skills of his people.'

'There's nothing like an indulgent father. Okay, down you go, collect one of those rifles, and keep the old man covered until I get there. Covered, mind.'

Claudine laughed, stooped, rolled the dead man over the lip, watched him plummet down to strike the ground at the feet of his father, and then followed, as gracefully as any trapeze artist. Jessica waited for her to reach the floor of the ravine and pick up one of the discarded weapons. Then she walked down the slope, the sun's heat smashing into her head like a physical force, the stones sharpening themselves on her bare feet.

At the bottom of the hill she came upon the camels, hobbled together. In front of them squatted the two women; their wrists had been bound behind their backs and then secured to a stake driven into the ground so they could not stand. They gazed at the almost naked white woman in alarm, mingled, she suspected, with amusement, and then with one movement shrugged their haiks from their heads. One was a Tubbu, plump and loose-mouthed; the other was a Negress, dark-skinned and disdainful; both were young and worth a second glance in any company.

Jessica untied their wrists but kept her rifle pointed at them as she beckoned them into the gully. They hesitated only for a moment, and then followed her, leaving the camels grunting and spitting. Claudine had regained her haik, and was seated cross-legged on the ground, her rifle on her knees, cleaning the bloodstained knife. The old man stood opposite her, hands clasped on his neck, gazing at the bodies of his sons. 'Tell these ladies that we mean them no harm,' Jessica said. 'And that they are at liberty to go where they please. We will take three of the camels and half of the food and water; they may have the other two.'

Claudine translated, and the Tubbu woman answered, vehemently. 'She says they have nowhere to go, Miss Jones, except with us. They say that they have lost their maidenheads and will not be welcomed back by their own people.'

'Well, suggest something.'

'It would be simplest to shoot them, Miss Jones.'

'Try again.'

'I do not understand you, Miss Jones. You have killed two men this morning already. What are two women? You are going to have to kill the old man in any event.'

'I don't think that will be necessary. And I personally have only killed one man, which I regret having to do. But the answer is still no. You tell them that we have no use for them, and that they must go their own way.'

Claudine shrugged, addressed herself to the Arab woman once again; the Negress screamed with laughter. 'That sounds promising.'

'I have told the Tubbu that you spit on her because her breasts are shrunken like dried dates, and her buttocks are bony like those of a camel, and she has the smell of a she-goat, and that if she does not take herself and her companion off you are going to shoot her in the belly.'

The Arab woman had already removed her haik and her tunic and was shaking herself to dispose of the first point; she was obviously about to attend to the others. 'Not dried dates,' Jessica said. 'Overripe pumpkins. But it's still no dice.' She shook her head. The woman scowled, and made a remark to Claudine. 'I won't ask what she said.' Jessica dressed herself, slung one of the Kalashnikovs, and pointed the other at the women. 'Tell them that we are going now. I have said that we will leave them two camels. But if either of them attempts to follow us I will shoot her.'

Claudine translated. The Negress sighed; the Tubbu rolled her eyes and made a suggestion. Claudine smiled, and then laughed. The old man dropped to his knees, hands clasped in front of his face, babbling at Jessica. 'She says, leave them the old man and they will stay behind.'

'He doesn't seem too pleased at that prospect. What will they do to him?'

'They hate him,' Claudine said. 'He has beaten them every day, and when they would not obey him he had his sons drag them through thorn bushes. They wish to kill him. Slowly.' She placed her foot on the old man's shoulder and pushed. He fell over, apparently still praying. 'It is what he deserves.' She shouldered the fourth rifle, picked up the knife, and stepped over his prostrate, gabbling figure.

'Where is the next water to the north?' Jessica asked.

Claudine shrugged. 'Several days.'

'Then tell the old boy to beat it.'

Claudine frowned. 'This man would have

raped you and then cut your throat, Miss Jones.'

'So I'm offering him sore feet and a big thirst.'

'Oh, he will get to the water,' Claudine said. 'He knows the desert as well as you know your own face. But he will not thank you for your mercy. He will hate you for killing his sons.'

'I'll add him to the bottom of the list. Now tell him.'

Claudine sighed, spoke to the old man. He gabbled something, scrambled to his feet, and hurried up the gully. 'I will just make sure he does not turn the camels loose.' Claudine glanced at Jessica. 'You do not wish me to shoot him? It would be best.'

'Just let him walk. What about these bodies? They should be buried.'

'No, no, Miss Jones. That would be a waste of time. They will be bones in a couple of days.'

Jessica supposed she was right; anyway, they had nothing to dig with. She faced the two women, who were still shouting and gesticulating. 'Now you just shut up and sit down, or I'll change my mind about the camels.' She pointed at the ground. 'Sit.'

They glowered at her, but sat down. Claudine returned, leading three of the camels, one of which was already laden with the folded tent, the sacks of food, and the skin of water. 'Ciao,' Jessica said, and walked behind her out of the gully.

Seven

The Police

'Where do you wish to go, Miss Jones?' Claudine asked.

'We are going to Kano, remember? At least to begin with.'

'Then you will return to Chad?'

'Just as soon as we have accumulated transport, clothes, and some usable hardware.'

'Then let us make haste before these women try to follow us.'

Jessica walked round the camels at a safe distance, but still managed to have what might have been a hose directed at her. 'You're going to have to teach me about these creatures. Do they do everything backwards?'

'Everything fundamental, Miss Jones. Two camels copulating make a most interesting sight. But this is not their breeding season.'

'Thank God for that. It seems to me that if there is anything wrong with this country it is that life is just too fundamental. What do I do first?'

Claudine shouted at the smallest camel, added a few pokes and thumps with the butt of her rifle, and he dropped to his knees, gazing at them with undisguised venom.

'Now you get on to the saddle, Miss Jones.'

'Famous last words. How's this?'

'Forward a little more. That is very good. Now kick him.'

'I wouldn't dream of it. Not while he's underneath me.'

'You must show him that you are his mistress.' Claudine swung her rifle, caught the unfortunate animal a savage blow across the rump. It stood up so promptly that Jessica nearly kept on going. Claudine scrambled on to hers, took the lead, clutching the halter for the third. Jessica copied her as best she could, but rapidly came to the conclusion that she had not by nature been designed as a camel jockey. But it beat walking through the sand sea; her feet no longer suffered. Against that, her stomach sagged and lurched along with her saddle, and sitting down was going to be difficult.

The rocks and boulders became larger and more numerous, and their progress began to resemble a drunken corkscrew. But now there was vegetation. They passed several suitable camping sites while the sun dropped into the western horizon, and still Claudine jogged along, head rising and falling with unchanging rhythm. 'Don't you think we could call it a day?' Jessica suggested at last.

'We must reach the water. It is not far.'

'We've enough for tonight, surely.'

Claudine looked over her shoulder; only her eyes showing above the fold of cloth across her nose and mouth. 'Do you not wish to be

202

clean again?'

'Well, if you put it that way...'

'We are here.' Claudine pointed. It was quite dark now, and for a few moments Jessica saw nothing, although her camel was certainly moving faster. Then they entered another of the long, narrow gullies between the rocks. Claudine halted her mount. 'You can get down, Miss Jones.'

'How do you recommend I do that?'

'You make it sit, like so.' She kicked and shouted at her mount, and it sank to its knees. Jessica tried the same intonations without success, until Claudine came to her aid. 'I will see to the camels and the tent. You would like a drink?'

'Where?'

'Just follow the cut, Miss Jones.'

Jessica descended the gently sloping rock passage, came to open ground with black earth, a scattering of palm trees, and a hole in the ground. She wasn't sorry the darkness prevented her from seeing anything more than that: this was water, and whether it was green or brown would not be apparent until morning. She lay on her stomach, rinsed her hair and neck, drank, wondered if she had sunstroke, as her scalp seemed to be lifting and falling with every breath. Claudine knelt beside her with the water-cans. She filled them, then drank in turn. 'Come.'

Jessica followed her to where the tent had been pitched, inside the gully itself. The camels were hobbled about fifty feet away, browsing on an incautious bush. 'This is the only oasis for some distance, Miss Jones, so we will not light a fire. In this ravine, no one will know that we are here.' She undressed, poured some water from a jerry-can into the drinking gourd, and with great care washed herself between the navel and the knee. 'Would you like me to wash you?' she asked.

'I think I can manage.' Jessica followed her example, although she also attended to her face and under her arms.

Claudine watched her. 'Now you wish to have sex with me?'

Jessica put down the gourd. 'It hadn't crossed my mind.'

'You are a handsome woman. I am a beautiful woman. Together we have survived much. Together we will accomplish much. It is fitting that we should also be lovers.'

'It's a powerful argument. Trouble is, I'm over-civilized. I only like to have sex in a soft bed between clean sheets and after a hot bath. I'd even settle for a cold shower. But lying on the ground with sand everywhere it shouldn't be doesn't turn me on.'

'You pretend to be effete. But I have seen you kill. You like to act a role, but you are as ruthless as I. We are two of a kind.'

'Close. But I wouldn't say entirely.'

'You still wish to arrest me for the destruction of the clinic.'

'Correction. I *have* arrested you for the destruction of the clinic.'

'You think you can do this? Did I not save your life?'

'I know you did. I am grateful. I am considering the matter.'

'Do you not know that I can kill you whenever I choose?'

'Your confidence amazes me. Would you like to do it now?'

Claudine gazed at her. 'I have the knife.'

'I think I should take care of it. Just to remove temptation.' Claudine's gaze seemed to have grown more intense. But the knife lay with her clothes, within reach, certainly, but then, she was within Jessica's reach. 'Just don't move,' Jessica warned. 'Because if you do, I will break your arm. I mean that most sincerely.' Claudine's breath hissed, but she remained still as Jessica picked up the knife and the two Kalashnikovs and laid them beside her own weapons. 'I really am sorry this had to happen,' she said. 'I thought we were going to work as a team until we can sort things out at the Centre of the Universe.'

Claudine continued to stare at her for some seconds. Then she said, 'I must agree, as I am your prisoner.' She lay down, and appeared immediately to go to sleep.

The spell of unity which had brought them out of the desert had definitely been broken. That had been bound to happen, of course, Jessica realized. She would have to sleep with one eye open from here on, with one caveat: Claudine certainly wanted to regain possession of her son, just as she desperately wanted

205

vengeance for her betrayal by Kanem. For both those reasons she needed to tag along with her. Afterwards ... Well, she'd face that problem when the time came. Because she wanted to return to the Centre of the Universe just as desperately, to rescue Andrea.

And the Followers of the Lord? Jessica had never considered herself to be a deep thinker on matters of philosophy or ethics, outside the uncompromising business of enforcing the law, and even that she was now bending to suit herself. But always there had been the case to be handled, or in more recent years, the client to be protected. She had been given a target, a job to be done to the best of her ability. Results had proved that her ability was considerable. It was only in the past year that she had ever paused to consider the guilt or innocence of the person opposing her. She brought them to justice, and provided the evidence. After that, it was in the hands of the courts.

The Followers of the Lord were outside of her experience. If Zobeir, Fodio and Kanem were three people she would cheerfully take on, not to mention the two pilots, were all the rest crooks? Or even fanatics? Or just innocent and rather stupid people who honestly thought that by sharing their thoughts and believing in abstractions rather than doing something concrete they could turn their lives around? She moved her hand to touch the assault rifles. Because whatever their true motivation, she could not doubt that they would close ranks about their lord. To go in there with all guns blazing was not really an option. And what of the Lord? Was he a true mystic, with possibly the seeds of greatness in him? Or a criminal charlatan who had become enormously wealthy through exploiting other people's weaknesses?

And all of those reflections left the decision on what to do with the utterly ruthless killer lying only a few feet away from her ... to whom she owed her life.

Jessica slept more heavily than she had intended, and awoke to the blaring of car horns. Claudine appeared to be still asleep, so she snatched a Kalashnikov and ran outside – to gaze at two jeeps blocking the entrance to the gully, and at least a dozen obvious policemen. One of these, apparently an officer, shouted at her, at the same time levelling his pistol. The odds were too great. Besides, these people had to be on her side. She dropped the rifle and raised her hands. Behind her she heard movement, and could only pray Claudine was not going to do something stupid. 'These are Chad policemen,' Claudine said. 'We must have strayed back across the border.'

Jessica had to wonder how much of an accident that had been. And on whose part. Claudine had certainly given the impression that she had always known just where they were. 'In which case,' she said, 'you had better leave the talking to me. *Bonjour, monsieur*. Are

207

we glad to see you.'

The officer came closer. He was a large, plump man, of medium height, light-skinned, and wore his cap, a French – type kepi, at a rakish angle. 'My God!' he commented, taking in Jessica's yellow hair, and more than that: the haik was now in rags. 'You are French?'

'English. My name is Joanna Smith. I'm a scientist. Perhaps you have heard of me?'

'Joanna Smith. The name has a familiar ring to it. But what are you doing here? And wearing Arab clothing?'

'I always wear Arab clothes. My jeep broke down in the sand sea. I'm afraid my papers and equipment are still there.'

'I am Faure.' Jessica shook hands. 'But we were not informed of your coming. That is not right.'

'Ah, well, you see, we were actually in Niger. They know all about me there. But when we were stuck, my companion' – she smiled at Claudine, who was hiding her face behind her haik – 'said she knew which way we should go, so here we are.'

'You walked out of the sand sea?'

'I thought our number was up, too. But she's very efficient.'

'Come here, woman.' Claudine advanced. Faure seemed to find her semi-naked body even more interesting. '*You* are French?'

'I am Miss Smith's assistant.'

Faure looked from one to the other; neither of them came much above his shoulder.

208

'Truly, Miss Smith, this is a most remarkable thing. And this young woman ... You did not by any chance buy her?'

Claudine tossed her head and pulled the haik from her head. 'I am not for sale. I am of the family of Ukuba.'

'Ukuba? Then I apologize. I only mentioned the matter because this is not a routine patrol. We are on the track of a notorious slaving gang. A father and three sons who have been selling women to the desert sheikhs. You are most fortunate to have avoided them, for our information indicates that they are travelling this way, and they will certainly stop at this water hole. Of course you seem to be well armed ... Do you know how to fire that thing?'

'Actually no,' Jessica confessed. 'But we felt it would be a good idea to have it along, to sort of wave at people, don't you know?'

'Ah. Yes. And the camels? Where did you find them? They are fine beasts.'

'Well, to tell you the truth, I think we took them off the men you are looking for.'

'You took them off the Touareg.' Faure nodded. 'Oh, yes, I understand, Miss Smith. I have met the English before. Always the jokes, eh? Now, I have a bottle of wine in my pack. Two, in fact. It is hot, and not very good vintage, but drinkable. Let us drink it while my men fill their canteens, and we will speak about this adventure of yours. And I would be honoured if you would join us, Princess.'

'I shall be pleased to do so.'

'Silly of me,' Jessica said in English. 'It never occurred to me that you would be a princess. Even if an adopted one.'

They breakfasted with the captain, and told him of their encounter with the slavers. Faure listened with obvious incredulity. 'This is the truth?' he asked when they had finished.

'It is what happened.' Claudine glanced at Jessica. 'She is good with the hands. And also the guns.'

'No one will ever believe such a report,' Faure opened his second bottle of wine. 'That two beautiful young women liquidated a slaving gang of Touaregs. Believe me, Miss Smith, my life is composed of reports, and red tape, and endless arguments with the people in Fort Lamy over what is and what is not possible in the desert. I have a proposition to make to you.'

'That is very nice of you, but I'm afraid I am committed to the princess.'

'Oh, you are a funny woman, Miss Smith. My proposition is that we say you had these camels all the time, walking behind your jeep, because you are a cautious woman, eh, and have driven in the desert before. And when I return to Mao, my headquarters, I will contact my opposite number in Niger and tell him we have heard a report of a gun battle at the oasis of Nzola, and let him take it from there. He will never relate it to you. This will save a lot of red tape. If you agree, I will give you food and water, and a paper which will allow you to continue on your way. Perhaps

210

you would be good enough to tell me your first destination?'

'Kano.'

'Ah. That is a long way by camel. Listen, when I return to Mao I will radio the police in Kano and tell them the situation, and ask them to pick you up at the border. Would you like that?'

'More than anything else in the world. May I ask you a question?'

'Of course.'

Jessica smiled at Claudine. 'We had been hoping to continue to Lake Chad.'

'Of course. You are the famous naturalist. There is much wildlife in the lake.'

'I suppose you could say that I'm a bit of an anthropologist as well. I also study animals and bugs, and even human beings. The princess keeps suggesting that we should visit some place called the Centre of the Universe. Have you heard of it?'

'Of course. And if the princess is of the family of Ukuba, then she must be related to the present Ukuba, who is known as the Lord.'

'I am a distant relative,' Claudine said.

'You say you know of it,' Jessica said. 'Have you been there?'

Faure shook his head. 'I only know of it by reputation. It is easier to approach from the Nigerian coast of the lake.'

'Which was our original intention, as I told you. But that was before my jeep broke down.'

'To take a jeep into the sand sea at all was a dangerous business, Miss Smith. But of course, you had your camels along as a precaution, eh? Very wise.' He chuckled to show that he was as capable of making jokes as the next man. 'But you can still go. It is simply a matter of crossing the lake. You must arrange for a boat. It would be a difficult task at the moment because there is little water. But soon the rains will come. It always rains, eventually. After you have been to Chad, will you be turning this way?'

'That depends on my transport situation. But I suppose I could. Why?'

'I would like you to come to Mao, and pay me a visit. I would like to know what you find in this Centre of the Universe.' He glanced at Claudine. 'But of course, you have been there.'

'No,' Claudine said. 'I have never been there. That is why I would like to go, and see my relatives.'

'Ah. You mean you are not a Follower of the Lord?'

'A Follower of the Lord? What is that? I am not a Christian, if that is what you mean.'

'Ah,' Faure said again.

Jessica decided to let Claudine play her own game for the moment. 'Why haven't you been there yourself, if you're so interested?'

'The island is situated somewhat in the Nigerian portion of the lake, and it would not be good for a Chad policeman to go invading it. Besides, many people, and my superiors are amongst them, dismiss any sect which can give its headquarters such an absurd name as not worthy of even our contempt. But, if you will excuse me, Princess, it is my opinion that the Followers of the Lord are a group about which every policeman, but more especially those in Equatorial Africa, should learn. I would greatly appreciate your views.'

'I understood they were a pacifist organization.'

'Oh indeed. Very pacifist, Miss Smith. But do you not find something disturbing about pacifism today? Something sinister? It is concerned with disarmament, with opposing globalization, with peace between peoples. These are certainly admirable objectives. But the methods employed appear to endorse, or at least be unable to control, a terrifying amount of violence, both to persons and property. I wonder if pacifism today is just a cloak for anarchy.'

As a policewoman, Jessica entirely agreed with him. But she contented herself with scratching her ear while glancing at Claudine, whose face remained impassive. 'And the Followers of the Lord are a pacifist group *par excellence*. Just how far the group extends, how many members it commands, is not known, but certainly it is widespread in Africa. And still we cannot be sure how widespread. Once upon a time, you see, the police reports from all the British – and French – controlled territories would have been correlated and could easily be accessed. Now we have more than a dozen rival nations, all determined to preserve their integrity, to guard their own archives, regardless of the possible cost. And the cost may be high.'

'You are accusing my grandfather of contemplating a continental revolution?' Claudine asked.

Faure did not appear to notice her slip. 'No, Princess. I believe your grandfather is genuine in what he preaches. But you cannot deny that he has many thousands, perhaps millions, of lives at his command. And he is a very old man. What if his successor decides to use this immense power? What could the authorities do to stop him if he should start leading mobs on marches of protest? Open fire? Then they would mow down thousands of unarmed men and women, and perhaps even children, and would immediately be condemned by world opinion. This is a new kind of warfare, Miss Smith, even more dangerous than the suicide bomber, although it too is waged with human bullets. Who knows; perhaps it has already begun. Who can say how many Followers of the Lord have taken part in the anti-globalization protests of the past few years, or the recent anti-war demonstrations? There is only one fact which is certain: our reports indicate that the number of Followers is increasing, almost every day, and the number of protesters throughout the world is also increasing, almost every day. Such numbers cannot be spontaneous. Nor can such huge numbers of ordinary people all afford to travel round the world to gather where it is considered appropriate. They must be receiving both direction and support.'

'That's quite a nightmare scenario,' Jessica remarked.

'Let us hope it remains only a nightmare, Miss Smith. To reassure myself, I would like to discover the true nature of the Followers of the Lord. I would like to know where they are going, what is their ultimate aim. I would like to stop them, if that is possible. So you come to Mao on your way home from the Centre of the Universe, and we will talk.' He stood up. 'And now, we must be on our way. The Nigerian border is but fifty kilometres away, and as I have said, as soon as I regain Mao I will radio Kano and make arrangements for you to be met. Is there anything else you need?'

'You wouldn't have any clothing to spare, I suppose?'

'I am afraid not.'

'I'd settle for a belt and a haversack.'

'I think we can manage that.' The belt was far too large for her, but Faure had his men punch appropriate extra holes. 'I will bid you goodbye, Miss Smith.' He kissed her hand. 'And you, Princess.' He kissed Claudine's hand in turn. 'You have made my day bright indeed.'

They watched the jeeps roll out of the gully and disappear into a dust cloud. 'Miserable bastard,' Claudine remarked. 'He could easily have sent us to the border in one of those jeeps. As for having to return to Mao to radio Kano, did you not see the aerial on his jeep? Or the cordless telephone on his belt?'

'I did,' Jessica agreed. 'But I would say he does not wish to be too closely identified with us until he has done some investigating. Our story was a little thin.'

'And if he investigates, and finds out that there has been no scientific expedition headed by a Miss Smith?'

'Then all he has to do is not make that radio call and let us fend for ourselves.'

'Bastard!' Claudine repeated. 'What he really wants is to destroy the Centre of the Universe.'

'Isn't that what you intend?'

Claudine glanced at her and then looked away again. 'My grandfather is a good man. Misguided, perhaps, but he wishes to do good.'

'I believe you. But what does happen when he dies?'

'My son will become the Lord.'

'Oh, really, Claudine. A six-year-old boy.'

Another quick glance. 'He will be the Lord,' she said stubbornly.

'Great. But with Zobeir pulling the strings. I don't think that will make friend Faure too happy.'

'He will be in my care.'

'Ah. Yes, I can see that would be an attractive idea. But you have to get hold of him first, right? Just as I have to get hold of Andrea, just as rapidly as possible. So let's

216

make a move.'

She found herself wondering how Faure, or anyone else for that matter – herself included – could live with the idea of a woman like Claudine controlling all of those obedient millions – supposing she could achieve that. But Andrea came first.

Claudine took the jerry-cans to the water hole and filled them. 'It is still two days to the border,' she remarked. 'And we do not know how often we will find water, even after we are in Nigeria.' She strapped the cans on to the supply camel, began taking down the tent. Jessica helped her. 'Do you not think it would be better for us to go directly to Chad?'

'The odds would be a bit heavy.'

'You have four automatic rifles.'

'With a total of maybe three magazines. Anyway, I hope you're not contemplating shooting your way in and then out again. As Faure said, that would be no way to win friends and influence people. Anyway, don't you think you already have enough deaths on your conscience?'

'Conscience!' Claudine snorted. 'I want my son. As you want your friend.'

'I'm still happy to see if we can get some assistance from the Nigerian police. So it's the border for us.' But she decided that she was over-armed, certainly when she only really had sufficient ammunition for one of the guns. She removed the three magazines –

217

each was about half full, giving her a total of about seventy-five rounds in addition to those in the fourth rifle – and then threw the empty weapons into the hole. The knife she stuck in her belt; the three spare magazines she stowed in her haversack.

Claudine watched her with smouldering eyes.

They made southwest through a stone desert, riding all day and pitching their tent for the night beneath a clump of acacias, which seemed able to exist without any visible water supply. 'There is water, deep down,' Claudine explained. 'These trees have very long roots.'

Before dawn they were awakened by a thunderstorm. The jagged shafts of lightning seemed to plunge into the desert not a hundred yards from where they lay, and the thunder was as continuous as a bombardment. Claudine opened the tent flap to gaze at the display. 'There will be wind,' she said. 'But the storm is good. It means the rains are here.'

She was right about the wind. It rose, steadily, until it was blowing a gale. They spent the morning huddled inside the tent, although for all the protection it gave them from the driving dust and pebbles they might have been in the open.

Towards noon the storm blew itself out, and Claudine went looking for the camels. She returned within half an hour with all three animals, and they repacked and were ready to move again when she suddenly waved violently at Jessica and ducked behind a tree. Jessica unslung her rifle, and saw a solitary camel, accompanied by two robed figures on foot, perhaps a hundred yards to the north. 'This is the most heavily populated desert I have ever known,' she remarked. 'Think they mean trouble?'

'It is those women. I told you that you should have shot them.'

Jessica squinted into the glare, realized that she was right. And the camel they had lost in the storm had carried their water. 'You'd better invite them in.'

'They will be both hungry and thirsty, Miss Jones. And therefore dangerous.'

'How far is it to the next water?'

'We should find some tomorrow.'

'Then we can spare them a drink. We're the ones with the gun, remember?' Claudine made a face and stepped out from behind the tree. She cupped her hands round her mouth and shouted. The women came towards them. Claudine pointed to the food and one of the jerry-cans. The women smiled at Jessica, and then attacked the food, using the knives they had taken from the dead Touaregs. Watching them, it occurred to Jessica that she was in the presence of three of the toughest women she had ever encountered; the two women lacked Claudine's terrifyingly amoral deadliness, but possessed instead the aggressiveness of women used to manual labour, and used, too, to disposing of their rivals with their hands rather than their tongues. She kept her Kalashnikov pointing at them. 'I think they've had enough to eat,' she told Claudine. 'Or they'll make themselves sick.'

Claudine barked an order, and they stopped eating, reluctantly. 'Now tell them to throw those knives over here. And tell them if I don't like how they do it I'll blow them apart.'

Another command. This time the women exchanged glances, but they could have no doubt that Jessica knew how to handle the gun and was prepared to use it. They tossed the knives on to the sand, and Claudine went forward. 'Don't pick them up,' Jessica said. 'Kick them over here.' She could not be certain of Claudine's loyalty, and she had seen her throw a knife.

Claudine considered for a moment, looked at the Kalashnikov, and then kicked the knives across the sand. Jessica picked them up and placed them in her haversack. 'Now tell them they can come with us as long as they behave themselves.'

'We have not sufficient food for four.'

'So we'll be on a diet. It can only be another day to the border.'

'You think the border is the answer to everything,' she grumbled. 'It is still half desert.'

But she spoke to the women, who seemed pleased, clapping their hands and shouting. Then they took turns at riding the camel, following Jessica, who turned in her saddle to wave them away whenever they got too close. But she knew she was in a dangerous situation: none of her three companions could be trusted, and she was getting very tired. So why *didn't* she shoot them? Shoot all three of them, in fact. She had no more need of them now. She had to shake her head, violently, to remind herself that despite Commander Adams' opinion, she was not a cold-blooded killer.

She had still not solved the problem of how she was going to get a night's sleep when Claudine indicated what she considered a suitable camping site. Jessica had no objection. The sun was still fairly high, but it had been an exhausting day on top of several even more exhausting days. She gladly dismounted, and Claudine set the women to erecting the tent. 'How are we going to handle this?' Jessica asked.

Claudine shrugged. 'It was your idea to bring them along. We will have to tie them up, or they will steal our camels and our food and leave us.'

Jessica considered. She didn't like the idea of tying them up all night, nor could she see it was a practical solution to the problem; they had no ropes, only the bridles and harnesses of the camels, and those could not be made fully secure. 'Tie them up with what?'

'We will make them take off their clothes, and use those.'

'Um, well ... What's she on about?'

The Negress was pointing at the sky. For a moment Jessica could not make out what she had seen, then Claudine snapped, 'The helicopter.'

Now Jessica could see it, flying low, obviously searching the land below ... and finding what it was looking for: it was heading straight for them. 'Take cover!'

'Why? They have seen the tent. Can you not shoot it down?'

Jessica looked at the weapon in her hands. Her memory went back to the Colombian jungle. But she did not ever want to do that again. And besides, she did not know who was in the aircraft. 'We'll wait till it lands.'

The four of them insensibly moved closer together, gazing at the approaching machine. 'That is not the Lord's helicopter,' Claudine said. 'It is too big.'

'You're right. It's a Chinook. And...' She squinted at the markings on the fuselage. 'That looks official.'

'It is the Nigerian police.'

Jessica ran forward, waving her arms as the helicopter settled on the ground. The first man down was Douglas Kahu.

Jessica threw both arms round his neck to hug him. 'Am I glad to see you.'

He wore a blue uniform and looked embarrassed. 'Sergeant Jones, you are one troublesome woman.' He held her away from him, and she remembered that her torn haik was not doing a very good job. 'I believe you know

Agent Smollett.'

Jessica's jaw dropped. Jackson Smollett was wearing a bush jacket over shorts, with matching khaki stockings and brown leather shoes. He carried a slouch hat in his hand. 'I'll go along with that,' he agreed. 'Ain't you going to hug me too, Sergeant? Maybe like after you've put down that Kalashnikov.'

Jessica looked from face to face. 'Someone has some explaining to do.'

'Someone sure has. Who're your friends?'

Jessica beckoned Claudine. 'How would you like to be introduced?'

'Who is this man?'

'His name is Jackson Smollett, and he is a CIA agent. He is presently trying to locate a woman involved in terrorist activities in the States. Name of Claudine Matthieu.'

'Hey!' Smollett complained. 'You're not supposed to go shooting that off.'

Kahu cleared his throat.

'I thought she might know of her. Princess...?'

'I am Princess Charmaine,' Claudine announced.

'Princess? Charmaine? Say, that sounds like something out of a novel.'

'It very probably is,' Jessica agreed.

Kahu appeared to be having trouble with his breathing. Now he asked, 'And those?'

'Two lost souls we picked up along the way.'

'Like maybe you rescued them from some slave traders.'

'Don't tell me Faure has actually been in

touch?'

'Why do you think we're here? Now the first thing is to get you ladies back to Kano.'

'Princess Charmaine,' Smollett said. 'Now there is something. You mind telling me where you fit into this, Princess?'

'I am with Sergeant Jones.'

Smollett scratched his head. 'I think we need to have a chat before we go rushing off to Kano,' Jessica said.

'You looked at yourself recently?' Kahu inquired. 'You need patching up, Sergeant. And you need a bath.'

'Well ... But there's so much to be done.'

'We'll talk about that in Kano. It's only a couple of hours.'

'Suppose I refuse to go?'

'Sergeant Jones, I can arrest you for indecent exposure. We are very strict about this in Nigeria. I can arrest you for carrying an unlicensed gun.' He looked at the knife in her belt. 'And other deadly weapons. In fact, you had better hand them over.' Jessica obliged, including the knives in her haversack, and he gave them to a waiting policeman. 'I can also arrest you, on behalf of the Niger police, for having engaged in a gun battle in their territory, using same unlicensed gun, in which three people were killed.'

'It was them or us. I fired in self-defence.'

'As you always do. But two of the men were killed with a knife. One of these knives, I would say. And whatever the reasons for what happened, the Niger police would still like to discuss them with you. There is also the matter of your illegal entry into Chad. However, all of these authorities are looking for a Miss Smith. Don't you think you will be safer with me? And incidentally, don't you *want* to have a bath?'

His logic was irrefutable. 'Actually, I would like nothing better than a hot bath. What about my friends?'

'I think the Princess ... Charmaine should accompany us. I am sure she has a great deal to tell us.'

Jessica glanced at Claudine, who shrugged. 'And the slave women?'

'Have you a use for them?'

'No. But I cannot abandon them.'

'Leave them the camels, and the food and water, and they will not consider themselves abandoned.'

Jessica had to agree that was the best possible solution. The women wailed and cursed, but when they realized they were, by any previous standard they had known, to become wealthy, they cheered up considerably, and even waved at the helicopter as it lifted off. 'How did you know it was me?' Jessica asked.

'When Faure described you, a very pretty, small, yellow-haired woman...'

'I liked him too,' Jessica said.

'Waving a Kalashnikov. Is there any other woman in the world who answers that description? Especially when I already knew you were in Africa.'

225

'Actually, I hated having to use that museum piece. It is too indiscriminate. But you didn't identify me to Faure?'

'Well, Agent Smollett had already arrived and put me in the picture, so I reckoned it would be best to have a chat with you first. You are really going to have to come clean, Sergeant Jones.'

They were seated at the rear of the cabin. Smollett had seated himself next to Claudine two rows forward, and the intervening row was occupied by two policemen. Smollett was engaging Claudine in animated conversation, but Jessica didn't suppose he was going to get anywhere, and as she couldn't hear what he was saying she didn't suppose he would be able to hear her. 'How did he get here, anyway?'

'Same way you did: by plane.'

'I mean, how did he know to come to Nigeria? To Kano?'

'That wasn't difficult. His people were keeping an eye on you. They followed you to Heathrow, chatted up the ground hostess and found you were off to Frankfurt. Their man on the ground in Frankfurt easily traced two such good-looking women ... Where is Miss Hutchins, by the way?'

'It's a long story.'

'She's not dead? Or hurt?' His voice was suddenly anxious.

'As far as I know, she's alive. As to whether she's hurt...'

'Tell me what happened.'

226

'Well, as you seem to know why we came here...'

'That is something else you have to tell me. I assume you know who Princess "Charmaine" really is?'

'Certainly.'

'So why are you so friendly, and alone in the desert?'

'First things first. Our business was to reach the lady, which is why we had to get into the house of her stepfather. Only she wasn't there. What did you do when we weren't waiting for you at the hotel?'

'I was pretty fed up.'

'It didn't bother you when we never returned?'

'The hotel received a message that you had gone away for a couple of days, and to hold your room. They are still doing so.'

'That's good news.'

'I would like to know where you went.' Jessica told him, and outlined briefly what had happened. She did not mention the boy Hercule, as she didn't reckon that was any of his business – yet. 'You are saying that Detective-Constable Hutchins has been kidnapped, for sexual reasons, by the man called Kanem?'

'She was certainly kidnapped. And he certainly liked the look of her.'

'You can say this so calmly? Was she not your friend?'

'Superintendent, I am not the least calm about what happened. I want her back, and I want something done about that whole outfit. Just as soon as you can.'

Kahu gazed at her for some moments. Then he said, 'And the Princess?'

'She saved my life.'

'According to Smollett, she is guilty of mass murder.'

'Are you going to arrest her?'

'I have no reason to do so, unless an application is made for her extradition from Nigeria. She has committed no crime here. Unless you wish to claim that you were actually kidnapped from Kano, and that she was a party to it.'

'We left Kano of our own free will, and she had nothing to do with it. Will you tell Smollett who she really is?'

'Do you wish me to?'

'Not right now. What I would like you to do is help me get Andrea back.'

'It is a difficult one. The island on which Ukuba has made his so-called Centre of the Universe is situated on the borders of three states. As you may know, we live in a volatile political climate. I do not think my superiors would agree to risk a police invasion of territory which from time to time is claimed by Chad and by Cameroon. It could lead to incalculable consequences.'

'You mean that you will—?' Jessica bit her lip as he raised a finger.

'Abandon a white woman to a fate worse than death? You must bring your thinking up to date, Sergeant. Sir Garnet Wolseley is

228

dead, over a hundred years. Rudyard Kipling is dead. So, sadly, is John Wayne. I am a great admirer of his movies. We live in the age of mass man, not heroic individuals. Even Stalin, with his "one death is a tragedy; a thousand is a statistic" is dead. A man, or a woman, who today starts a war to rescue one individual, however beautiful, however precious, would be condemned as a criminal.'

'As you say, Inspector, I never have come up to date. Maybe that's because I prefer the old-fashioned sense of values. But I thought you, and your superiors, might be interested in discovering just what goes on inside the Centre of the Universe, and what plans those who succeed Ukuba may have for the mass of humanity you value so highly.'

'I am indeed interested, Sergeant, and I regard what you have had to say as most useful. But these people have committed no crime, against Nigeria, at any rate. As to the part they may have played in the destruction of the De Groot Clinic, that is outside of my jurisdiction until, as I have said, we receive an official request for the extradition of the person, or persons, the United States government considers to have been involved. However, should Detective-Constable Hutchins return to Kano and lay an official complaint against this Kanem, it may be possible to take the matter further.'

'And if I tell you that I intend to get her out of there, no matter what it takes to do so?'

He gazed at her for several seconds, then looked out of the window.

It was ten o'clock and utterly dark when they landed. A police car was waiting for them. 'He will take you to your hotel,' Kahu said.

'And then?' Jessica asked.

'I suggest that you go to bed and have a long sleep. I will stop by tomorrow.'

'Why?'

'I shall require a full statement of everything that you allege to have happened.'

'Then I suppose you will require me to leave the country.'

Kahu looked at Claudine. 'That will depend on your statement. You have tonight to consider what you wish to say. I will see you tomorrow. Mr Smollett?'

'I'll go with the ladies.'

'We'd rather be alone, if you don't mind,' Jessica said. 'We're very tired.'

'Oh, well ... How about dinner?"

'Smollett, we are going to bed.'

'You could join us for breakfast,' Claudine said, surprisingly.

'I'll do that.'

'Are you out of your tiny mind?' Jessica asked as they were driven away. 'That man is out for your blood.'

'He doesn't know who I am.'

'You can be pretty sure he's going to find out.'

'Are you going to tell him?'

'Of course not.'

'Because you regard me how – do you say? – as your pigeon?'

'Because I need you to get back into the Centre of the Universe. Hell, I forgot. Don't you want to go to your stepfather's house?'

'I don't think that would be a very good idea, right this minute. They will have telephoned him from the island and told him the situation.'

'Right. So he thinks you are dead. That could give us a handle.'

'Why are you interested in my stepfather? He is nothing. When Hercule begins to rule, he will be less than nothing.'

'I'm sure you're right, but I can't wait that long. I need to go to your stepfather's house because I was forced to leave my important gear there. That includes my passport, airline ticket, money ... and a weapon.'

'You are the famous Sergeant Jones. There is a British consulate in Kano. You go to him and tell him you have lost your passport and he will issue a new one.'

'After requesting identification from London, which could be dicey. Anyway, I have to have money, and that weapon.'

'That is not a problem, either. I have money.'

'You? Where?'

'In my bank account, here in Kano. I am a millionairess.'

'Silly of me not to realize that.'

'I will draw whatever you require tomorrow. And when we have done that, we will buy

231

whatever weapons you require.'

'Not from Mr Masud, I hope.'

'No, no. He is a Follower. I know another source. A better source.'

'Great. Claudine, you do know that you are under arrest? That it is my job to take you back to England to stand trial?'

'For what? I have committed no crime in England.'

'When it comes to acts of terror, we work pretty closely with the United States. If friend Smollett has a warrant...'

'How can he have a warrant? He does not know who I am. You did not identify me when you met in England, did you?'

'He told you about that?'

'Oh, yes. He told me everything. He thinks you know who Mrs Matthieu is, and where she can be found. That is why he followed you. He wants me to help him get the information out of you.'

'This seems to have been a very rapid liaison.'

'Oh, well, you see, he would like to – how do you say? – get his hands in my knickers.' She giggled. 'Only I do not wear knickers.'

'I can see that you are going to be a great trial to me,' Jessica said, and became aware of a very loud noise. 'What in the name of God is that?'

'Rain, Sergeant Jones.'

It was the heaviest rain Jessica had ever known on land, heavier even than in South

America, only to be compared with the typhoon she had experienced in the Pacific. By the time she and Claudine got from the car into the hotel lobby, a matter of perhaps twenty yards, they were both soaked.

The resplendent doormen, who were sheltering – Jessica presumed they were afraid their armour would rust – stared at them in consternation. The reception clerk was appalled as puddles gathered around their feet. Fortunately at this hour the lobby was deserted. 'You cannot enter the hotel,' he protested.

'Listen, buster,' Jessica said. 'It's me, Miss Jones, remember? The one who has, and is, seriously considering breaking your neck. Give me my key.'

'Oh. Miss Jones. But ... your clothes!'

'Are a matter I intend to take care of now.'

'But ... this lady...'

'Has replaced the other lady. The key. Or shall I come round there and get it?' He rolled his eyes and handed over the key. 'Thank you. Now, I would like you to send up a bottle ... What have you got in the way of champagne?'

'There is Bollinger. But it is very expensive. One hundred pound a bottle.'

'Send up two bottles, and put it on Mr Matthieu's account.'

'I do not think I am authorized to do that, madam.'

'Don't be silly. This is Mrs Matthieu. She will sign for it.'

The clerk goggled at Claudine, who smiled

at him. 'Do as Miss Jones wishes,' she said. They went up in the lift, found the bedroom exactly as Jessica had left it. 'This is very comfortable,' Claudine remarked.

'And the beds are soft, too. Although, do you know, I haven't actually slept in one yet. Do you want the bath first?'

'You go ahead.' But she came in to watch her. Jessica didn't mind. Nothing had ever felt so good, even if she was discovering fresh bruises, bites and scratches every place she soaped. 'You are a very handsome woman.'

Jessica watched her let her haik fall to the floor. 'And you are quite exquisite.'

'Do you know, no one has ever said that to me before? That is a large tub. There is room for me, too.'

'Ah.' But after what they had shared ... 'All right. I'll just let some water out.' Jessica sat up, and Claudine daintily lowered herself, facing her.

'What do we do first, tomorrow?'

'Get you some clothes. Then use your money to equip ourselves. Then work out the best way to get back to the Centre. And out again.'

Claudine turned her head to look at the window, and the teeming rain. 'It is going to be difficult.'

Jessica was busily washing her hair. 'Nothing is quite so difficult as worrying about it. Oops, there's the door. Our champagne.'

'I'll get it.' Claudine climbed out of the bath, scattering water.

'For God's sake put something on.' Claudine pulled one of the towels from the rack and wrapped it round her waist. 'You can't...' Jessica protested.

But Claudine had already left the bathroom and was opening the door. 'Why Inspector,' she said. 'What a pleasant surprise.'

Eight

The Fishing Trip

'I really am sorry...' Kahu's voice fell silent: he was clearly enjoying the view, or at least struck dumb by it. Jessica scrambled out of the bath. Her dressing gown still hung on the back of the door, and she wrapped herself in this, grabbed a towel for her soaking hair, and went into the bedroom.

Kahu still stood in the doorway, carrying a tray on which were the two bottles of champagne in an ice bucket and two glasses. 'I seem to be always busting in on you when it isn't convenient,' he said. 'But I happened to encounter the waiter with this tray, and I thought I'd save him the journey.'

'Then you'd better come in. Claudine, there's another dressing gown in the bathroom. Why don't you put it on?' Claudine retreated. 'She's an odd mixture of sophistication and primitiveness,' Jessica explained. 'But she certainly knows her survival techniques, at least when it comes to deserts.'

She closed the door, and Kahu placed the tray on the table. 'Don't you think I should go?'

'Not now that you're here, sir. Maybe you could open a bottle.' Kahu did that, and the pop brought Claudine back out of the bathroom, wearing Andrea's dressing gown, which was several sizes too large for her and trailed on the floor behind her. Jessica filled the glasses, gave one to Kahu, drank from her own, and handed it to Claudine. 'I had no idea you lived in this hotel, Inspector.'

'Well, actually, I don't.'

'Do sit down.' She indicated the one chair, and sat herself on her bed. Claudine crossed the room to lie on hers. 'But I suppose it's none of my business to inquire what brings you back here at eleven o'clock at night.'

Kahu sat down. The chair creaked. 'The fact is, Sergeant, when I got home I started to think, and, well ... Maybe I was a little bit negative on the trip back.' Jessica took the half-empty glass from Claudine's hand, drained it, got up, refilled it, and passed it back. 'Don't get me wrong,' Kahu said. 'What I told you was the truth of the matter. For me to go busting into Chad would cost me my job. But what the hell. The thought of that real nice girl...' Jessica got up again, refilled his glass. 'It would have to be completely unofficial, and I couldn't take any of my people, but ... Are you as good as they say you are?'

'She is better,' Claudine said.

'And you, Princess?'

'She's good enough,' Jessica said.

'Do you think Smollett would bend the book?'

'Isn't that what the CIA does all the time? But do we need him?'

'Didn't you say there were about forty of these Followers in residence?'

'Forty-three,' Claudine said. 'But they are not armed. I know this. Ukuba does not permit guns on the island. There are some bows and arrows for shooting fish, and of course most of the men carry knives...'

'Which means they could still be a threat. So another reliable man would be useful.'

'The trouble is, Douglas ... You don't mind if I call you Douglas, sir? If we are going to tear up the books.'

'I'd like you to call me Douglas, JJ. What is your problem?'

'If we involve Agent Smollett, and take him with us to the island, he will discover who Princess Charmaine really is.'

'I thought we'd agreed to leave that until Andrea is rescued.'

'*I* agreed to leave it. I'm not sure we will be able to persuade Smollett to do so. The Americans are inclined to have tunnel vision where terrorism is concerned, and she didn't save *his* life.'

237

'I think we could do a deal with him. From what he told me, Washington considers Matthieu as the true perpetrator of the crime. With another man. They regard you, Mrs Matthieu, as an accessory, certainly, but of immediate importance only as a possible supplier of proof against your husband. Would you be prepared to do that?'

'I can tell you what happened. But Henri will tell a different story.'

'Well, that is a problem for the future. If we tell Smollett that the proof lies in the Centre of the Universe, I think he will play ball.'

'He won't,' Jessica said. 'If we rope him in for a pretty dicey operation, on the grounds that Mrs Matthieu is in the Centre, and when we get there he discovers that she has been sitting beside him all the time, he is going to abandon all idea of any future cooperation, with us or with her.'

'But I can deliver Matthieu's accomplice,' Claudine said. 'The actual bomber.'

Jessica snapped her fingers as she remembered the scene in the hut. 'Of course! Kanem!'

'That fellow again?' Kahu remarked. 'He is someone I just have to meet.' He finished his champagne. 'Okay, ladies. I reckon you could both do with a good night's sleep. I'll get us organized and pick you up tomorrow morning. This trip could take a couple of days, so pack a small bag each.'

'We don't have a small bag. Mine is at Kwarism's.'

'I'll send a couple of holdalls over first thing in the morning.'

'Are we taking weapons?'

'I think that would be a good idea. I suppose you'd like your Kalashnikov back.'

'I told you, it's not my favourite toy. You wouldn't have an M-16? Mark Two if possible.'

'No. How does a Minimi grab you?'

'Just great.'

'I'll bring one along. And you, Claudine?'

'I know nothing of guns.'

'But she's just as deadly with a knife,' Jessica said. 'You have ours.'

'Ten o'clock.' Kahu closed the door behind himself.

'That is the first policeman I have ever met I could possibly like,' Claudine remarked.

'I see.'

'You are a police *woman*,' she pointed out. 'You, I could love.'

'Not tonight, Claudine. I'm too tired. Just let's finish these bottles and go to bed.'

It was the heaviest sleep Jessica had ever enjoyed. When she awoke she felt as if she was climbing out of a deep, dark, but entirely peaceful cavern. She opened her eyes, blinked at Claudine, who was standing above her, wearing jeans and a shirt.

Jessica sat up. 'What the hell ... Those are mine.'

'So what else am I supposed to wear? I think they're a very good fit. And you have

239

another pair.'

Jessica supposed she had a point, and their shopping spree was obviously going to have to be postponed. 'Actually, they suit you. What time is it?' Her watch was still at Kwarism's house.

'Just gone nine.'

'My God! We only have an hour!' She threw back the covers, leapt out of bed, and discovered that all the aches and pains that had been lurking seemed to have come together, from the top of her head to the tips of her toes, aided and abetted by the amount of champagne she had drunk.

'The holdalls have arrived, and I've ordered breakfast,' Claudine said, and turned to the knock on the door. 'Here it is now.'

Jessica dashed into the bathroom. A cold shower made her feel better, and the food improved matters further. 'I am very excited,' Claudine said.

'About going home?'

'It is no longer my home. I do not think it ever was, really. I am excited about getting back to Hercule.'

'I can understand that.'

'And settling with that bastard Kanem.'

'I can understand that too. But you do realize that if this is going to work, Kanem has to be arrested and handed over to the CIA?'

'It would be better if he were killed.'

'Your solution to everything.'

'If he is not killed, he will testify against me.'

240

'Just keep thinking about your son. I'm looking forward to meeting him, if he is as bright as you seem to think.' Claudine did not reply, so Jessica drank her coffee and then looked up. 'Did I say the wrong thing?'

'My son is very bright,' Claudine said. 'We had better go downstairs and wait for the police.'

'I gather plans have changed,' Jackson Smollett said as they got into the police jeep for the drive to the airport. 'And that you guys have an important lead.' He looked from one face to the other.

'The people you seek are to be found in the so-called Centre of the Universe,' Claudine said.

'You know them?'

'I know them.'

Smollett looked at Kahu, who was seated in front beside the driver. 'And we can bring them out?'

'I think that may be possible,' Kahu agreed.

Another police car waited for them at the airport, and Kahu shared out the weapons, pistols for himself and Smollett, and two Minimis; one he took himself and the other he gave to Jessica. 'Say, you know how to use that thing?' Smollett asked.

Jessica stroked the Belgian-made gas-operated assault rifle. 'I've fired one.' She checked the box; it was full, and she knew it had a thirty-round capacity.

Kahu gave her another box to put in her

haversack. 'It's sighted up to six hundred yards.'

Jessica nodded. The Minimi, which out-ranged both the AK-74 and the Armalite M-16, was a favourite weapon of the SAS.

'Nobody told me we were aiming to start a war,' Smollett grumbled.

'Hopefully, none of these guns will need to be fired,' Douglas told him. 'They're along to get us in, and get us out. Let's go. It could be a long day.'

They took the same route as Jessica remembered from five days previously. Only today it was overcast with occasional heavy showers of rain. Looking down, she felt she could almost see the country beginning to turn green. 'Is this good or bad for us?' she asked Douglas.

'On the whole, good, I would say.'

'Tell me why.'

'The more water there is in the lake the better, as we have to cross a bit of it.'

'We're not going to drop in by this chopper?'

'I don't think we can risk that. This is a government machine, and clearly marked. If it is spotted flying over Chad territory we'll have that international incident we need to avoid. There's a small village called Baga just on our shores of the lake. We'll be set down there, and I have arranged a boat for us. Officially, I and some friends are going fishing.'

'With assault rifles?'

'That lake is full of trouble, from hippos to crocs. The crocs mostly hibernate during the dry season, but once the rains start they get active. You ever encountered an active croc?'

'No. But I have encountered a very active, very large alligator. In fact, several of them.'

'What did you do?'

'I shot one of them; Andrea shot another. And then we beat a strategic retreat.'

'You are really something, Sergeant Jones. So is Andrea. You reckon she will have been able to handle whatever has been happening to her?'

'I would say so. But it will have been more traumatic for her than for most.'

He frowned. 'She married?'

'She is not married. Nor does she ever intend to.'

He stared at her. 'Shit! That lovely girl...'

'She is still a lovely girl, Douglas. Her personal point of view is her business. Nobody else's.'

'And you?'

'I have a partner.' Jessica smiled. 'A male partner.'

'Who lets you go around the world shooting up alligators. Or slave traders.'

'He doesn't have any choice. We're in the same business.'

He blew through his teeth. 'You ever encountered any situation you couldn't handle?'

'Not till this trip. I wouldn't have been able to handle the desert without Claudine. And I have never taken on an unarmed opposition. Up till now it has always been straightforward: guys with guns who have to be put out of business. I have never shot, or even shot at, an unarmed man.'

'Well, keep your fingers crossed. But JJ, let me tell you something. I would have counted my life a complete failure if I hadn't had this opportunity to work with you. So don't go soft on me now.'

It was late afternoon when they landed. From the air they had seen the lake in the near distance, the water glimmering, the reed banks dark, the tree-dotted islands even darker. It was not possible to make out the Centre of the Universe, and it came as something of a surprise to Jessica to remember that she had never seen the island in daylight. They had been surrounded by heavy cloud throughout the journey, and almost the moment they landed it began to rain. Baga was a surprisingly large village, and despite the weather the people turned out to look at the helicopter. There was a local police station-cum-border post, and to this they were hurried, being soaked in the process. 'The boat is ready, Inspector, sir,' said the sergeant. 'But it is late, and the weather is bad. May I suggest you spend the night here and start your trip tomorrow?'

'I'll say amen to that,' Smollett agreed.

Douglas looked at Claudine. 'Princess?'

'You say it is ten miles to the island?'

'Is that correct, Sergeant?'

'There are many islands, sir.'

'I am speaking of what is called the Centre of the Universe.'

To Jessica's astonishment, the sergeant crossed himself. 'You wish to go to the Centre of the Universe?'

'We wish to go fishing, Sergeant. But we thought, as we are so close, we might stop by. This lady is a distant relative of the Lord, and she has never met him. What do you know of the place?'

'It is said to be a bad place, sir. Much ju-ju.'

'We'll bear that in mind. Ten miles?'

'As a bird might fly, sir. But the reed banks, and the other islands ... More like twenty.'

'But this boat has an engine?' Claudine asked.

'It is an outboard motor, madam.'

'Then tomorrow morning will do.'

'Very good,' Douglas said. 'You have accommodation for us?'

'Well, sir, I have three empty cells.'

Douglas and Jessica looked at each other, and burst out laughing at the same time. 'It'll be an experience I should have had years ago,' Jessica said.

The cots in the cells were surprisingly comfortable, certainly for people who had spent three of the past four nights sleeping on the ground, and the station food was surprisingly good, while the constables could not do enough for them. And still the rain teemed

245

down, not heavily, but in an unending thick drizzle.

'Now it's started, will it ever stop?' Jessica asked Douglas as they sat together on the station porch after supper staring at the darkness.

'It will, sometime.'

'But if it doesn't, tomorrow...'

'We will get wet. But again, it can be to our advantage. It may enable us to approach the island unobserved, do what we have to do, and leave again, perhaps unpursued. Did you see what sort of boats they had?'

'I didn't really see a thing. We arrived after dark, and left again before dawn. I got the impression, though, that the only way in or out was by helicopter.'

'I still think they will have some boats. You cannot live on an island and not have a boat.'

She glanced at him. 'Are you regretting coming?'

'Why should I do that?'

'Well, from your point of view, I got the impression that this was to be strictly a rescue mission.'

'Is that not also your point of view?'

'Ah ... not entirely. What I am trying to say is, I got the idea that you were intent on getting Andrea out of there because, well, you felt there might be something in it for you. Forgive me. I have a nasty habit of speaking my mind.'

'It is a very good habit. And now you think I should forget about your friend because

246

there *cannot* be anything in it for me. I still intend to rescue her.'

'Actually, you know, it might not be quite such a dead end as I first thought. I've been remembering that she took quite a shine to you, too.'

'You're trying to make me feel optimistic. Then I will be optimistic. But I am interested in what you said. This woman is your close friend. But getting her out is not the only reason you are going back? You mean you are still on the trail of the Princess? You have her; whenever you wish to use the handcuffs, I will give them to you.'

It was a tremendous temptation to tell him the truth of why she was there, but it had to be resisted, at least in full. 'There is something else.' He waited, patiently. 'There is something strange about her son.'

'She has a son?'

'That is why she is so anxious to get back there. She wishes to regain possession of him.'

'That is not unreasonable, for a mother.'

'Not at all. But I can't escape a feeling, from what was said, both by her and by others, that there is something special about this boy.'

'In what way?'

'I have no idea. He is only six years old, yet no one seems to have any doubt that he will be the next Lord.'

'That also is not unusual. Think of the Dalai Lama.'

'Agreed. In many religions or sects a new

leader is chosen almost at birth and is educated to his position. Claudine seems to feel that her son is capable of taking up that position now.'

'There are lots of mothers who overestimate their sons' capabilities. Ninety-nine out of a hundred, in fact.'

'From what I have seen of Claudine, she doesn't have a sentimental bone in her body. She wants possession of her son, but not to hold him tenderly to her bosom. There is something more. Something that has been bothering me from the start of this business. Claudine was inside the De Groot Clinic, minutes before the explosion that destroyed it, when she was six months pregnant. According to the CIA's reckoning, her condition was the reason for her husband and Kanem to be able to get into the building in the first place, in order to destroy it. I thought to myself then, what kind of woman would expose herself to such a risk when six months pregnant with her first child?'

'You could say she's a fanatic.'

'Claudine isn't a fanatic. She is utterly amoral, certainly, and I don't believe she really gives a damn for her son, as a son. But she desperately wants to regain possession of him. So does her husband.' She paused, aware of her slip, but he didn't seem to notice. 'What is more, the De Groot Clinic, perhaps the most famous transplant hospital in the world, did not deal with maternity cases. I don't even think it had a maternity unit. So why did they take her in, and, co-incidentally, on such a day?'

'What are you driving at?'

'Simply this. Smollett and his colleagues are working on the theory that Matthieu intended to destroy the clinic, and De Groot, or maybe Coleby, for some reason they haven't yet been able to discover. But just suppose they're completely off the track? Suppose Claudine was actually the centrepiece, in the clinic to have some kind of a transplant performed? Suppose the destruction of the clinic, and the operating surgeon, De Groot himself, was necessary to keep the nature of the transplant secret?'

'That's quite a theory. Who would this transplant have been for? Mother or child?'

'I would say child, which is why everyone who knows of it wants to keep hold of him.'

'You're saying a transplant operation could have been carried out on a six-months-pregnant woman, on the child in her womb?'

'Why not? We know that such operations have been carried out to correct heart defects in foetuses.'

'Okay, supposing you're right, what could have been done to the boy? In what way is he abnormal?'

'I have no idea. I've never seen him.'

'And you don't think this could have been one of those corrective surgeries?'

'A fairly routine operation, needing to be carried out by the world's leading transplant surgeon?'

'Point taken. And what about this guy Coleby? You don't think they were after him?'

'There doesn't appear to be any connection. Seems that he was just unlucky enough to be in the next theatre when the place went up.'

'Hm,' Douglas commented, and looked up as Claudine and Smollett appeared out of the darkness, wearing borrowed raincoats and hats, although the rain itself had all but stopped ... and holding hands!

'You guys must be eaten alive,' Jessica commented, while her brain did handsprings.

'We used bug spray,' Smollett said.

'Which both stinks and stings,' Claudine said. 'There's something we'd like to discuss with you.' Jessica stared at her, open-mouthed; she could not believe that Claudine had revealed her true identity to a man determined to bring her to justice. 'We'd like to share a cell,' Claudine explained. 'Get to know each other better. Do you object?'

Jessica looked at Douglas. 'I'll move out,' he agreed, showing no emotion.

'You could move in with Jessica,' Claudine pointed out.

'Ah...' Douglas looked at Jessica. 'There is another cell available.'

'And I think I need a good night's sleep,' Jessica said.

The rain started again in an hour, waking her up, and she lay beneath her blanket listening to it pounding on the roof just above her head. She wondered if she'd passed up a

250

great experience. But he was really only interested in Andrea.

Dawn brought about as perfect a day as Jessica had ever seen. The sky was a brilliant and cloudless blue, it was too early for the sun to make itself a nuisance, and round them the forest was filled with cheerful birdsong. And waiting for her was a formidable if unusual breakfast of eggs and fish.

'Caught in the lake,' Douglas explained, pouring coffee.

Jessica looked at Claudine, who looked back, face expressionless. Then she looked at Smollett, who also looked back, and flushed. She wondered how he was going to resolve *his* conflicts of interests. 'Is the rain gone for good?' she asked.

'It will be here again by ten o'clock. I'm sorry, but we are going to get wet.'

'It'll make a change to being parched.'

After the meal, it seemed that the entire village escorted them to the rickety wooden jetty, situated at the head of a small creek which wound its way between the trees. Douglas's policemen were loading their gear and food supplies into the boat, together with jerry-cans of boiled water and petrol. The boat was actually a somewhat large flat-bottomed punt. They were equipped with the promised outboard, but this was tilted up, because there was no water, just an expanse of soft mud. 'The water is not far,' Douglas said. 'The next rain storm will bring it even

251

closer.'

'Great,' Jessica said. 'Do we wait?'

'We go to it.' He indicated the four long poles laid across the thwarts.

'Holy shit!' Smollett remarked. 'We do that?'

'It will not be for long,' Douglas assured him.

'But why can't we take a couple of these guys?'

The watching policemen were all big, strong men. 'They have work to do, while we are on holiday, remember?'

'Shit!' Smollett muttered.

'You happy about this, JJ?' Douglas asked.

'No. But if that's the way the cookie crumbles.'

Claudine was already on board, and waiting with a pole. Jessica joined her, and the men followed. 'It will be hard at first,' Douglas said. 'But once we get a momentum going, we will slither across the surface, right?'

'I hope to God you are,' Smollett remarked, picking up his pole rather like a vaulter determined to break the world record.

'Ladies in the bow, you and me aft. All together now. And do remember to bring the pole out after each thrust.' Jessica thrust her pole over the side and was taken by surprise, as it only went in about four feet. But their combined efforts moved the punt perhaps two feet with a tremendous squelching sound. The villagers cheered.

Douglas had been correct in his estimate

that it would be hard. For the first fifteen minutes they scarcely seemed to move more than a few inches for every push, while Jessica's arms were already beginning to ache and her clean shirt was soaked in sweat. But when she looked back she saw that they had actually travelled about thirty yards, and the village was almost out of sight behind the trees. Douglas was also right about the proximity of the water. Another fifteen minutes and they rounded a shallow bend and were suddenly floating – just. 'Half an hour and we can put down the outboard,' Douglas promised.

Jessica sighed with relief and glanced at Claudine, who was poling with the same grim determination she had revealed in the desert. Suddenly she remembered that Claudine had been about to tell her the reason behind the bombing of the clinic when they had been interrupted, and they had never got back to the subject. Then she realized that it had become distinctly cooler; as well as darker. She looked up and saw that the sky was completely overcast, the clouds low and black. A moment later it began to rain.

As usual, the rain came down in solid sheets, obliterating everything more than fifty feet away, immediately starting to fill the shallow bottom of the boat. This was clearly something outside of Smollett's experience. 'Holy shitting cows!' he commented, shipping his pole.

'Keep poling,' Douglas told him. 'We want

253

to get to deep water.'

'But we're gonna sink.'

'Ladies, will you bail? Smollett, we'll move a little forward.' Thankfully Jessica and Claudine shipped their poles, knelt in the water, which was already two inches deep, grasped the bailing cans and began work. Jessica looked over the side. The mud was dissolving before her eyes into huge pools of water, and she could feel the boat gathering speed as if on a rising tide. 'There are waterproof capes under the bow seat,' Douglas said.

Jessica looked down at herself; she seemed to have developed a second skin. 'Let's save them for the next time we're dry,' she suggested.

The rain stopped just before noon. 'Okay,' Douglas said. 'Lunch time.'

The sun had immediately appeared, and the punt began to steam, principally from their wet clothes and bodies.

'Do you think we should change?' Jessica asked.

'I wouldn't bother. The sun will have you dry in half an hour.'

Jessica took off her sodden hat. 'How do I look?'

'Like a drowned rat. But a very attractive drowned rat. Let's see what we have here.' He unpacked the food bag, handed out cardboard containers of cold couscous and dates. 'There's nothing hot, I'm afraid.'

'But the beer is hot,' Smollett complained, opening a can.

'There's water, if you prefer.'

Smollett drank the beer while they drifted, perhaps a mile from the shore, bobbing on the surface of an utterly calm sea, for the moment even free of the reeds, although they could see that they were actually surrounded, a couple of hundred yards to each side.

'What next?' Jessica asked.

'Princess?'

Claudine grasped Jessica's shoulder to stand up and peer into the heat mist; the entire lake seemed to be steaming. She pointed. 'Over there.'

'How can you be sure?'

'There are trees. That is the first of the islands.'

Smollett took off his own sodden hat to scratch his head, and Jessica held her breath: Claudine, as Charmaine, had claimed never to have been to the lake before. But the American did not say anything. No doubt, she reckoned, he was realizing that it was too late to turn back ... and too early to start something. 'How far?' Douglas asked.

'About eight miles. But it will be longer. The Centre of the Universe is surrounded by reed beds.'

Douglas nodded. 'We'll get as close as we can as quickly as we can.' He thrust his pole over the side, brought it up. 'Five feet. That's ample for the outboard.' He went aft, lowered it into the water. 'Now, if everyone would like to sit comfortably.' Smollett snorted, but sat on the midships thwart. In normal circumstances Jessica would have expected him to want to sit beside Claudine, but he clearly wanted to think about things. So she sat beside her herself, on the forward thwart, three feet back from the bow. Douglas pulled the cord, and the engine chattered into life. The punt move forward at surprising speed, the brown water parting before it.

'As Andie would say, wowee!' Jessica said. 'Won't the noise announce our presence?'

'Not yet,' Claudine said. 'It is too far.'

But the chatter of the engine did provide them with privacy. 'How was friend Smollett?'

'I made him happy.'

'And what did he do for you?'

'He was very passionate.'

'Um. I have a feeling that right now he's doing his sums.'

'You won't let him interfere, at least until after we have regained Andrea.'

'And then?'

'Let us regain her first. And my son.' Which sounded somewhat ominous, but before she could think about it Claudine suddenly waved her arms. 'Hippo!'

Douglas had been sitting down, but he immediately put the outboard tiller hard over, causing the punt to slew to the left and nearly unseating Smollett. 'What the shit...!'

Jessica gazed at the three enormous creatures, only their heads and backs visible, disturbing the water as they turned to watch the stranger rushing by. 'Are they dangerous?'

'They can be, if disturbed. Anyway, to run into one of them would sink the boat.'

'Well spotted, Princess,' Douglas said. But he reduced speed.

Half an hour later they were up to the reeds. By now the last of the mist had cleared, and they could see the various clumps of trees quite clearly. 'That looks about two miles,' Douglas commented, cutting the engine so they glided to a gentle halt a few feet short of the reed forest. 'Where do we go from here?'

'We go through the reeds.'

'The outboard will never cope.'

'I know. We must pole.'

'Isn't there a channel in?'

'Yes. But if we use it they will see us coming.'

'If we go through the reeds they'll certainly know we are coming.' He pointed; already quite a few disturbed birds had risen and were fluttering to and fro. 'We might as well ring a bell. So, we are looking for the best possible means of surprise. How far is this channel?'

'About a mile from here.'

'And how long is it?'

'Only about a hundred yards. The Followers keep it clear.'

'Right.' He restarted the engine, and steered away from the reeds and the islands out into the centre of the lake until any trace of land was only a shadow. Then he cut the engine again and the punt drifted to a stop.

'Now we'll anchor and wait out the night, and move in just before dawn tomorrow morning. Now remember that we don't want any violence if it can be avoided, and with our firepower, unless these people are raving fanatics, there shouldn't be any. We want, first of all, Miss Hutchins. Then we want Kanem, both for kidnapping Miss Hutchins and for his possible part in the De Groot bombing.'

'We want Hercule,' Claudine said.

'Certainly Princess. Once we have those three, we regain the punt and leave.'

'And if they follow?' Jessica asked.

'I think we can discourage them.'

'We're also looking for this Matthieu dame,' Smollett reminded them. He had not apparently yet made a decision either on Claudine's knowledge of the lake or the fact that she apparently had a son in a place she had never been.

'I hadn't forgotten.' Douglas gazed at Jessica with a quizzical expression. 'Would you throw the anchor over the bow.' She obeyed, and the punt lay quietly.

'It's going to be a long afternoon,' Smollett commented. 'Anyone got a pack of cards?'

'Wouldn't do you much good,' Douglas said. 'We haven't had our afternoon rain shower yet.' He pointed at the darkening sky, and a few minutes later it opened.

Nine

The Centre of the Universe

'I was just beginning to feel dry,' Jessica remarked, replacing her hat, although she didn't know why, as it offered no protection. 'Is it back to bailing?'

'We'll do it,' Douglas said.

Smollett did not look very pleased, but he took a can and got to work, while Jessica and Claudine sat together and felt the water flooding their hair, and then their shirts, and then penetrating their jeans. 'How long does this last?' Jessica asked.

'Maybe an hour.'

Jessica hunched her shoulders.

The rain lasted longer than that, but stopped about dusk. 'At least there shouldn't be too many bugs out here,' Douglas said. 'Let's eat.'

Dinner was the same as lunch. 'What happens when we finish at this Centre place?' Smollett asked.

'We get back to Baga just as fast as we can. If all goes well we should make it in a couple of hours.'

'I'm glad of that. The idea of having to eat this stuff again for lunch tomorrow does not appeal.' He surveyed the calm surface of the lake. 'Anyone object if I have a swim? I'll keep my drawers on.'

'You know, that might not be a bad idea,' Jessica agreed. 'This rain hasn't exactly made me feel clean.'

'I don't recommend it,' Douglas said. 'Princess?'

'Definitely not,' Claudine said.

'I said I'd keep my pants on,' Smollett protested.

'That wouldn't make any difference to him.' She pointed. There was movement in the water. Jessica had seen it before, several times, a faint ripple caused by something swimming just beneath the surface; she had assumed it was a fish of some sort. But this movement was quite close, and now she saw that it was actually caused by a pair of eyes, raised above the head to which they belonged, surveying the evening as it moved.

Smollett had seen it too. 'Holy shit! Is that what I think it is?'

'That is a crocodile,' Claudine said.

'How big?'

'I have no idea. They can grow to twenty feet.'

'Shit! You reckon he's gonna attack us?'

'Not unless provoked. From his point of view we're too big to be comfortable.'

Smollett opened his haversack and took out his pistol. 'Put that away,' Douglas commanded. 'Like the Princess said, he won't trouble us unless we trouble him. But unless you can hit him in the eye or the open mouth, your bullets will simply bounce off, and even if you kill him, he can still sink us with a single swish of his tail.'

'Big deal,' Smollett remarked. 'You expect us to sleep tonight?'

'Crocs aren't normally active at night. They're cold-blooded creatures, so they get their energy from the sun, not from their blood. No sun, lethargy sets in.'

'Well, I sure hope you're right.'

The sun disappeared with its usual tropical decisiveness. 'Actually,' Jessica said, 'sitting here in a sodden mess isn't very conducive to sleep either. How cold does it get?'

'It may be chilly. Do the best you can.'

'And don't sneeze,' Smollett requested.

Jessica and Claudine settled beside each other. 'Do we still need him?' Claudine whispered.

'For God's sake, wasn't he in your arms just twenty-four hours ago?'

'He wanted it.'

'Have you no morals at all?'

'Has it never occurred to you, Miss Jones, that morality was invented by men, for the protection of certain ideas they consider important? Different groups of men have created different concepts of morality, which they always claim have been given to them by whatever they call their god. Women are expected to conform to that morality. Has any woman ever been allowed to lay down a morality to which all men must conform? Our only duty is to please men and protect our young. Well, then, that is my morality.'

'I think we had better go to sleep before you convert me,' Jessica suggested.

To her surprise she actually slept; despite the fact that it rained again during the night: there were still residues of exhaustion hovering on the edge of her consciousness. But she was awake when a dawn breeze, which was distinctly cold, swept across the surface of the lake. 'Check your weapons.' Douglas said. 'Make sure they're loaded.'

'I thought we weren't meaning to shoot anybody,' Smollett said.

'We aren't. But you know as well as I, Mr Smollett, that if you ever threaten anyone with a gun, if push comes to shove and you have to use that gun, and you can't, you're in for a hiding. That's basic police training, at least in this part of the world.'

As with the previous dawn it was a cloudless sky; there was still an hour to sunrise. Douglas used the outboard to close the reed beds again, then followed Claudine's pilotage until she said, 'The entrance to the channel is close.'

He stopped the engine and tested the depths of the water; it was down to four feet. 'We'll use the poles. Try to make as little noise as possible.'

They took their positions, thrust the poles down to the bottom, and moved forward, parallel to the reeds. It took them about twenty minutes to gain the entrance to the channel, which they reached almost at the same time as the sun rose. As they turned into it, they heard the clanging of the triangle. Smollett immediately shipped his pole and reached for his pistol. 'They have not seen us,' Claudine said. 'That is the call to breakfast.'

But they might as well have been seen, Jessica realized, as people began emerging from their huts. She also noted that the helicopter was on its pad. She was pleased about that; she felt she owed the pilots a thing or two.

'All together now,' Douglas said, and they surged forward. Almost immediately people began pointing, and shouting, and then running down to the water's edge. Jessica made out the bulk of Golightly, somewhat to the rear, but at that moment the punt grounded and she nearly went over the bow.

Douglas leapt over the side into knee-deep water. He carried his Minimi with his pistol stuck in his belt. Smollett was at his shoulder, pistol drawn. Jessica laid down her pole, slung her haversack, picked up her rifle, and followed, Claudine at her heels.

'What is the meaning of this?' Zobeir came through the throng. 'You? You have dared to return?'

'We couldn't keep away,' Jessica said.

'Don't get too close to them,' Douglas warned, and they halted, ankle-deep in water,

263

about thirty yards from the shore. 'Where is the Lord?'

'The Lord sleeps,' Zobeir said. 'But he will be most displeased at this intrusion into our privacy. And with guns! This is not permitted without the Lord's permission.'

'It will have to be retroactive,' Douglas said. 'Now, we don't mean to cause any trouble, so please don't start any. We have come to take some people away from here. Firstly, Miss Andrea Hutchins.'

'Miss Hutchins is not here.'

Jessica levelled her rifle. 'If anything has happened to her...'

'You know what happened to her, Miss Jones. She was taken into the desert, with you. Is she not with you now?'

Jessica looked at Claudine. 'Kanem!'

'He's someone else we want,' Douglas said. 'Bring him out. And his brother.'

'They are not here. Kanem has not yet returned. His father is seriously ill. He telephoned Fodio and Serene to come to him, and they left, four days ago.'

'They will be in Kano,' Claudine said.

'Kano?' Jessica shouted. 'Where in Kano?'

'At Kwarism's house.'

'But Kwarism...'

'Is their father.'

Of course, Jessica remembered. Ukuba had referred to Kanem and Fodio as his grandsons. 'And Serene is his daughter,' she said thoughtfully. 'Did you know that Kanem has kidnapped Miss Hutchins?' she asked Zobeir.

264

'I know nothing of this. I do not believe you. He and Fodio, and Serene, will return when their father is well again.'

'We seem to have been following the wrong trail,' Smollett remarked. 'Let's get the hell out of here. These people give me the creeps.'

'No one leaves the Centre of the Universe without the permission of the Lord,' Zobeir said.

'Bring me my son,' Claudine said.

The crowd of people rustled. 'The Lord comes,' they whispered. Jessica turned her head, sharply, as the people parted to allow a small boy to pass through them.

'Hercule!' Claudine splashed forward.

'Don't go into them!' Douglas shouted. Claudine ignored him to reach the land and drop to her knees before the boy. 'Shit!' Douglas snapped.

'Hercule!' Claudine shouted, reaching for him. 'Mummy has come back for you.'

Jessica studied the boy. He looked perfectly normal, his features very like his mother's with just a slight heaviness inherited from his father, but they were absolutely cold as he gazed at Claudine. But ... the Lord? 'I think we may have a problem,' she muttered to Douglas.

'Call her back.'

The boy was speaking. 'You were sent away from here, Mother. Why have you come back? You should not have done that. It is an eternal sin to disobey the Lord.' A six-year-old boy? Jessica felt as if a sudden shaft of lightning had penetrated her brain. Her brain!

'I have come back to take you away from here,' Claudine said. 'Away from these people.'

'How can I leave these people? They are my people, my Followers. I am the Lord.'

Claudine stood up. 'You are dreaming. Where is Ukuba?'

She looked left and right. The Followers exchanged glances. Jessica couldn't make out Lennon, but Golightly towered above his companions, staring at her, his features twisting. There was no sign of either of the two pilots, which she found disturbing. 'Ukuba has left us,' Zobeir said.

'Left you?' Claudine demanded. 'You mean he is also in Kano? Very well, I will take Hercule and go to him there.'

'Ukuba is not in Kano.'

'Then where is he?'

Zobeir waved his hand. 'I do not know. He went for a walk, out there.'

Claudine stared at him in horror. 'You sent the Lord into the lake?'

'He did not attempt to resist the will of the Lord.'

Claudine looked at her son. 'You executed Ukuba?'

'I sent him into the lake, Mother. I did not execute him. He may still be alive.' Jessica thought of that crocodile, swimming just below the surface, and shuddered.

'You are a murderer!' Claudine shouted.

'And what are you, Mother?'

'I killed for you! To give you your powers.'

'And I removed Ukuba because he had outlived his usefulness, because the Followers no longer wished his rule, because his absurd ideas were out of date, because he controlled so much power and would not use it.' A six-year-old boy!

'Looks like all of us make mistakes,' Smollett remarked. 'He's some kid, eh? But are you telling me I had that woman at my side ... Shit!'

'This is a fuck-up,' Douglas said. 'Princess, come back here. Quickly.'

'No,' Hercule said.

Instantly several of the Followers closed on Claudine, seizing her arms, plucking the knife from her belt. Golightly was amongst them. Jessica brought up her rifle again. 'Let her go.' The men looked at her, and then at the boy. Claudine stopped struggling.

'What are you going to do?' Hercule asked. 'Miss Jones, isn't it? Sergeant Jones. Are you going to shoot us all, Sergeant Jones?' Jessica hesitated, and bit her lip. 'There are only forty of us here,' Hercule said. 'I am sure that with all those guns you have more than forty bullets.'

Jessica looked at Douglas. 'Like I said, a fuck-up,' he remarked. 'Okay, Lord, or whatever you are, what do you want us to do?'

'I give you permission to leave, and not come back. You have no business here, and no jurisdiction.'

'We might just do that. Just send the Princess back to us.'

'The Princess belongs here. So she will stay here.'

'I'd say he has a point,' Smollett said.

'Well...' Douglas turned to Jessica. 'If she *is* guilty of mass murder...'

'They will kill me,' Claudine shouted. 'As soon as you are gone, they will send me into the lake.'

'Oh, come now,' Smollett said. 'You're the boy's mother.'

'I don't think that matters a damn,' Jessica said. 'I'm sorry, Douglas, but whatever her crimes, she saved my life. I'll happily see her go to prison. But I won't stand by and watch her be eaten by a crocodile.'

'So what do you aim to do?'

'What I do best. Will you back me up?'

'Say the word.'

Jessica drew a deep breath. 'You,' she called. 'Zobeir! There's a stone at your feet. Pick it up, and throw it into the air above your head.' As she spoke she adjusted the Minimi for a single shot.

Zobeir looked at Hercule, who shrugged. Slowly Zobeir stooped, picked up the stone, which was about the size of a tennis ball, weighed it in his hand, and then threw it above his head. Jessica had taken another deep breath, and this she held so that her body was totally controlled as she raised the rifle, sighted along the barrel, and squeezed

268

the trigger. The stone disintegrated.

'Holy shitting cows!' Smollett remarked. Douglas just stared. The Followers seemed to sway to and fro.

Jessica kept her rifle levelled. 'Now,' she called, 'I'm not into shooting innocent people, Zobeir, but in my book, as you condemned me to death, you are not innocent. Unless you tell those people to release the Princess, the next thing that gets blown apart is going to be your head. I'll give you three seconds. One.'

Zobeir stared at her. The Followers continued to move, restlessly. 'Two.' Zobeir licked his lips. Jessica caressed the rifle with her cheek as she sighted. She had closed her mind to any thought but that of hitting her target. 'Three.'

'Let her go!' Zobeir shouted.

As he spoke, a shot rang out. Douglas turned, sharply, to look at Jessica, but she was looking at the spurt of water that had spouted only a couple of feet from where she stood. 'Down!' she shouted, and fell full length into the water. The Followers scattered, led by Zobeir. Freed, Claudine scooped Hercule from the ground and ran towards the punt.

'Put me down!' Hercule commanded. 'Put me down, wretched woman!'

There was another shot, this one hitting the earth just in front of the running woman, causing her to trip and fall full length, the boy flying from her arms. 'So guns are forbidden,' Jessica snapped. 'The big hut. Cover me.'

She had seen the flash of the second shot, and now Douglas sent several in reply at the eating-house. Jessica scrambled up, scattering water, slinging her rifle as she did so, cast a quick glance at Smollett, who was also prone in the shallows, and ran towards Claudine. Both she and Hercule were getting to their feet. Hercule was already turned to run towards his Followers, but Jessica caught up with him and swept him from the ground. 'Let me go!' he bawled.

'You are coming awfully close to a clip around the ear hole,' she panted, carrying him to the shelter of the nearest trees, where she fell beside him. 'And you are going to get one if you move a muscle.'

Claudine joined them, just in time, for if momentarily silenced by Douglas's burst, the people in the hut had resumed firing. Douglas had now taken shelter on the far side of the landing area, with Smollett close behind him. 'How do we handle this?' Douglas called.

Jessica considered the situation. Time was not on their side. The Followers were for the moment scared and disorganized. But they would recover, and Zobeir would rally them. While the people in the eating-house, almost certainly the two pilots, controlled the embarkation area. On the other hand, as far as she could figure out, they did not possess automatic weapons, nor had she heard anything sounding like a rifle, while both she and Kahu possessed mini-machine-guns. But the

270

Zimbabweans – or, she supposed, Rhodesians, as they would prefer to be called – were working to a plan. Even as she considered the situation, they opened fire again, this time aiming at the punt. Holed in several places it moved to and fro, still on the bottom but gradually filling with water. 'Talk about being up the creek,' Smollett complained.

'They will send us all into the lake now,' Claudine whispered.

'And I will watch you drown,' Hercule said.

'He's your son,' Jessica pointed out. 'Can you handle him? I'll look the other way if you feel the need to belt him one. Douglas.' She raised her voice. 'You still with me?'

'All the way, Sergeant.'

'So let's sort this out. Smollett, covering fire.'

'You got it.'

'Right. You in there. You have ten seconds to come out with your hands up, or we are going to blow you apart. Counting now.'

'Come and get us, bitch.'

'Fuck that,' she muttered, stopped counting, stood up, and emptied her entire magazine into the side of the hut. The grass walls seemed to dissolve beneath the hail of bullets. Jessica ran forward, discarding her empty magazine and replacing it as she did so.

To her left, Douglas also emptied his gun, and reloaded as he reached the entrance to the hut at the same time as her. They burst inside, blinking in the gloom, but it was less dark than usual because of the torn walls.

Both the pilots were dead, their bodies shattered. 'You know these guys?' Douglas asked.

'We've met, briefly. They're the ones who dropped me off in the desert.'

'They didn't know what they were playing with. What happens now? We seem to be isolated, and those Followers aren't going to be happy.'

'Haven't you got a mobile?'

'I left it in the station in Baga. Just to resist temptation. Even if I had it, I wouldn't like to use it. What would happen if it got out that a Nigerian policeman was involved in a shoot-out on foreign territory?'

'Then, as Smollett said, we could be up the creek, unless we can access one of their boats.'

At that moment Smollett joined them. 'Holy shitting cows! You guys are really something. I think we had better get the hell out of here.'

'We couldn't agree with you more. If we had any means of doing that.'

'What's wrong with that chopper?'

'Nothing. Save that we don't have a pilot.'

'No problem. I'll fly it.'

'You know how to fly a helicopter?'

'I have a licence that says I do. Part of my training.'

'Smollett, I could grow to love you. What are we waiting for?' She stepped outside, waved her arm. 'Claudine, let's go. Bring the boy.'

Claudine came towards them, dragging

272

Hercule by the arm. 'There is no boat.'

'Agent Smollett is a man of hidden resources.' She escorted them to the helicopter,
and pushed them in. Douglas and Smollett
followed, Smollett going up to the flight deck.

'Now what have we here,' he said, sitting
down and surveying the instruments.

'Don't take *too* long,' Jessica suggested.
'The natives are about to become revolting.'

The Followers were gathering on the edge
of the trees, staring at them. Jessica again
easily identified Golightly, and almost called
out to him. But he was making no move
towards them or trying to attract her attention, and a moment later they were lifting.

'Where to?' Smollett asked. 'Back to Baga?'

'Tricky,' Douglas said. 'Maybe not.'

'We left some gear there.'

'I can always send for that. Will this thing
take us back to Kano?'

Smollett checked his fuel gauge. 'Nope.'

'There is fuel at Gwala,' Claudine said.

'Of course,' Jessica agreed. 'That's where we
stopped on the way out.'

'Gwala,' Douglas said thoughtfully. 'I know
it. But it is just an isolated farm.'

'You don't go there often enough,' Jessica
suggested.

'So show me where this place is on the
map,' Smollett requested.

'Ah...' Douglas opened various lockers.
'Shit!'

'No map? How about a direction?'

273

'You got any ideas?' Douglas asked over his shoulder.

'Something like due west,' Jessica said. 'We should be able to recognize something.' She looked down, but when they had flown over this on the way in to the Centre of the Universe it had been dark. 'You must have made this trip often,' she suggested to Claudine.

'I have never paid it much attention. You remember where Gwala is, don't you, Hercule?'

'I shan't tell you.'

'You really have mothered a monster,' Jessica remarked. 'Care to tell me about it?'

Claudine sighed. 'It was Kanem and Henri. Kanem knew that Ukuba would never pass the leadership on to him, both because of his lack of education and his character. Hercule was always designated as the next Lord, before he was even born. I told you, that is why Ukuba made me marry Henri. He wanted my child to succeed him.'

'As I *am* the Lord,' Hercule declared.

'Be quiet,' Jessica recommended. 'So?'

'Both Kanem and Henri wanted the next Lord to be their creation, their puppet, but I wanted him also to be the most brilliant brain of his time. I supposed it would have to be done by education, but we were all afraid that before that could be completed, before Hercule could grow up sufficiently to become the Lord, Ukuba would die, and would be replaced by Zobeir.'

274

'And what would happen then?'

'The Followers would disintegrate. Zobeir is no leader. He has no charisma. He has no knowledge.'

'Zobeir is a great man,' Hercule said. 'He is my friend.'

'You *do* have a problem,' Jessica remarked. 'I still don't quite get what you achieved. What you wanted to achieve. How? Was De Groot in on it?'

'Only medically. Henri read an article by him in which he claimed that it was possible to transplant any part of the human body into any other human body. I was just pregnant. So we arranged a meeting with De Groot when he was in England on a lecture tour, and discussed possibilities. He said he could do it, as soon as the foetus was sufficiently developed.'

'He was going to transplant an adult brain into your baby?'

'Only certain parts of it: knowledge and memory and speech. And not any brain. It had to be the best brain we could find.'

'Coleby! And De Groot agreed to this?'

'We paid him ten million dollars.'

'But what was to happen to Coleby?'

'Well, without a brain he didn't have much to live for.'

'God Almighty! Just like that. But why did you have to destroy the entire clinic?'

'De Groot signed a confidentiality clause. The operation had to be kept a deadly secret, don't you see? If it had got out, the press would have been on our necks. Hercule would have been a celebrity freak from the moment he was born. We couldn't have that. But when the operation had been completed, De Groot wanted to renegotiate. He said the operation would make him the most famous surgeon in the history of medicine. When we pointed out that he had signed a contract, he then asked for another twenty million. That was blackmail.'

'So you blew him up. And what was left of Coleby. And the staff. And a hundred other people. As friend Smollett would say, holy shitting cows! But wait just a moment. That was a massive bomb. Not something one carries about in your pocket for use in emergencies. You went there *intending* to destroy him and his clinic.'

'Well, we knew he would betray us sometime.'

'I have met a lot of villains, but you are in a class of your own. And your husband, of course. And Kanem, right? So tell me what went wrong. Why did you leave Matthieu?'

'He changed his mind about taking over the Followers. In the beginning, we didn't know how successful the operation would be, or if it would be successful at all. But when Hercule got to be three and then four, we realized that he was already thinking like an adult, and talking like one too. I supposed that everything was going according to plan. But Henri was already having other ideas. He felt that returning Hercule to the Followers to

276

become their leader would be to lose control of him. He began to think of him as a freak who could be used for so many things. Not least to make us more money. I do not believe he was ever a true Follower.'

'Just a mass murderer. Like you.'

'You won't forget that I saved your life.'

'And I saved yours, just now. From this monster of a son you have.'

'I am the Lord,' Hercule declared. 'My word is the law. All those who oppose my will shall be cast out.'

'Including your own mother?'

'I need no mother. I am a child of eternity. And my so-called mother is a criminal. She has just confessed this to you.'

'Tell it to the judge. What the...'

The helicopter was enveloped in a huge, rattling sound. 'It is raining,' Claudine said.

The machine was being thrown about by a sudden strong wind, but Jessica released her seat belt and climbed the steps to the flight deck. 'Can't we get above this?'

'It seems to stretch pretty high,' Douglas said. 'It's a damned nuisance. I was just beginning to pick out some landmarks.'

Jessica looked down; there was nothing to be seen save driving rain mist. 'How's the fuel?'

'Half an hour, maybe,' Smollett said.

'You said you had some landmarks.'

'We crossed the railway line twenty minutes ago. Gwala is north of the line, maybe fifty miles.'

Jessica looked at the air speed indicator. They were flying at a hundred and fifty miles an hour. 'Then we should be just about over it.'

'If we've been following the right line. But for this rain we should be able to see it.'

'So we're about to overshoot,' Smollett said. 'Which way should I turn, left or right?'

'Right,' Douglas said. 'I think we've been west of the line.'

'Can't we go lower?' Jessica asked. 'Your altimeter says seven hundred feet. There are no big hills around here.'

'I'm not sure that is an accurate setting. I think we're a lot lower than seven hundred.'

Douglas grinned at her. 'We'll make it. These storms seldom last more than half an hour.'

'Which is the amount of fuel we have left.' The needle on the gauge was certainly hovering close to zero. 'But it's already been raining for ten minutes,' Douglas reminded her. As he spoke, there was a flash of lightning and a tremendous peal of thunder. The helicopter slipped sideways and Jessica lost her footing, only preventing herself from tumbling down the steps by hanging on to the rail. 'Look, go back to your seat and strap yourself in,' Douglas said. 'We don't want you to get busted up.'

The machine had steadied, and Jessica regained her seat. Hercule was crying. 'We're going to die,' he wailed. 'I don't want to die.'

'So he's not entirely an adult,' Jessica

278

remarked. 'Try bending your mighty brain to something else. How about multiplying ... a hundred and nineteen by two hundred and fifty-one. That should keep you busy for a while.'

'The answer is twenty-nine thousand, eight hundred and sixty-nine,' the boy replied with some dignity.

'I sit corrected, and apologize.' Lacking a calculator, she had no means of telling if he was right, but he had answered without hesitation.

'If that lightning had hit us...' Claudine said.

'We'd be cooked. But ... Shit! I think it did.' There was a distinct smell of scorching from aft. Jessica released her belt and went to the steps. 'We're on fire.'

'Eh?' Both men spoke together.

'Check it out,' Smollett snapped.

Douglas left his seat, came down the steps, and made his way into the rear of the cabin. 'Yes, we are. Where's the extinguisher?'

'Haven't a clue,' Jessica said. 'Where is the fuel tank? Or isn't there enough in there to be dangerous?'

'There's enough fumes, to be sure.' He returned forward. 'Take her down, Smollett. Quickly.'

'I can't see.'

'Fuck that! Take her down. Get belted, JJ. But get out the moment we're down.'

Jessica sat down. 'Are we going to die?' Claudine asked.

'Who do you usually pray to?'

Hercule burst into tears.

They could almost hear the flames crackling now, and by looking over her shoulder Jessica could see them bursting through the door to the empty baggage compartment. It was a matter of whether they got down before the fire reached the fuel tank. Jessica remembered the Colombian drug helicopter hovering above her, the men looking through the open door, one of them holding a bomb, having already dropped two. She had fired instinctively, certainly intending to hit the aircraft, but without any knowledge of where the fuel tanks had been situated. And then, a huge fireball, plummeting to the earth. How ironic if she was to go the same way...

They were certainly plummeting to the earth as Smollett descended. 'I see! I see!' he bawled through the intercom.

'Brace yourselves,' Douglas shouted.

Jessica put her head between her knees, but was yet taken by surprise as the impact seemed to encompass her whole body. Claudine screamed, as did Hercule, but his was a disturbingly choked sound. Then there was nothing but disjointed noise. Jessica didn't know whether she was hurt or not, but she did know she was seated next to the door. She wrenched it open, grabbed Claudine by the arm. 'Out!' she screamed. 'Out!'

Claudine had not released her belt. Jessica did so, held both her arms, and threw her out of the door. Claudine screamed again.

Hercule had also not released his belt. Jessica did it for him while he stared at her with wide, uncomprehending eyes. Blood was dribbling down his cheek. She threw him behind his mother, then jumped herself, thinking as she did so, been there, done that. She struck the ground and rolled, then buried her face in her arms as behind her there was a great *whoompf!*

Again memory flooded back, of the bomb blast in Alicante when she had lain just like this, with her hands over her head, feeling burning cinders dropping on her; there were still faint marks on her back, nearly three years later. Now again there were little objects pounding on her back, only these, she realized, were not cinders, but pouring rain. She had forgotten about the rain. And the thunder, which continued to rumble, setting off vivid flashes of lightning.

She got to her knees and looked behind her. The remains of the helicopter still burned, but the flames were already dying down. She looked the other way, and saw Claudine. She was also on her knees, hugging Hercule against her. 'You okay?' she shouted.

Claudine raised her head to stare at her with enormous eyes. Jessica took that for a yes, at least for the time being: she had to find the men. She stood up, staggered to and fro. She became aware of pain. Nothing sharp, just a general ache. Her body was telling her that it was getting fed up. She didn't blame it.

She stumbled round the front of the helicopter to the pilot's door. But this no longer existed, because the flight deck no longer existed. It had been torn apart, a jumble of disintegrated instruments and gauges. But no men. She looked left and right, took a few steps, and fell over a body. On her knees, heart lurching, she bent over Douglas. He lay on his back, his face impassive.

'Hey,' she shouted. 'Hey! Wake up.'

Now she saw the bruise on his forehead, the seeping blood constantly washed away by the pouring rain. 'Hey!' she shouted again. 'Don't die on me, Douglas.' Still there was no response. She panted, lowered her head, and bit the lobe of his ear.

'For Christ's sake!'

'Thank God!'

He blinked at her. 'You look wetter than yesterday.'

'I am wetter than yesterday. Where's Smollett?'

'God knows. He was thrown out, forward.'

'Through the window?'

'Don't panic. They're Perspex.'

'Can you manage?'

He struggled to a sitting position, began feeling himself. 'I'm getting there. How about the Princess and the boy?'

'They're alive.' She stood up, did a little more staggering, and went towards the front of the wrecked aircraft. Still the rain pounded on her head and shoulders, but this was refreshing her. Then she saw Smollett. He lay on his face, some thirty feet in front of the

282

helicopter's nose. The distance he had been thrown indicated the force of the impact.

Douglas was at her shoulder. 'He was in such a hurry to get out he released his belt before the impact. I saw him go.'

Jessica went forward, stood above the American. There was no movement, and more blood than even the rain could cope with. She dropped to her knees. Theirs had been an uneven relationship, but he had never shirked his duty. So she'd never know if he would have arrested Claudine once they regained civilization. But then, she didn't know what she was going to do about that, either.

And first, they had to get back *to* civilization. The thought of another trek through the desert curdled her blood, although she didn't suppose water would be a problem on this occasion unless there was too much of it.

'Do you have any idea where we are?' she asked Douglas.

'Only that we're at least fifty miles north of the railway line.'

'Are there any towns around here?'

'No. We're pretty close to Niger, and the desert.'

'What about Gwala?'

'That's a small village. And if what you say is correct, they'll be hostile. All our hardware went up in that smoke.'

'Shit!' She'd forgotten that. 'So what do we do?'

'First thing, we wait for the rain to stop.

Should happen any moment now. Let's see how the princess is.'

They splashed round the now smouldering wreckage. Claudine still sat, Hercule in her arms, rocking to and fro and moaning.

'Where does it hurt?' Douglas asked.

'I am not in pain.'

'Is it the boy?'

Claudine didn't reply. Jessica knelt beside her. Hercule's head rested on his mother's shoulder; tears dribbled from his eyes. And there was quite a lot of blood, constantly being washed away by the rain. 'He's had a knock.'

'He is hurt,' Claudine said. 'He bumped his head.'

'Where? Let's have a look.'

'Don't touch him.'

'Claudine, you are being hysterical. That's not like you. I'm trying to help.' She touched Hercule's arm, and he jerked.

'Looks like he's suffering from shock,' Douglas suggested.

'Hercule,' Jessica said. 'Can you hear me?'

Hercule stared at her.

'Maybe he's gone deaf,' Douglas said.

Hercule turned his head.

'He's not deaf. Hey, Hercule, wake up. Do some multiplication. How about three hundred and four multiplied by two hundred and seventeen.'

Hercule stared at her.

'How do you expect a six-year-old kid to be able to work out something like that?'

Douglas asked.

'He could do it just now. I think we need to get him to a doctor.'

'I think we all need to get to a doctor. But as we don't know where the nearest doctor is, we'll have to be patient. We could have a long walk ahead of us.'

'Tell me about it.' Jessica sat on the ground beside Claudine. Suddenly she was thirsty, but she solved that problem by simply opening her mouth and tilting her head back. She was also hungry; breakfast seemed a very long time ago. And she was worried, and not just about the crash. This whole thing had gone terribly pear-shaped. 'How do we handle this?' she asked Douglas.

'It'll be tricky, until we find out just where we are, how far from civilization.'

'I meant, this whole thing. We've stolen a helicopter and then smashed it up. We've killed two men and managed to lose a CIA agent. When the news gets around...'

'I have an idea it's not going to get around, unless we spread it. I don't think your friend Zobeir is in a position to bring charges. He'd have to explain the kidnapping of you and Andrea, not to mention the princess, and the dropping of you in the middle of the desert. More important, he'd have to explain the disappearance of Ukuba. Even if he got away with that, the publicity could be fatal to his ambitions. The Followers were founded by Ukuba. If his death becomes known there could well be a considerable fall-out. The last thing Zobeir will want is an investigation of the Centre of the Universe, whether it's done by me, or by Faure, who, as you know, is already anti. And when we get back to Kano and I allow it to become known that his helicopter crashed, killing everybody on board, I have an idea he will just breathe a sigh of relief and say, blessed be the Lord! Smollett, now, will have to be explained. We'll have to work on that.'

'But there is still Andie. And we still have to get back.' It was now five days that she had been in the hands of Kanem, and possibly his brother as well. Anything could have happened to her. She could even have been killed, if she had resisted them strongly enough. At the very best ... She sighed, and hunched her shoulders, and realized the rain had become a drizzle and the thunder had faded into a distant rumble.

'Hallelujah!' Douglas said.

'The rain's stopping,' Jessica told Claudine. 'We'll soon be on our way. We may need you.'

Claudine ignored her, continued to hold Hercule close. She really does love the boy, Jessica thought. And what was to be done with her, and him, was now squarely in her lap, with Smollett gone. And the boy could hardly be considered innocent – he had condemned Ukuba to death, or at least acquiesced in that condemnation. He could never be put on trial, because of his age. But if he did have the brain of a thirty-year-old genius...

Douglas stood up, looked around himself.

The rain had stopped altogether, the clouds were rising and breaking, and the sun was coming through, with the inevitable result that the ground was beginning to steam, creating an immediate mist that limited visibility even more than the rain. 'It'll clear,' he said.

'What time is it?'

He looked at his watch. 'Eleven. Seems like this day has been going on forever.'

Jessica also got up. Her clothes were now steaming as well, as were everybody's. The ground around them was sodden, with little pools of water everywhere; she had a sudden thought that they should drink some of it before it evaporated.

And the helicopter still smouldered.

'What about Smollett?' she asked. 'We can't just leave him there.'

'We sure can't bury him. We don't even have a knife. When we get back I'll send a squad out to pick up the pieces and bring him in for burial.' He frowned. 'Someone's coming.'

'What?' She turned, blinking into the mist, but for the moment seeing nothing. 'Give them a shout.'

'Hold on! We don't know who they are. This is a frontier, JJ. They could be Touaregs. And we have no weapons.'

'So what do we do?' It was so easy, and such a relief, to hand over both responsibility and command.

'Let them come closer so that we can have a look. Take cover.'

He knelt and she followed his example, staring into the mist. Now she was beginning to make them out. Four camels, two mounted by women.

'Like you said,' she remarked. 'Hallelujah!'

Ten

The Family of Evil

The women had now made them out as well, and halted. Jessica went forward. 'JJ!' Douglas warned. He had not recognized them.

'We're old friends,' Jessica said. 'Don't you remember?' She advanced towards the women, remembering to take off her hat and attempting to fluff out her sodden hair, which was plastered to her scalp. 'Remember me?' she called.

Apparently they did. They pointed at her, broke into laughter, and gabbled. 'Can you understand them?' Jessica asked Douglas. 'I know the princess can.'

'Come on, Princess,' Douglas said, heaving Claudine and the boy to their feet. 'I can get the drift, but you may have to talk.'

'Remind them that we saved them from slavery and gave them those camels,' Jessica

288

said. 'Now we would like three of the camels back.'

Claudine exchanged remarks. 'They want to know what we are doing here.'

'Tell them we fell from the sky, and ask them what *they* are doing here?'

Another exchange. 'They say they are going to Kano, and were sheltering from the rain when they heard the sound of the crash and saw the flames, and were curious.'

'To see what they could pick up, I have no doubt. Ask them why they are going to Kano.'

The women were voluble. 'They say they are going to the city to sell the camels, and be rich.'

'What a brilliant idea. Tell them we will buy their camels at twice the going rate, if they will let us accompany them and ride the beasts.'

Claudine translated, and the women appeared to be discussing the offer. 'They say, why should they help us?'

'For one thing, because we helped them. For another, tell them that they will not get as good a price anywhere else but from us, so they will be even richer. And thirdly, tell them that if they do not help us, I will deal with them exactly as I dealt with the Touaregs.'

This time the discussion was brief. 'They say they will accept your offer.'

'You, JJ, are quite something,' Douglas said.

'Sometimes a reputation comes in handy,' she agreed. 'And nearly always, casting your bread upon the water brings results.'

*   *   *

By the following evening they had regained the railway line, and by the next morning they had reached a station. By then they were entirely out of food and water, but the stationmaster and his wife fed them, attended to their various cuts and bruises, and gave them beds, while Douglas telephoned Kano and arranged for the police helicopter to pick them up first thing next morning, and to bring with it the agreed fee for the camels. He also, at Jessica's request, arranged a separate room at the hotel for Claudine and Hercule. 'You'd better arrange an appointment with a doctor,' she suggested.

'Where's the damage?'

'I'm thinking of Hercule. He does nothing but weep and hug his mother.'

'Like I said, he's suffering from shock.'

'Maybe. But I think it's more serious than that. Now tell me what we are going to do about Andie.'

'Well, the first thing is to get a warrant to search Kwarism's house. Hopefully.'

'What do you mean, hopefully?'

'As you may know, there is a great deal of corruption in this country. Kwarism is a wealthy man, and a popular one. He almost certainly has several of our magistrates in his pocket, and his links to the Followers of the Lord are well known and have never been considered illegal. So we may have a little trouble over the warrant.'

'But if his sons have kidnapped Andie...'

290

'We have to convince people that they have.'

'I saw him do it.'

'With respect, JJ, in Kano the testimony of an English police woman, unsupported, is not going to get too far against the denial of Mahmood Kwarism.'

'The princess was there.'

'Do you reckon she is really on your side? And Kwarism is her stepfather.'

'She despises him.'

'What do you reckon she feels about you?'

'Whatever it is, it's not contempt. But perhaps we could do a deal. Her support in getting inside Kwarism's house in return for mitigating evidence at her trial.'

'What trial?'

Jessica stared at him 'Douglas, the woman is a mass murderess.'

'Do you have a warrant for her arrest?'

'Of course I do not.'

'Can you wire Scotland Yard and get one?'

'It would be tricky.'

'Quite. Because she has committed no crime in England. So you cannot arrest her, and you cannot force her to leave Nigeria if she does not wish to go. Nor can I interfere. She is a citizen of this country, and she has not committed a crime here.'

'Shit,' Jessica said. 'Shit, shit, shit! Well, tell me this: are you going to help me get Andie back?'

'That is my intention, certainly. If it can be done legally.'

Jessica wondered what he might do if he

discovered that she was not here in an official capacity, but was actually working for Matthieu.

It was mid-morning when they reached Kano, having left behind them two very happy women, who had both been paid for the camels and retained the beasts.

The police car dropped them at the hotel. 'I reckon you should go to bed,' Douglas said. 'I'll be in touch as soon as I have something to tell you. Princess, you have an appointment for Hercule to see Dr Nanko this afternoon at two o'clock. I suggest you also have some rest until then.' The car drove off.

'What is this appointment with a doctor?' Claudine asked.

'Don't you want Hercule to see a doctor? He's not well.'

'Ha,' Claudine commented, and went into the lobby, past the saluting doormen, holding Hercule by the hand.

'Mrs Matthieu,' said the receptionist. 'Are you all right?'

'You have a room for me and my son.'

'Oh, yes, indeed.'

'Then shut up and give me the key.'

He gulped and obeyed, and she stalked off. He tried his luck with Jessica. 'Miss Jones, every time I see you, you look worse than before.'

'It must be the climate,' Jessica said. 'Is breakfast still on?'

'Breakfast ended fifteen minutes ago. But it

292

is only two hours to lunch.'

'I shall be asleep. I would like breakfast sent up to my room, now.'

'But breakfast is finished.'

'Then unfinish it.'

Achmed made a face. 'Is the other gentleman with you?'

Douglas would have to handle that one. 'You'll have to ask him when you see him.' She went upstairs, slowly removed her clothing; it seemed glued to her body, and she also discovered some cuts and bruises she hadn't been aware of.

She was still examining herself when the meal arrived. She received it in her dressing gown, handed over her filthy and still wet clothes to be laundered, ate, and then wallowed in a hot tub before going to bed, and into a deep sleep, to be awakened by a knock on the door.

For a moment she was disoriented, then she sat up. 'Who is it?'

'I have a message for Detective-Sergeant Jones.'

The voice was familiar, although she could not place it. And he seemed to know who she was. She got out of bed, put on her dressing gown and opened the door.

'Miss Jones,' said Henri Matthieu. 'What have you been doing to yourself?'

Trying to shut the door was a waste of time; he was already inside. Nor, in her half-awake and undressed mode, did Jessica feel capable

293

of taking him on at the moment. She backed across the room. 'What the hell are you doing here?'

'Trying to discover exactly what is going on.' He closed and locked the door behind him.

Jessica gathered the dressing gown round herself. 'I think you had better leave. I will get dressed and meet you downstairs.'

'I prefer to speak in private. You have not forgotten that you are working for me, I hope? And as you have rather skilfully managed to extract a quarter of a million pounds of your fee, I am sure you will understand that I feel in need of a progress report.'

Jessica sat on the bed, and began getting her brain into gear. 'Only a quarter of million? Shit.'

'Indeed. Your little ploy took some time to permeate the upper regions of the various banks we were employing. But two days ago I received a telephone call from the manager of the Guernsey bank, asking me if I was aware that you had established a standing order for a daily transfer of ten thousand pounds and if this sort of arrangement was what I had in mind when I set up the accounts. Isn't it reassuring to know that our finances are protected by the eagle eye of our bankers? I immediately cancelled the facility, of course.'

'And came here? I thought you said it was too dangerous for you to do so.'

'Circumstances appear to have changed. My agent informs me that the Centre of the

294

Universe is in chaos, that Ukuba is dead, and that my son was abducted by his mother and a yellow-haired woman who is absolutely deadly with guns.'

'Your agent,' Jessica said. 'You do know that Masud is also working for Ukuba. Or I suppose he is working for Zobeir now.'

Even as she spoke she realized there was something wrong with what she had just been told, but there was no time to pinpoint it.

'Masud is irrelevant now,' Matthieu said. 'The kidnapping of my son took place three days ago. He should have been back in England by now. Yet the jet is still waiting at Kano airport, and I find you in bed. I have come for my son, Sergeant.'

Jessica considered. It occurred to her that she was being offered an exit route. She had no idea what to do with or about Claudine and Hercule. If she reunited the family now, she could simply walk away from the entire business, and whatever happened between them could be regarded as an act of fate. Providing she straightened one or two other matters out at the same time. 'I can tell you where your son is,' she said. 'But only on conditions.'

'You are in no position to make conditions.'

'Are you threatening me, Mr Matthieu?'

He gazed at her while trying to make up his mind. He could tell that she was not armed at the moment. And he no doubt felt that he could cope with her physically. But he could not be sure. 'What are these conditions?'

'The first is that you reinstate my credit transfers.'

'I will do that when you take me to my son.'

Jessica shook her head. 'There is hotel notepaper in the drawer on that table. Sit down and write four letters, one addressed to each relevant bank manager, informing him that you have spoken with your daughter, that she has reassured you as to her intentions, and that her orders regarding the money are to be reinstated immediately.'

'You think you can give me orders?'

'Yes, Mr Matthieu. If you wish to see your son.'

He glared at her for several seconds, then went to the table and began writing. Jessica used the opportunity to collect some clothes – she had to wear a dress, as all her shirts and jeans were either at Kwarism's house, in the hotel laundry, or on loan to Claudine – and went into the bathroom to dress and brush her still damp hair. Then she returned to the bedroom and read the letters. 'I think these are satisfactory.'

'Where is my son?'

'About fifty feet away from you.'

'What?' He looked left and right.

'I'm not sure of the room. I'll just find out for you.' She picked up the phone, called the desk. 'This is Miss Jones. Would you give me the number of Mrs Matthieu's room, please. I assume she has returned from the doctor by now.'

'You mean she is here in the hotel? With

Hercule?' Matthieu said. 'And I did not know?'

'Doctor, Miss Jones?' the clerk asked.

'Never mind. Give me the number of her room.'

'But Mrs Matthieu is not there, Miss Jones. She is not in the hotel.'

'Then I want to know the moment she gets back.'

'She is not coming back, Miss Jones. She has checked out.'

'Checked out? To go where?'

'She called a taxi, to take her to her father's house.'

'Oh, fuck it!' Jessica replaced the phone. 'She's gone back to Kwarism.'

'You had her, you had Hercule, and you let them go?'

'I had no means of stopping her. Here in Kano she's a free agent. But if she ever leaves ... And the same goes for you, Matthieu. Claudine made a confession, and as you are not a Nigerian citizen...'

'But as you are not on official duty, you can't touch me, JJ. I'll have those letters back.'

'You won't, you know.'

He stepped towards her, and she picked up the phone. The front desk was a matter of pressing R. 'Hello, Achmed. Would you be a dear and get me Inspector Kahu? Ask him to come over here immediately. Tell him it is very important.'

She replaced the phone, and Matthieu

297

glowered at her, his hands opening and shutting. 'Who is this Kahu?'

'A close friend. He runs the show around here. Don't panic. He's a reasonable man. And he may be the man to get your son back for you. Amongst others. Why don't you sit down?' She called room service and ordered tea. 'By sending me to Masud you set me up.'

Matthieu sat down. 'I knew you could handle it. As you obviously have.'

'Not without one or two unfortunate experiences. So your real agent was Golightly.'

'One should always have more than one string for one's bow, JJ.'

'Absolutely. And presumably he had a mobile concealed in that stick of his.'

'Of course.'

'So what happens to him and Lennon now?'

'I have instructed them to remain on the island for the time being. They seem to be well integrated. And they will keep me informed as to the situation there.'

'So what exactly is, or was, your plan? To take over the Followers yourself, through Hercule?'

'That is an intriguing idea, is it not? Until you let him slip through your fingers.' The tea arrived. 'Tell me,' Matthieu said when the waiter had withdrawn. 'What do you propose to do with my wife's confession? I assume you have it written down?'

'No, I do not.'

'Then it is useless.'

'Not if Claudine can be persuaded to repeat

it. There is also Kanem's testimony.'

'He would be implicating himself.'

'I think he might be persuaded to become a prosecution witness. Unlike you and your wife, you see, he has actually committed a crime here in Nigeria, for which he could go to prison for a very long time.'

'What crime?'

'More tea?' Jessica poured, and listened to feet outside her door. 'It's open,' she called.

Douglas entered, and stopped at the sight of Matthieu.

'You haven't met. Inspector Kahu, this is Henri Matthieu, the husband of Claudine Matthieu and the father of Hercule Matthieu. And, incidentally, the man who blew up the De Groot Clinic in Chicago.'

Slowly Douglas closed the door. 'What is he doing here?'

'Looking for his son.'

'There is no law against that,' Matthieu said.

'Not in this country.'

'Unfortunately,' Jessica said, 'Claudine has done a bunk. I don't know if she went to the doctor or not, but she called a taxi to take her to her stepfather's house.'

'Where Kanem is? Why should she do that?'

'I don't really know. I do know that she's bewildered and feeling very isolated. And having got Hercule back, I think she just wants to roll up into a ball and drop out while she considers her options. So what have you got for me?'

Douglas sighed. 'As I suspected would be the case, the magistrate to whom I applied would not give me a search warrant. He pointed out that Kwarism is a model citizen, as well as a wealthy one. He also points out that we have no evidence that this kidnapping ever took place, save the testimony of, in his words, "two hysterical women", and we can't even count on Claudine now. In fact, if she's gone back to her stepfather, I would say definitely not.'

'I do not understand,' Matthieu said. 'Who is accused of kidnapping?'

Jessica ignored him. 'What are we going to do?'

'There is nothing we can do. Legally.'

Jessica gazed at him.

'As for illegally,' he said, 'well, I'd be putting my career on the line.'

'Not if we find Andie in there, surely.'

Douglas stroked his chin.

Jessica turned to Matthieu. 'Tell us about this house. You must have been there.'

'Oh, I have been there. You are thinking of forcing an entry? That is crazy.'

'Your son is in there, Matthieu. Don't you want to get him out?'

'Of course I do. But what you are proposing is crazy. That is not a house; it is a fortress. You would need an army.'

'But it is possible to get in without using the front door.'

'There is no other entrance.'

'Oh, come now. There has to be a tradesman's entrance. How do heavy goods get in?'

'There are panels to either side of the small door which can be opened.'

'And these goods are carried into that small entry hall?'

'The inner wall also opens, to give access to the courtyard.'

'So it's the front door or nothing. Okay, we'll have to play it rough.'

'Just what do you have in mind?' Douglas asked.

'To force an entry, get in, find Andrea and Claudine and the boy, and get them out of there.'

'Who is this Andie?' Matthieu asked.

'My partner, remember?'

'The other woman, yes. So she has got herself into trouble. Do you realize that Kwarism has a staff of at least thirty men, not to mention the harem? The men will all be armed. And if you break into his house, they will be entitled to use their arms.'

'Life is full of little problems. Douglas?'

'Well...'

'So I'm putting your career at risk all over again. But if we find Andie, and we know she's there, won't you be in the clear?'

'Well, you thinking about just you and me?'

'And him, for starters.'

'Me?' Matthieu cried. 'I cannot be involved.'

'You are involved. It's your son, remember? And we need you to get us in. That fellow Abdullah, Kwarism's doorkeeper, knows me.'

301

'Do you not suppose he knows *me*?'

'Sure, but he'll open the door for you if you tell him you wish to speak with your wife.'

'I will be killed.'

'Hopefully not, with me looking after you. Tell me what you can give me, Douglas.'

'I've no more Minimis to spare. It'll have to be pistols.'

'Fair enough. I'm not aiming to do any more damage than I have to. What sort of pistols?'

'Our standard issue are Brownings.'

'Year?'

'Well, they ain't new.'

'Not pre-World War II, I hope.' The Browning Hi-Power automatic had been developed in the 1920s.

'No, no. These are about thirty years old.'

'Right.' The Browning, with its thirteen-shot magazine and massive stopping power, had been a favourite weapon of the SAS for years, until superseded by the lighter and handier Sauer. 'And any additional support?'

'I think I can raise a few volunteers. What exactly is your plan?'

'Henri here is going to draw us a plan. Aren't you, Henri? Just sit at that table again, use one of those sheets of hotel paper, and sketch the interior of the house.' He did so, Jessica and Douglas standing at his shoulders.

'That is very good,' Jessica said. 'It had also better be very accurate. Does Claudine have her own room? Or will she be in the harem?'

302

'She has, or she had when she lived there, her own apartment. Here.' He made an X.

'Um. That's virtually the other end of the house from the harem. Okay. I imagine you'd like to handle her end of things. We'll let you have a gun, but bear in mind that if you shoot your wife you will be charged with murder.' She looked at Douglas. 'What do you do with murderers in these parts?'

'Oh, we hang them. Publicly.'

Matthieu gulped.

'So be careful,' Jessica recommended. 'Your business is to get your wife and child out with as little fuss as possible.'

'Suppose they refuse to come with me?'

'Be masculine. Just remember that I want Claudine alive.'

'So that you can hang *her*.'

'Sadly, we don't do that any more in England. Anyway, I promised to do what I can for you. Okay, that's your angle. Now tell me where Kanem is likely to keep a woman. In the harem?'

'No, no,' Matthieu said. 'The harem is for his father's women. He would not be allowed in there.'

'So where would he keep her?'

'I have no idea. In his own apartment, I should think.'

'Show me.'

'I cannot. I do not know where it would be. It is a big house.'

'All right. I'll find it.'

'By yourself?' Douglas asked.

303

'Give me two pistols. I don't reckon on too much trouble getting in. Getting out I hope to have Andie with me.'

'And what do you have in mind for me and my people?'

'Back-up. You'll keep our line of retreat open. The whole thing should be done in fifteen minutes. Have a car waiting to take us to the airport.'

'I will take you to the airport myself. What time does this happen?'

'Make it midnight.'

He nodded, and stood up. 'You are something, Sergeant Jones. What about him? Shall I take him with me and lock him up until it is time?'

'You cannot do that,' Matthieu snapped.

'He can, you know,' Jessica said. 'But he's not going to. Leave him with me, Douglas. He's on our side, at the moment.'

'I'd better go and rest up,' Matthieu said.

'No, you don't,' Jessica said. 'You are staying right here. Don't you want to spend a couple of hours with me? I seem to remember you inviting me to spend the night with you last week?'

'Well...'

'You're not in the mood for sex. Relax. Neither am I. But I'm not in the mood for trusting people, either. Besides, you have something to do.'

'What?' He was immediately suspicious.

'You have to telephone your pilot, and tell

304

him to obtain flight clearance and then stand by, because you are leaving Kano sometime around one o'clock tomorrow morning. Do it now.'

He obeyed, and appeared to obtain a satisfactory response. Well, she reflected, it was his life as much as theirs that was on the line.

Then they waited. Neither was in the mood for conversation, either. Jessica had no doubt that his brain was teeming. She could not imagine a man like Matthieu tamely returning to England to be arrested and extradited to America. She didn't know if the State of Illinois retained the death penalty, but she did know that in the United States, unlike England, a life sentence was liable to mean just that. Therefore he would be planning to make a break. But he would not do that until after he had secured Hercule. Hercule was not only the reason for his past, he was the key to his future. She wondered how Claudine would react to the unexpected appearance of her husband. But as she had thought earlier, it was up to them to sort out their domestic differences, and if they did it at the point of a gun, that might solve a great many problems. She was at least certain that neither of them would willingly hurt the boy.

And herself? She was totally concentrated on getting Andie out of whatever hell she was presently in. Time to wonder what came next when she had done that.

She ordered dinner, served by waiters who rolled their eyes at the idea of this man and this woman apparently sharing this room when they knew very well they were not married. They also brought up her laundry, and after the meal she retired to the bathroom and changed into her shirt and jeans. The rest of her stuff would obviously have to be abandoned, but both she and Andie should have their shoulder bags and original clothing waiting at Kwarism's, if they had not been destroyed.

The hours drifted by. 'Are you not afraid?' Matthieu asked.

'Doesn't seem much point.'

'Because you have done this so often it means nothing to you anymore.'

'It always means something to me, Henri. A week ago I thought I'd given it up. Maybe after this one I'll be able to hang up my gun.'

'Maybe you will not have the opportunity.'

'Could be.' She looked at her watch. 'Eleven thirty. Let's go down.'

They waited in the lobby, watched suspiciously by the reception clerks. Achmed was apparently off duty, but he had clearly briefed the night staff regarding the eccentric Miss Jones. However, Douglas arrived ten minutes later. In the van were six policemen, wearing civilian clothes, as was he, and only just suppressing their excitement.

The policemen were armed. Douglas handed Jessica her two pistols and gave one to Matthieu. 'Don't shoot yourself,' he recommended as Matthieu took the gun, somewhat gingerly. He also gave Jessica two spare magazines.

'Don't I get one of those?' Matthieu demanded.

'We'll be covering you.' Jessica pulled her shirt out of her pants, thrust the first gun into her waistband, and the second again into her waistband, but in the small of her back. The magazines she put in her pockets, and began to feel extremely overloaded. But, she reflected, it wouldn't be for very long. 'Okay?' Douglas asked.

'Okay.'

The streets were dark and deserted, save for stray dogs. There was no moon. The van stopped a block short of the square dominated by Kwarism's fortress. 'Now,' Douglas said, 'you all know what you have to do. Let's go. Nammu,' he told the driver, 'stay awake, and when we emerge, come and get us.'

'I'll be waiting, Inspector,' Nammu agreed.

They walked round the square, keeping in the shadows. Dogs barked, but they had been barking anyway. They stood against the wall, pistols drawn, while Matthieu went up to the door and pulled the bell rope. It was answered surprisingly quickly, considering the hour. 'You have business?'

'I am Henri Matthieu.' His voice was surprisingly resonant. 'I have come to see my wife.'

'Ah, Mr Matthieu. Welcome. Enter.'

'Shit!' Jessica muttered. Abdullah, or whoever it was, had clearly been expecting him.

But it was too late to change their plans now. The door was already swinging in, and Douglas was leading his men through in a rush. She had to follow. To remain outside and have the door close again would leave her with no means of entry, and no back-up either.

She ran into the entry hall, blinked in the gloom, watched the policemen jostling each other as they made for the inner doorway, and the lights came on. She checked, her back against the wall, while the door slammed shut. She blinked at the several men lining the walls, each armed with a Kalashnikov. Whether these were 47s or 74s did not seem relevant; they were good enough to destroy the intruders. Standing in front of the inner door were Kwarism and his two sons, as well as Serene; all were fully dressed, and both the younger men were also armed.

'You bastard!' Douglas snapped at Matthieu.

Matthieu's mouth opened and shut.

'He did not betray you, Inspector,' Kwarism said. 'Do not the Followers of the Lord know everything? Lay down your weapons, gentlemen. Cleaning up your blood will be such a tiresome task.'

The policemen looked at Douglas, who hesitated just a moment before nodding. Matthieu had already dropped his pistol.

'And you, Miss Jones,' Kwarism said. 'Come forward where we may see you.'

Jessica stepped through the policemen, the
308

pistol hanging at her side. Her brain was seething, but only with the white-hot fury, the determination to destroy the opposition regardless of what happened to her, that made her so deadly.

But these people did not know that, nor did they know about her second weapon, nor did they know her capabilities.

'Take her gun, Kanem,' Kwarism commanded.

'I will do it,' Fodio said. 'I claim this one as my own.' He grinned as he stepped forward.

Jessica reversed the pistol, brushing her hand over the safety catch as she did so, and held it out. Fodio took the gun, and then stepped against her, reaching for her shirt with his free hand. Jessica thrust forward with all her strength. The pistol and Fodio's hand thudded into his belly and he gasped and pulled the trigger, as she had known he would. But the safety catch prevented a shot. She thrust him away from her, stepped round him, drawing her other pistol as she did so, wrapping her arm round Serene's waist and presenting the pistol to her head. 'Move, and she's dead!'

As she spoke, she stepped backwards, carrying the girl with her, so that she was clear of Kanem and Kwarism. Taken by surprise, Serene did not react for a moment, then she screamed and made a convulsive effort to get free. Jessica rapped her across the head with the pistol butt, and she subsided, moaning, held up by Jessica's left arm.

There was an enormous ripple round the room and one of the men swung his Kalashnikov towards Jessica. She levelled the pistol and shot the gun out of his hands, shattering his fingers as she did so. He gave a scream of agony. Jessica swung the pistol to and fro. 'You want to remember,' she said, 'that I have twelve shots left, and there are only eleven of you. Drop your weapons.'

All the heads turned towards Kwarism.

'Oh, you'll be first,' she told him.

'Put down your guns,' Kwarism said.

'And I suggest your boys pick them up, Douglas,' Jessica said.

Douglas signalled his men and the servants were disarmed.

'That's good,' Jessica said. 'Now, can you hold these guys here while Matthieu and I do our stuff?'

'You do not wish a back-up?'

'I think we can manage. Let me have that other Browning.'

Fodio had dropped it. One of the policemen picked it up, and Jessica thrust it into her waistband 'Okay, Matthieu, on your way. Just find Claudine and Hercule and bring them here. No violence.'

Matthieu had also picked up his gun and went through the inner doorway. Kwarism had regained his nerve. 'You will suffer for this,' he snarled. 'If you harm my daughter...'

'Don't count your chickens. Move, Serene.'

The girl was just starting to recover from the blow on her head, which had left a trace of

310

blood showing through the dark hair. Still holding her arm, Jessica pushed her through the inner doorway. 'Take me to Andrea. Miss Hutchins.'

'I do not know where she is,' Serene muttered.

'Little girl, do you wish to have another clip around the ear?'

'She is in my brother's apartment.'

'So take me there.'

'It is across the courtyard.'

'Is it guarded?'

'Not at this time.'

'So let's go.'

Serene opened the door and they stepped into the night. There was no wind and Jessica could smell the fetid odour of the crocodile pit, while she could hear restless movement from down there as well. Douglas had said that the reptiles were not very active at night, but even if he was wrong, the gate at the top of the ramp was securely closed. Even so, remembering her experience in Bolivia made her skin crawl. There was also considerable agitation from the right-hand wing of the house, on the upper floor. 'The women have been awakened by the shot,' Serene said. 'They will clap their hands when you die.'

'You people do have one-track minds,' Jessica remarked. 'Don't you ever talk about living?' They reached a flight of stairs on the far side of the yard. 'Just remember,' Jessica said. 'Try to pull a fast one and you will have

311

a close encounter with your favourite subject.'

Serene went up the stairs, Jessica immediately behind her. They reached a verandah, and Serene led her past two doors to a third. 'This is Kanem's apartment.'

'How many rooms?'

'There is the reception room, and the bedroom, and the bathroom.'

Jessica tried the door. It was locked. 'You in there, Andie?' she shouted.

'JJ? Is that you? Oh, thank God!'

'Where are you?'

'In the bedroom.'

'Stay there.' Jessica levelled the pistol and fired three shots. Wood splinters flew, and Serene gave one of her little shrieks. But the lock was shattered. Jessica pushed the door in, stepped into blackness. She grasped Serene's arm. 'Switch on the light.'

The room glowed.

'Thank you. Is that the bedroom door? Open it.'

Serene crossed the room and opened the door.

'You!' Andrea shouted.

'Don't worry,' Jessica said. 'She's with us, reluctantly.'

Serene switched on the light and Jessica gazed at Andrea, who lay on the bed, naked, her wrists bound together and secured to the bedpost above her head. There were marks on her body but none that looked very serious. 'Oh, JJ,' she said. 'I knew you'd come for me.'

'I'm sorry it took so long. We had some problems.' She turned to Serene, who was sidling to the door. 'Come back here. Lie down on your back, legs apart.'

Slowly Serene obeyed her, obviously wondering what was coming next. But once she was down and spread-eagled she could not get up in a hurry. Jessica laid down the pistol and untied Andrea's wrists. 'Whoosh!' Andrea rubbed her hands together.

'How long have you been tied up like this?'

'Since we were at the island, on and off.'

'That's almost a week. You have been tied up for a week?'

'He released me to eat and go to the loo. But you were in the desert with the Matthieu woman.'

'We found that we had a lot in common. How do you feel?'

'I would like to kill someone. Preferably Kanem.'

Jessica gave her the other pistol. 'I don't think you should shoot him out of hand. But you can have a go at encouraging him to resist arrest.'

'And how.' Andrea slowly got out of bed.

'Where are your clothes?'

'Kanem liked me better like this.'

Jessica nudged Serene with her toe. 'Are our clothes still in that room?'

Serene licked her lips. 'I think so. We have had no instructions from the Centre of the Universe, and no news either, until today, when Claudine came here.'

313

'And who told you we were coming?'

'Matthieu's pilot. He is a Follower. He told Papa you were leaving tonight, with Matthieu. Papa knew that if Matthieu was in Kano it was because of Hercule, and that he would not leave without him. So if he was leaving tonight, we knew to expect him before then. We also knew that he would not come alone.'

'Isn't life simple when you have people in the right places. Okay, get up and take us to where our clothes are.'

'You are going to have to tell me how you got in here,' Andrea said. 'With Matthieu?'

'We have friends. Douglas Kahu is downstairs.'

'Kahu?!' Andrea positively squeaked. 'He can't see me like this.'

'You'll be dressed in a moment. Come along, Serene.'

Serene led them out of the apartment on to the verandah, and turned to the right, away from the harem. She opened a door to allow them into the main house, and there was a sudden explosion of sound from in front of them. Jessica recognized Claudine's voice, shouting. 'Seems like Matthieu has found her.'

'What do we do?' Andrea asked.

'Treat it as a domestic squabble. What the...'

There was another explosion of sound, this time from downstairs, shouts and several shots. Jessica ran back to the verandah to look

314

down, and Serene suddenly charged her. Jessica heard her coming and sidestepped. Serene vaulted the rail, and jumped the twenty feet to the courtyard below. She landed on her feet, but staggered and went down, and stayed there, rolling to and fro in agony.

'What do we do now?' Andrea asked.

'She'll have to sweat it out. Come on.' She ran through the open door and into a darkened corridor.

'Which room?' Andrea shouted.

'Fuck that! Our boys are in trouble.' She couldn't imagine how it had happened.

She ran along the corridor to the stairs, and a door opened beside her. She checked, turning, pistol thrust forward, and Matthieu staggered out of the doorway, a knife sticking out of his chest. 'Help me!' he gasped. 'Help me.'

His shirt-front was a mass of blood, and even as he spoke his legs gave way and he fell to his knees and then on to his face. Jessica looked past him at Claudine, standing by the bed, clutching Hercule against herself. 'You!' she snarled. 'You brought him here! To take my son!'

'I recommend that you stay exactly where you are,' Jessica said. 'Until I sort one or two things out.' She took the key from the inside of the door, closed it and locked it from the outside.

'Bitch!' Claudine shrieked.

'JJ!' Andrea muttered.

Several men were coming up the stairs. They were definitely not policemen, and they

315

were armed with knives. They checked at the sight of the two women, even in the gloom able to see that Andrea was naked.

'Scatter!' Jessica told them. 'Go! Disappear!'

They gave a shout and ran at her. Both she and Andrea fired at the same time, and two of the men went down, writhing and screaming.

'That makes me feel a whole lot better,' Andrea said.

The remainder had decided to obey Jessica's instructions, and were tumbling back down the stairs, to be met by more gunfire. They screamed and threw away their knives, dropping to their knees and raising their hands in the air. Douglas appeared in front of them.

'Oh, my God!' Andrea muttered, stepping back into the darkness and retreating to the top of the stairs.

'What happened?' Jessica asked.

'These characters suddenly burst in on us. We hadn't reckoned on so many servants. So the guys we were covering also made a grab for their weapons, and, well, it was pretty nasty. One of my men is dead; two are wounded. I have to get an ambulance here.'

'What about the Kwarisms?'

'They're in the building somewhere. They ran into the courtyard.'

'They could be anywhere. This place is a rabbit warren.'

'Do we care where they are?'

'Of course we do, Douglas. Kanem, anyway.

316

He's our reason for being here, remember?'

'Did you find Miss Hutchins?'

'I found her.'

'And...' He peered past her to the top of the stairs. 'Andrea?'

'I'm not presentable right now. JJ, can't we find my clothes?'

'I think we need to find Kanem and his brother first. They could be lurking anywhere, and we don't know what other resources they have. You with me, Douglas?'

'As soon as I've offloaded this lot.'

'Stay there, Andie. I'll get back to you in a minute,' Jessica said, and followed Douglas into the entry hall, which was indeed a shambles. Four of Kwarism's servants were on the floor, and two looked dead. And as Douglas had said, three of his policemen were also down. He used his mobile phone to call for an ambulance as well as reinforcements. 'Will there be trouble?'

'Not now. They attacked us. Questions will be asked, I reckon. It's up to us to have the answers. Where is Matthieu?'

'Matthieu is dead.'

'Not you?'

'His wife stabbed him.'

'And she is...?'

'Locked in upstairs with her son.'

'Now there's a tricky one. I am going to have to charge her with murder.'

'Let's talk about it. When we've settled with the rest of her family.' She went to the door to the courtyard.

317

'Careful,' Douglas warned.

Jessica threw it open, flattening herself against the wall beside it. 'Kwarism,' she called. 'Come down, with your sons.'

'Leave my property, woman. Take your people and go. You are defiling the house of the Lord. Leave, or I shall destroy you.'

'He sings a slightly different tune than poor old Ukuba. That won't work,' she shouted. 'There are more policemen on their way. If you force another shoot-out it is you who will be destroyed.'

'Me, destroyed? See my power!'

'There is someone in the yard,' said one of the policemen, watching through the window.

'The girl, Serene. She jumped from the verandah. Don't shoot. She is innocent.'

'There is someone else. By the pool.'

Jessica had been looking at Serene, who had in fact not yet got up, as if she had hurt herself more seriously than she had supposed by her fall. Now she looked at the pool, and saw a shadowy figure at the top of the ramp.

'My God!' Douglas said from immediately behind her. 'They're opening the gate.'

'Jesus!' Jessica stepped outside. 'Your sister!' she shouted.

Several shots rang out, smashing into the wood around her, and Douglas grasped her arm and jerked her back inside. 'You trying to die?'

'That girl! Serene!' Whoever had opened the gate was apparently still unaware that Serene was lying on the ground, and had

318

darted back into the shadows on the far side of the courtyard. But out of the now swinging gate there emerged one huge snout, and then another. 'Oh, shit!' Jessica said. 'We must get her!'

'Those are killers!'

'So am I. So they say.'

Douglas took a deep breath. 'Open fire,' he commanded.

'On the crocs, Sir?'

Douglas looked at Jessica.

'One on the crocs. The others on the verandah.' Jessica drew a deep breath herself, and ran out of the door. Again she remembered her experience in Bolivia, but these creatures were altogether larger than Ramon Cuesta's pet caiman, with thrashing tails some six feet long which she knew could break every bone in her body with a single blow.

For the moment the three of them were looking around themselves, confused by the noise and their unexpected freedom. Already several more shots had been fired from the verandah, fortunately very inaccurately, and now the three policemen opened up, spraying the night with fire from the captured assault rifles.

Jessica raced across the yard, and reached Serene just as she sat up, clawing at her ankle. Jessica grasped her arm, and she looked up, and shrieked, striking at Jessica's face.

'Behind you!' Douglas shouted, firing as he did so.

Jessica released Serene to turn and see one of the crocodiles, having identified a victim, move towards her at tremendous speed. She drew her pistol, but had no time to aim as she threw herself sideways, sprawling in the dust and forcing herself to lie flat as the gigantic tail swished above her head. Then she rolled over and sat up. She knew that pumping bullets at the reptile's armour-plated skin was a waste of time; as Douglas had said, it had to be eyes or mouth – and she was now behind it. As was Douglas, and the crocodile was still turning away from them as it sighted Serene. The girl had got to her feet, and was hobbling, trying to reach the verandah. But she would never make it; another of the crocodiles had come round the back of the pool; and was directly in front of her. The girl stared at it in horror, turned back, and found the other reptile immediately behind her. She screamed, and four shots rang out. The second crocodile seemed almost to rear in the air as the bullets were poured down its throat, and it uttered a roaring sound as it rolled over on to its back.

'Holy Jumping Jesus!' Douglas exclaimed.

Jessica looked up to where Andrea stood at the verandah rail, looking down. But she wasn't pleased with her marksmanship. 'Look out!' she shouted.

For Serene, glancing over her shoulder at the reptile behind her, had turned back again, and decided to escape round the dying beast, forgetting that it was still dying. The huge tail still thrashed, and now it swung sideways to strike Serene across the thighs, sending her flying with another shriek of mingled dismay and agony, hurling her to the ground in a crumpled heap.

Jessica scrambled to her feet and ran towards her, followed by Douglas. The firing had ceased as both sides watched in horror. The first crocodile turned towards Jessica. Andrea fired again, several times, but the angle was wrong and the bullets merely bounced off the scaly skin. Jessica realized she would have to handle this one herself, turned to face the creature while Douglas burst past her to reach the stricken girl. The crocodile's mouth was closed; there were only the eyes to aim at. And if the range was very close, the beast was again travelling at tremendous speed.

'JJ!' Andrea screamed.

Jessica levelled the pistol, held in both hands, and squeezed the trigger several times. At least two of the nine-millimetre bullets struck the crocodile in the eye, and it collapsed, its jaws only feet from where Jessica stood.

Douglas came towards her, well away from the thrashing tails, carrying the girl in his arms. 'She is dead.'

'Oh, shit!' Serene might have hated her as the prospective destroyer of her family, but she had found no reason to hate the girl.

'But that shooting ... both of you...'

'We practise.'

There was a shout, and Kwarism and Fodio came running down the stairs and across the yard.

'Hold your fire!' Douglas shouted at his men.

The father and brother, carefully avoiding the third crocodile, who was by itself on the far side of the pool looking somewhat bewildered, ran towards them. 'Serene...'

'Is dead, Mr Kwarism,' Douglas said. 'Killed by your senseless opposition to the law.'

Fodio stretched out his arms, and Douglas placed the dead girl in them. 'Where is Kanem?'

'I do not know.'

There was another shout from above them, and they looked up to see Andrea in Kanem's arms, wrestling against the verandah rail; he had obviously taken her unawares, and she had dropped her pistol.

'Goddammit!' Douglas raised his gun, but he knew he was not a sufficiently accurate shot to risk firing.

Jessica, slamming the spare magazine into her Browning, swung to face the verandah. Kanem held a knife under Andrea's chin, so that for all her skills she dared not move, make any attempt to free herself.

'Leave this house!' he commanded. 'Free my father and brother and go. Or I will cut her throat.'

Douglas looked at Jessica, his face a mask of appeal. She drew one of her deep breaths. Kanem's head was quite visible, looking

322

round Andrea's. But in the darkness it was still indistinct, and there was the knife. Success would depend not only on her skill as a markswoman but on the speed of his reactions. Yet she knew she was going to do it, just as she knew Andrea would expect her to. She threw up the gun, sighted with her years of experience and practice, and squeezed the trigger. Struck in the middle of the face, Kanem was blasted backwards, his head virtually disintegrated, the knife slipping from his lifeless fingers.

'Sergeant Jones,' Douglas said. 'You are *something*!'

'How do you feel?' Jessica sat on a chair beside the bath in which Andrea was soaking. It was two o'clock in the morning, but the adrenaline was still flowing.

'I'm not sure,' Andrea said.

'I mean, about what happened. With Kanem.'

'I'm glad you didn't miss. But you don't ever miss, do you, JJ?'

'I have, in the past.'

'Now you tell me.'

'You still haven't answered my question.'

Andrea stood up, and Jessica handed her a towel. 'He was a brute. But...'

'Ah. Was he really the first since you were twenty?'

Andrea towelled vigorously. 'He was the first.'

'Oh, hell. I am so sorry.'

'It made him very happy.'

'Will you tell Josie?'

'Shit, no. In fact, I'm thinking of giving Josie the push.'

Jessica decided not to comment on that.

'What's going to happen, JJ?'

'That depends on Douglas. He'll tell us at the meeting this morning. But I have some ideas.'

'And Claudine? The way she screamed when they took Hercule away from her...'

'That depends on Douglas, too. Let's get some sleep.'

'As I have been obliged to make a report,' Douglas said, 'I felt it might be as well to make it a very full one, covering what we know of what went on in the Centre of the Universe as well as at Kwarism's house. There will obviously now be a hearing to decide what action needs to be taken there, but I think, given Colonel Faure's point of view, that the governments of Chad and Nigeria may be able to take joint action. There can be no doubt that Zobeir at least is responsible for the death of Ukuba.'

'Then what will happen to the Followers?'

'That is a problem. If we break up the Centre of the Universe it'll leave several million people rudderless. If we allow it to continue, the odds are its control will fall into the hands of someone as unscrupulous as Zobeir was.'

'Or Kwarism or Fodio.'

'There's no chance of that. They're on criminal charges. I don't know if we can make murder stick, but kidnapping is certain.' He looked at the two women seated before his desk. 'You are both of course material witnesses. However, as the case will certainly not come up for several months you are free to leave the country, on condition you return when required. In this regard, I will be forwarding a copy of my report to New Scotland Yard to put them in the picture.'

Jessica and Andrea exchanged glances and he raised his eyebrows. 'You have a problem with that?'

'The fact is,' Jessica explained, 'we weren't sent to Nigeria. We came.'

Again Douglas looked from face to face. 'I think you need to explain that.'

Jessica looked at Andrea, who waggled her eyebrows, clearly indicating that it was up to her.

'Well,' Jessica said, 'the fact is' – she gazed at him, her eyes enormous – 'we were approached, in a private capacity, by Matthieu to locate his son. We both had a bit of leave coming up, you see...'

'And you accepted the job? From a man like Matthieu?'

'Well, we didn't know anything more about him than that he was a man whose wife had gone off with his son. He painted a pretty horrific picture of the life the boy would have to lead, suggested that Claudine was involved in international terrorism. We had to be interested in that, but we hadn't actually decided yet, when…'

'Why didn't you take it to your boss at the Yard?'

'We didn't have any proof. Only what Matthieu told us.'

'He offered you money?'

'Well, there was a small retainer…'

Andrea scratched her ear.

'But as I was saying, before we had come to a decision, Smollett showed up and put us in the whole picture. That sort of made up our mind for us.'

'But you still didn't go to the Yard.'

'Smollett wasn't keen on that. He didn't think they'd be any help. Neither Matthieu nor Claudine had committed any crime in England.'

'But he came to you.'

'He knew we were on leave, and wondered if we'd like to come along.'

'Just like that? In preference to his own people?'

'He knew of Matthieu's approach. He had him under surveillance, and he saw us together. He found out who I was, and thought I might have some information to give him. He didn't know where to go looking for Claudine. We did. But we didn't tell him. What he had told us, though, made us realize that this was something big. So we decided to see what we could do on our own. I think he took offence.'

Douglas gazed at her for several seconds.

'I'm not sure that you aren't as good a liar as you are a shot, JJ.' He tapped the folder on his desk. 'This has to go to the Yard. To your superior. Commander Adams, is it?'

'That's the man.'

'So?'

'Well, perhaps you could put it as I say. Only indicate that we came here as part of Smollett's set-up. How are you handling his death, anyway?'

'A flying accident.'

'And Claudine?'

'She murdered her husband, JJ.'

'I am sure it was self-defence.'

'She also blew up a hundred people. And also despatched a couple of Touaregs.'

'That also was self-defence. I will testify in her favour.'

'What is this with you and her?'

'She saved my life. And taught me a lot about guts and determination that I didn't know I lacked.'

Douglas sighed. 'Well, your feelings do you credit. But they can't do her any good now.'

'I have said I will testify at her trial.'

'JJ ... Claudine Matthieu hanged herself in her cell just before dawn this morning.'

'Oh, my *God*!' Andrea cried.

'Our people were careless. She should never have been left alone. But maybe it was for the best.'

'And the boy?' Jessica's voice was low.

'He becomes a state orphan.'

'He's probably the greatest genius in the

327

world.'

'What makes you say that?'

'Well, the way he talks. His mathematical powers. His ... You saw him; you heard him.'

'I didn't, actually. I know you chatted him up. But the fact is, the doctor who saw him said that, apart from the bump on the head when the helicopter went in, which might have caused a mild concussion, he is in every way a normal boy. At my suggestion he tried him with a couple of mathematical questions, but he obviously didn't have a clue.'

'The bump on the head,' Andrea muttered. 'It must have wiped out...'

'We'll never know for sure.'

'But Claudine knew,' Jessica said. 'My God! That's why she killed herself. All those deaths, all that mayhem, all that scheming to gain control of the Followers ... all for nothing.' She sighed. 'Well, I think we'll be heading home. By scheduled flight.'

'There won't be one until tomorrow. You ladies promised to have dinner with me, remember?'

Jessica looked at Andrea, who waggled her eyebrows. 'You take Andie,' she said. 'I'm for an early night.'

'Well,' Commander Adams said. 'What an amazing story. You are an incredible woman, JJ. You do realize that what you did is quite unacceptable.'

'In what way, sir?' Jessica wore uniform and was her usual spic-and-span self.

328

'Well, working with the CIA without my permission.'

'With respect, sir, I was on vacation. When I was approached by a most likeable CIA agent requesting my support, I found the idea intriguing. It's all there in Inspector Kahu's report.'

'I suppose I cannot command what you do in your spare time, JJ, but this sort of, shall I say, moonlighting is most irregular, and I should not like to have it happen again.'

'It hardly can, sir, if I am to be in records.'

'Ah. I have been considering that, after consultation with my colleagues. And reading this report. They feel, well, that you may yet be an asset to the force in the field. I'm afraid they also feel that perhaps your promotion should be put on hold, for a little while yet. Tell me, how many men did you dispose of this time?'

'Two definitely. Possibly four. And one large crocodile.'

'Amazing. I hope you weren't looking for a handbag. Ha ha ha.'

'Ha ha ha, sir.'

'But to be serious, we have a task for you, which we feel may be right up your street.'

'Thank you, sir. May I ask...'

'We'll discuss it when you return from holiday. You still have ten days to go. And JJ, please spend them somewhere very quiet, and if possible, in this country.'

'You always seem to fall on your feet,' Mrs

Norton remarked.

'Despite various efforts,' Jessica agreed. 'By the way, did you read Inspector Kahu's report?'

'Yes, I did.'

'And not even a black armband?'

'I have no idea what you mean.'

'Well, isn't it customary to wear some kind of mourning when a close friend dies?'

Mrs Norton glared at her. 'You have no proof.'

'I'm a detective. I deduce things. It could only have been you who gave Matthieu such a thorough file on me at such short notice.'

Mrs Norton licked her lips, and glanced at the closed door to Adams' office. 'He'll never believe you.'

'Do you know, I think he might. But I won't tell him, if you'll tell me why. And how.'

'Well...' Another circle of the lips. 'We met at a party, and became friends.'

'Good friends, as the gossip columnists put it?'

Mrs Norton blushed. 'Well...'

'I'm not criticizing. I'm just registering surprise at some people's tastes. Yours and his. Now tell me why.'

'He told me he wanted someone, a woman, to undertake a special mission for him. He said he would pay her well. I knew you were at a loose end. I thought I was doing you a favour, JJ. I had no idea it would be dangerous. How much did he pay you, anyway?'

'That,' Jessica said, 'is my business.' She

went to the door. 'And only my friends call me JJ, Mrs Norton.'

'I think we're in the clear,' she told Andrea as they shared a taxi home.

'And the money?'

'I think we'll be able to collect the rest of it.'

'I mean, do we keep it?'

'Don't you think we deserve it?'

'Absolutely. But suppose Adams learns of it?'

'There is no reason why he should, providing we don't start spending high, wide and handsome. It's for our retirement.'

Andrea giggled. 'But I can buy some expensive underwear. From time to time.'

'I think that's reasonable.'

'And I can get rid of Josie. I won't need a flatmate anymore.'

'Right. But won't you find it lonely, all alone in that flat?'

'Well, it won't be *that* lonely. Douglas is coming to England in a month's time, and I told him I'd give him a bed.' She glanced at Jessica's open mouth, and flushed. 'Just don't say it.'

'I was going to say, it couldn't happen to a nicer guy. Or girl.'

'And you?'

'I am going to make a special effort to make Tom happy, for a while anyway. I've been feeling somewhat isolated, emotionally, these last few weeks.'

'But when you're an inspector...'

'That's been put on hold,' Jessica said. 'Adams actually thinks he's punishing me for moonlighting. So, are you on for whatever comes next? Providing it doesn't interfere with your love life, of course.'

'I'm on,' Andrea said.